Penguin Books
The Egyptologists

G000047328

Kingsley Amis, who wa[...]
was educated at the Ci[...]
John's College, Oxford[...]
lecturer, a keen reader[...]
enthusiast. His novels include *Lucky Jim* (1954), *Take
A Girl Like You* (1960), *The Anti-Death League* (1966),
Ending Up (1974), *The Alteration* (1976, winner of the
John W. Campbell Memorial Award), *Jake's Thing*
(1978), *Russian Hide-and-Seek* (1980), *Stanley and the
Women* (1984), *The Old Devils*, which won the 1986
Booker Prize, and *Difficulties with Girls* (1988). Among
his other publications are *New Maps of Hell* (1960), a
survey of science fiction, *The James Bond Dossier*
(1965), *Colonel Sun* (1968, under the pseudonym of
Robert Markham), *Rudyard Kipling and his World*
(1975) and *The Golden Age of Science Fiction* (1981).
He published his *Collected Poems* in 1979 and his
Collected Short Stories in 1980. Many of his books are
published in Penguin. He has written ephemerally on
politics, education, language, films, television and
drink. Kingsley Amis was awarded the C.B.E. in 1981.

Robert Conquest was born in 1917 and educated at
Winchester and Magdalen College, Oxford. His career
has been varied. He has served in the light infantry and
the diplomatic service, receiving an O.B.E. Since then
he has worked as a freelance writer. He has been a
research fellow at the London School of Economics;
lecturer in English at the University of Buffalo; literary
editor of the *Spectator*; visiting fellow at a number of
universities and institutions; and research associate at
Harvard University. He has written numerous books of
poetry including *Poems* (1955), *Between Mars and
Venus* (1962), *Arias from a Love Opera* (1969), and
New and Collected Poems (1987); and a science fiction
novel, *A World of Difference* (1955). His other books
include *Where Marx Went Wrong* (1971), *Kolyma: The
Arctic Death Camps* (1978), *Inside Stalin's Secret Police*
(1985), *The Harvest of Sorrow* (1986), *Tyrants and
Typewriters* (1988), *Murder of the Century* and *The
Great Terror Re-examined* (1989).

Kingsley Amis
and Robert Conquest

The Egyptologists

Penguin Books

PENGUIN BOOKS

Published by the Penguin Group
27 Wrights Lane, London W8 5TZ, England
Viking Penguin Inc., 40 West 23rd Street, New York, New York 10010, USA
Penguin Books Australia Ltd, Ringwood, Victoria, Australia
Penguin Books Canada Ltd, 2801 John Street, Markham, Ontario, Canada L3R 1B4
Penguin Books (NZ) Ltd, 182–190 Wairau Road, Auckland 10, New Zealand

Penguin Books Ltd, Registered Offices: Harmondsworth, Middlesex, England

First published by Jonathan Cape 1965
Published in Penguin Books 1968
10 9 8 7 6 5 4 3 2

Made and printed in Great Britain by
Cox & Wyman Ltd, Reading
Set in Monotype Times

To Charmian

Contents

1 The Inner Ring

Their lives were built on caution.

They simply could not afford any prolonged contact with alien, or even inquisitive, 'elements', as the Secretary was inclined to call them. Article 22 of the Constitution laid down a standard procedure for dealing with the present type of emergency, and this had so far always proved adequate, but to draw comfort from such reflections was as false and illogical as to cheer oneself up in the line of battle by the thought that one's skin was still intact. A single mistake, the equivalent of breaking cover a second too soon or neglecting to aim off for wind deflection, could be lethal.

It was not the Treasurer's way to brood, but he ruminated briefly along these lines as his taxi elbowed and jostled its way down William IV Street. He was already a little late for the weekly meeting of the Committee of the Metropolitan Egyptological Society at which the ominous Lee Eddington Schwartz matter would doubtless head the agenda.

The weather was beastly cold. The early-evening rendezvous at Bragg's Wine House off the Strand had turned out to be inconvenient to him after all. This was through no fault of that organizing genius, the Secretary. It had just happened unexpectedly that the Treasurer had spent the afternoon, not at the great draper's shop in New Oxford Street of which he was manager, but negotiating with another firm in the depths of Mayfair, and the taxi had a cramped and difficult route.

Dismissing Eddington Schwartz and other immediate concerns for the moment, he huddled back into the cushions. As the taxi nudged slowly forward he was soon in what amounted to a dream. In it, he was on a golden tropical beach in the Seychelles Islands, clad in one of those cabana sets he had seen in Austin Reed's window, drinking a tot of palm wine and accompanied by a dusky but rather plain girl. The Treasurer considered himself a devotee of realism, and as the picture formed it held true to the authorities he had so often read. These described the islands as ideal in every way but one: the unattractive appearance of the race inhabiting them. And yet, no matter how highbrow the higher faculties of the mind, the lower remain hopelessly pop. As the Adelphi slid past unseen, the piggy near-triangles of the girls' eyes expanded, her hair softened, stains and snaggles disappeared from her teeth.

The taxi braked sharply behind a stationary car with a French registration plate and gave an angry hoot. The Treasurer emerged from his set-piece, feeling refreshed. The taste of a dreary afternoon's draping had been expunged and, it occurred to him belatedly, even in her original, authentic form the dusky girl had at least not been his wife.

Entering the dark wooden depths of the wine hall a few moments later, he saw the President and the Secretary ensconced as usual in the practically eavesdrop-proof alcove in the far corner. Before them stood a bottle of claret and three glasses, some bread and biscuits and a large Stilton cheese.

This was usual too. On just such an occasion as this, a couple of years previously, a rush of the President's Friday-evening eloquence had carried him unexpectedly to that imaginative triumph, the idea of the Society. The Committee as then constituted was *ad hoc*, but its composition had been regularly confirmed by the small, slow-growing membership.

The President was not now in that state of extreme euphoria. Under an electric glow so dim as almost to suggest candlelight, his dramatic face was at least comparatively calm, though its long oval under the dark wavy hair bore some trace of ill humour. The Secretary, as extreme a contrast as ever, hardly looked up from the file he was turning through, merely gesturing at the bottle. But the President, an instinctive host, half rose to welcome the stocky, brown-haired, undistinguished figure of the Treasurer, poured him a glass at once and with a flourish of his free hand.

The Secretary found the paper he had been looking for. He sat, perfectly impassive, as though prepared to cope even with a public inquiry into the doings of the Society. His bullet head, as round as some Maya or Toltec demon's, was not so easily divisible into cranium and face as that of the President. It was all of a piece, the

10

strong and pale pudginess of the cheeks, surmounted by thick circular glasses with wire frames, blending almost imperceptibly with the short, nondescript-coloured hair. He gave every impression of keen intellect and powerful character – too powerful, if anything, but such qualities were absolutely necessary in keeping an organization of their sort united and dedicated, and in overcoming the breathtaking crises which occasionally shook it to its very foundations.

He now brought up the Eddington Schwartz matter. In his level voice, so dry as to suggest extreme physical dehydration, he said, 'My feeling is that this is a bone fide inquiry. But that wouldn't make it any less potentially dangerous, of course. Remember Professor Armitage the year before last?'

The President shuddered.

'Anyway . . . "I came across the name of your Society when looking up the telephone number of the Metropolitan Ear, Nose and Throat Hospital in the Directory."' The Secretary removed his glasses momentarily. 'If you remember, I opposed our choice of title on the reasoning that just this sort of thing was bound to occur some day. But never mind that for the moment. What is slightly cheering, at this stage of the case, is that no really malignant, uh, element . . .'

'. . . would use such a thin tale,' put in the Treasurer.

'Exactly.'

'That is the purest guesswork,' intoned the President through pouted lips.

The Secretary stared irritably at him. The President's inspiration had certainly provided the whole basis of the Society, but such flashes of the perverse as he had just manifested (he was always doing it) seemed to call in question his long-term reliability, his basic drive. He smiled and frowned back at the Secretary, then raised his eyebrows, as, still looking at him, he drank daintily from his glass.

The Secretary turned abruptly back to the Treasurer. 'Well, who's going to tackle him?'

'I will if you like. After the last three or four I'm more or less used to it.'

'Good. Remember, if you can't head him off completely, give him the narrowest front you can.'

11

'Of course. Tombs and royal sculpture at Thebes and Amarna, eighteenth Dynasty.'

'Is that narrow enough?'

'You bet.'

'What made you pick it?'

'Just took it at random. No, wait a minute: it's Nefertiti's period, I remember now.'

The Secretary sat still for a moment, his molars grinding together silently, his eyes glittering in phase with his glasses. Then he said, 'How do you know that?'

'I looked it up.'

The President rolled about in his chair, laughing.

'I see,' said the Secretary. 'Well, don't start discussing her, simply because she'll be there upstairs.'

'What do you take me for?'

'All right. Now, you'd better have his letter. I should drop him a line right away – don't telephone, of course – and arrange to see him tomorrow: he says he can come along any time. The sooner he's disposed of the safer for everyone.'

The Treasurer glanced at the sheet of notepaper. 'Bags of politeness, eh? Getting on for bloody smarmy, in fact . . . I say, he's an American. Spells "honour" without a "u".'

'Let me see that.' When the Secretary handed the sheet back, he was smiling thinly. 'That is very observant of you,' he said with something approaching cordiality in his tone. 'Well, that should make your task easier. You can be eccentric to him. Americans expect Englishmen to be that. It pleases their sense of the fitness of things.'

'Tell him to get the hell out and he'll be tickled to death?'

'Not quite that, perhaps, but you're likely to find –'

'Do you mind if we move on?' asked the President. 'I have to get home so that my wife can take me out to dinner.'

'Ring up and arrange to meet her where you're going,' suggested the Treasurer.

'I have to get home,' the President repeated at half speed, 'so that my wife can take me out to dinner. And I naturally assumed from the very beginning,' he went on *a tempo*, 'that the fellow was an American. How many Englishmen are called things like Lee Eddington Schwartz?'

'Very few, I imagine,' said the Treasurer. 'We need another bottle, by the way.'

'No more for me, thank you.'

'Thank me, hell, it's your turn.' Since last month, the Treasurer said to himself.

'Oh, sorry.' The President looked briefly and vainly about for the waiter. 'Anyway, what's next on the list?'

The Secretary said, 'Furze. He's acting up again.'

Furze was the Society's only employee, a small man with white hair and a black moustache who was responsible for keeping its premises clean and orderly and who intermittently acted as caretaker. Although half crazed, he was thoroughly efficient, and his loyalty and discretion had never been questioned. An ex-company-sergeant-major, he had been the President's platoon sergeant in the Italian campaign.

'Ladies' Night, I suppose,' said the Treasurer.

'He says he simply couldn't stand another one.'

'The last one was just about the most –'

'A great success,' said the Secretary authoritatively. 'What I can't understand is why he always insists on coming.'

'Sense of *duty*,' said the President with a large 'projecting' gesture.

'Well then . . .'

'You don't understand. The only way he can not come with a good conscience is to hand in his notice.'

'Get Cambuslang on to him,' said the Treasurer.

'Furze doesn't like Scotsmen. Supposing I have a word with Mordle?'

'Quite unsuitable,' snapped the Secretary.

The Treasurer silently agreed. Mordle, a newish member introduced by the President, had a habit of unfocusing his eyes and trancing occasionally before answering a question, even a simple request for agreement, as if unable to provide a reply from his own resources and so compelled to proceed in his astral body to some distant library or card index to refresh his memory of the original source material. This did give him a scholarly look which was a distinct asset to the Society in its public activities, but he would be no good as an audience for Furze's tirades.

The problem was solved by the Secretary. 'I'll circulate a

directive to all members,' he said, making a note, 'instructing them to listen to Furze as much as possible and take a long time sympathizing. Perhaps I can work out some sort of rota. We should all share the responsibility.'

'What about this drink question?' asked the Treasurer.

'A very good point,' said the President eagerly. 'Have you ordered it?'

The Secretary raised his spherical head. 'Ordered what?'

'The *drink*, my dear boy,' cried the President with another of his manual sweeps, going so far this time as to spill the last half-inch of Pauillac mistakenly borne aloft in his gesturing hand. As it trickled up his sleeve, he added more restrainedly, 'For Ladies' Night.'

While the Treasurer reflected on the paucity of this self-inflicted punishment for a blatant piece of side-tracking, the Secretary answered, 'But of course. Half a dozen South African sherry.'

'Some of those aren't too bad,' said the President.

'This is a Rich Golden blend.'

'Oh. You know, some comedian person was on television the other day saying that what he called a cream sherry from Cyprus was most frightfully good for you. Six bob a bottle kind of thing.'

'I think that might be going too far. And we have ourselves to consider.'

There was a short pause as a carrot-haired woman with long turquoise earrings crossed the length of the hall and went out by the Maiden Lane door, letting in a large draught. Women were rarely seen in Bragg's. Then the President and Treasurer nodded and mm-ed respectively.

'Mordle was telling me,' said the Secretary in a quiet but loaded fashion, 'that he knows something about the law.'

'Not much, I fancy,' said the President. 'He only read it in his first year at Oxford and he was drunk all the time then.'

'What a pity.'

The Secretary's observation sounded pointless, but no doubt he was still hankering after reconstructing the Legal Committee of the Society. This body (quite superfluous as far as the Treasurer could see) had actually got round to producing Society Pamphlets 3 and 5, rather unreal documents which at best seemed to be fair light reading. It had in any case more or less disintegrated, now

14

that Chester, its Chairman and mainspring, so seldom appeared.

'We've never had a real lawyer,' muttered the Secretary.

'We've never had anyone who would ever have considered being a lawyer,' said the Treasurer, 'if it weren't for –'

The President interrupted animatedly, 'If it weren't for the forces which got us all into our present situation and keep us at our jobs!'

The Treasurer wished, in a way, that he had one of their jobs instead of his own, much as they loathed them themselves. The Society, his 'hobby' as his wife called it, was a great compensation. He turned to the President and said, 'Of course, you'd like to be an actor. Isham wants to be a painter. I've got my Seychelles, but –'

'What about our Secretary here?' put in the President.

What indeed? the Treasurer thought.

The Secretary himself smiled and made no answer.

The President smiled too, a little maliciously, and said, 'I expect he would like to be a social reformer.'

The Treasurer said quickly, 'What about Froald? I bet he wants to drive an engine.'

Interested as ever when there arose one of those personality questions on which the whole basis of the Society depended so directly, the Secretary leant forward. Signalling inattentively at the waiter's back, he said, 'I think your estimate of Froald is a little mistaken. He is not quite so naïve as he sometimes appears.' Passing from the particular to the general, as usual, he took off his glasses and let himself indulge in what the Treasurer always hoped was mere speculation. He felt that instead of treating the Society's business, complicated enough by any reckoning, simply as it came, the Secretary was inclined to long-term ideological theorizing which spelt trouble. He was now launched on one of his 'I see us as' disquisitions. What he was seeing the Society as today was one of those groups which, 'starting in a small way', brought 'seminal ideas' into the community – 'like, say, the Freemasons in one of the clerical autocracies of the nineteenth century.' His voice boomed uneerily from the woodwork.

All this philosophizing made the Treasurer uneasy. If it was only a way of explaining the life-patterns of the membership, a desire to make motives explicit – well, that might pass. But it had a certain air of special pleading. It seemed a bad sign, perhaps a sign of a bad conscience, that any necessity of justifying their actions, even to one another, should arise.

The waiter Jones, whose bony face and half-shut eyes gave him the look of a knowing corpse, had moved forward to one of his usual rest positions – as if by calculation, either just within or just beyond overhearing range. As far as anyone could tell he was quite harmless, except optically, and even the security-obsessed Secretary did not halt in his discourse, though it seemed to become a little more general and non-committal.

Chewing at a lot of cheese on a small biscuit, the Treasurer wondered whether to call Jones over himself. To be reminded thus crudely, and for the third time in five minutes, of his obligations was the sort of thing that annoyed the President, or caused him to put on a show of annoyance. At the moment, having evidently forgotten his desire to leave, that official was keeping a faraway look on his face as he rather obviously 'played the unaccustomed role of' listener to the Secretary's diatribe, like Sir John Gielgud doing Bottom in a charity performance.

Jones was normally insensitive to any summons subtler than a shaken umbrella or a wave involving the whole top half of the body, but now he caught the Treasurer's eye and bustled forward almost with civility. His arrival coincided with the end of a paragraph from the Secretary, and the President had no choice but to order up. He did it with fair grace, but again stated that he wanted no more himself. Laughing boyishly, he then said, 'No other business, is there?'

'Actually there is,' said the Secretary. 'Last night's report: a nil one, so that's that. A couple of hand-outs, but they can wait until I've had them typed. Now . . . last item. You'll be pleased, I think.' He flashed his glasses at each of them in turn. 'I was notified this morning that planning permission for the additional entrance and staircase has been granted. This means, of course, that the Isis Room project can proceed. I shall look about for a suitable contractor in the next few days.'

'Splendid,' said the President heartily. 'Splendid. How did you manage it?'

'Fire insurance angle. I said as things were the premium for the valuable and irreplaceable contents of the premises was impossibly steep and that we reckoned we'd get the money for the alterations

16

back within five years. I threw myself on the fellow's mercy as a man of culture.'

There was laughter and mutual congratulation, at the end of which the Secretary said he had nothing further. At this, the President started laughing boyishly all over again. He said, 'I was having drinks with my wife's brother and his wife the other day. Not such a hopelessly bad chap really, I suppose. Very chummy with this fellow Eric Lasker who works on "This Evening".'

'That's a name to conjure with, isn't it?' put in the Treasurer.

'What, "This Evening"?'

'No, Eric Lasker. Try conjuring with it and see –'

'You've lost me, I'm afraid,' said the Secretary. 'What's this about this evening?'

'You know, "This Evening",' explained the President tolerantly, '– that TV show where they interview sterling blokes whose houses are going to be knocked down to make room for motorways and things.'

'TV again,' said the Secretary. 'Don't you ever do anything else?'

'You of all people shouldn't need to ask that.'

'All right, go on.'

'Well, Egyptology came up, you see, and there was a bit of a discussion in the course of which –'

'A *bit of a discussion*?' The Secretary's chronic pallor lessened slightly. 'How did that come about? A *bit of a* . . .'

'I couldn't choke them off straight away, it would have looked too –'

Shaking his head violently, the Secretary said, 'I sometimes wonder why I bother at all, why I don't just . . . sit back and . . . Christ, here I am sweating my guts out, putting Pamphlet 2 together, distributing the bloody thing, and sods like you tell me they can't choke off nosey bastards because it would have looked too something or other, so they settle down to a *bit of a discussion*. It's enough to drive a –'

The return of Jones broke off this diatribe, but the Secretary was able to mime its continuation by at once pouring out a fresh glass and savagely attacking it.

The Treasurer took the chance. 'Well, anyway, what happened?'

17

The Secretary frowned. The President paid. Jones left. The President went boyish again and said, 'Quite extraordinary. My brother-in-law seemed to think that the Society would be right up Lasker's, uh, street. Promised to have a word with him about it. They were having lunch together today. It'll be interesting to see...'

Even the President noticed the quality of the silence he had produced. The Secretary sat as if carved out of soap. The Treasurer tried to lighten things by saying, 'So we're in the same class as sterling blokes who are going to have their houses knocked down to make room for a motorway, are we?'

'Clearly,' half-shouted the Secretary. 'A very appropriate image for the future of the Society.'

'Rather a pessimistic one, isn't it?' asked the Treasurer.

'How do you feel about it after being told that little lot?'

Silence again. The President just knew better than to do any more laughing, but his tone was still untroubled when he said, raising an upturned palm as if it bore a small cannon-ball, 'Why all the excitement? Lasker will laugh himself sick at the idea. And even if he doesn't, it's the simplest thing in the world to block him. The place is closed for cleaning. For repairs. For staff holiday. Or if they want a discussion in the studio we're ill, we're abroad, we ask a hundred guineas a man. Nothing to it.' He looked for agreement at the Treasurer, who nodded his head.

The Secretary was shaking his again. Perhaps his powerful neck had been developed by all the exercise it got in this way. He said, 'It isn't *that*. The chances of serious embarrassment from this source are, I should say, negligible. It isn't *that*.'

'All right, what is it, then?' asked the Treasurer.

'The attitude. A threat that, if it were to be realized, would mean the end of the Society and of much else besides, and we get laughter. Facetiousness. Everything we've always sworn to avoid.'

The Treasurer was far more disturbed at the Secretary's air of deep distress than by any shortcoming of the President's. He said gently, 'But you yourself just said that the threat won't be realized. What's wrong with a carefree attitude when there's no need to care? Just because we have to take our work seriously doesn't mean we have to have faces like death all the time. Aren't you getting things a little out of proportion?'

18

The Secretary sighed and ran a hand over the nap that covered the top of his skull. 'Perhaps I am. I have been really quite worried about this Lee Eddington Schwartz business. Now that you point it out I can see the cases aren't really parallel. But I do wish I thought everybody saw us as clearly as I do that, if we ever are exposed, it'll be because one of us has made an avoidable mistake, not because of some supernatural ill fortune. Perhaps everyone does see it like that. I certainly hope so.'

Soon afterwards the President made his farewells and left for his dinner. He gave the performance less production than he usually did, but shook hands with both the others, in compliance with the often expressed wish of the Secretary, who held that the ritual encouraged right thinking.

The latter had been cheering up somewhat. He smiled as he said to the Treasurer, 'Now, don't think me an old woman, but our friend gave us a first-class example of what you've got to avoid with Schwartz. No bits of discussions. Don't let yourself be drawn into any chats about . . . about the Delta. You don't know anything about the Delta.'

'Not an iota.'

This brought a momentary return of the Secretary's suspicious manner, but the area roughly identifiable as his brow, had cleared before he spoke again. 'Bit odd that our esteemed President opted out of a drink, don't you agree?'

'He was trying to opt out of buying that bottle, too.'

'Perhaps he's saving up for something.'

'A RADA course?'

'A what?'

'Royal Academy of Dramatic Art. Acting joint.'

'Oh, I shouldn't think so.'

'I don't really, either.'

'No, it'll be the usual,' said the Secretary. 'Well . . . good luck tomorrow night.'

'I probably won't need it.'

Jones sidled up for another order, but it was time to return to unreality.

2 Preparations for a Visitor

ENOBARBUS: It is a place
           The look of man not lights thereon, nor woman
       Untutored fronts it.

The present home of the Society lay in the intricate recesses of that region where all the streets are called Westbourne something-or-other, and only natives know which is which. Near the centre of this labyrinth there is an area of a dozen blocks or so, complicated by a reach of the Regent's canal, where the streets are curved and cornered in such a way that what seem to be three right-angled turns take the traveller through a full 360 degree circuit or, in other cases, through only 180 degrees. Complicated by an irregular knot of crescents and quincunxes, the total effect makes it notoriously possible, even when heading for a house one has visited already, to find oneself back at one's starting point. Taxi-drivers are sometimes reduced to reconnoitring on foot, and will often ask for an oral route-card when summoned from the local rank by telephone. Even by daylight long stretches of pavement hold no idler or passer-by of whom inquiry may be made, or yield only a group of aphasic children, a monoglot Hungarian, a couple of Negroes, probably African rather than West Indian, fluent and courteous but accented beyond intelligibility. The noise of traffic in Harrow Road, fierce enough at close quarters, never penetrates even the northern edge of the maze. Dead-ends abound, often ending in a manner suggestive of suicide, on the gloomy waters of the canal.

Any inquiring stranger who managed finally to present himself at the threshold of the Society's premises (thereby defeating one of the Secretary's most finely conceived and executed security precautions) would find himself a little overwhelmed by the heavy, rather formal granite of the Badgett Street house, small though it was and carried between larger buildings clashing in design, but admittedly similar in mood. On the dull brass of the plaque, *Metropolitan Egyptological Society* was inscribed in special hard-to-read lettering designed by Isham.

Having gained entry, if anything a more difficult feat on the part of an outsider than finding the house, one moved down a short flagstoned corridor giving access to the Lecture Hall on the left and, by way of the staircase, to the main Club Room. Here, twenty-four hours or so after the meeting in Bragg's, Cambuslang and Isham were chatting over pink gins.

Their chairs formed a triangle with a small pedestal on which stood the statue known as Nefertiti. It was not full length, only going down to the waist. Its composition, or at least its colour, was terracotta. An expert might have been surprised at its deviation from the norm of Egyptian royal statuary in the matter of clothing. For it had none, apart from the elaborate head-dress and a curiously decorated band round the neck. The latter in fact covered the point at which the head had been added to the torso. There had been much varied discussion before the statue was put up. Froald, with his defensive attitude, had maintained that nakedness was to be avoided, on the grounds that there was no need to risk arousing the slightest suspicion, however unconscious and off the mark, in the mind of what he described as 'the wrong sort of visitor', who might conceivably penetrate to the room. To this point the Secretary had replied that, on the contrary, all-male premises of any sort would look extremely odd if they did *not* contain some naked representation of the female form. He had instanced the pleasant and sexy Venus at the top of the stairs in the Travellers' Club. The presence of such a decoration, particularly in the formalized manner of a Roman goddess, or an Egyptian queen, would be reassuring to an accidental intruder rather than otherwise. It would tend to remove that faint subliminal air of homosexuality which many outsiders seem to scent in men's clubs. A more serious objection was the obvious non-authenticity of the sculpture. But the Society could not be expected to possess expensive originals of this size, and it would not be difficult to answer any inquiry by explaining that the object had been willed to them by an eccentric Egyptologist of the last generation and tolerated as amusing and decorative.

Its real origins were different. The torso had been carved by Isham. The head, originally a hollow shell, had been picked up cheap in an odds-and-ends shop in St Martin's Lane. When Isham had seen it on the Secretary's desk something had impelled

21

him to measure its neck. The result had led him to retrieve the torso from the attic of an uncle, the resting-place of many of his contributions to the visual arts. And, having filled the head with plaster, he had cemented the two together and painted the torso a terracotta shade. In the circumstances, the Secretary had put it at a General Meeting, he could not recommend the Society's rejection of this remarkable artefact from the hands of one of its members. So there it stood now, its only defect the tendency of the paint to come off on the fingers. Isham would not hear of varnishing it.

At the moment its part-author was gazing at Cambuslang with a vague resentment. The general unity of the Society was scarcely that of a monolithic collective, however profound its basic emotional solidarity. Some jarring of temperaments was often observable. For instance, Cambuslang found it hard to stomach Froald's naïveties, unable to see him in the way Isham and the Treasurer did, as a sort of Candide. 'D'you know,' the Scotsman was saying, 'he told me there was a man called Vane in that meteorological office of his and asked me to guess what his nickname was? He was quite offended when I told him he talked a lot of weather . . .'

Froald entering at that moment, Cambuslang broke off, and started a vague tirade against Egyptians.

'Start with the obvious. Brother-and-sister marriages. Now I quite readily admit that I had it pretty rough growing up in Renfrewshire, but that doesn't affect the general point. A more repulsive – '

'I don't see how it could,' said Isham, 'unless you married your sister there, which I reckon we'd have heard about long before now.'

'To hell, I'm sorry. I meant I grew up with a sister older than me with a face like a haggis who took every opportunity of beating hell out of me.'

'Isn't that rather trite? I don't mean the experience, I mean the comparison. Haggis.'

'Trite maybe, but apt, as you'd agree at once if you saw her. That bursting look. The whitish patches. And the dirty greasy surface texture. I don't like haggis either. I mean as well as sisters.'

'The treatment doesn't seem to have done you any harm, anyway,' said Froald, coming over from the drinks cupboard to

22

join them, his mind as usual on the last remark but two. Nevertheless he was right: the sometime victim had turned out heavy-boned and grizzled, a strong and steady Celt among volatile Englishmen like Isham. But Cambuslang gave Froald a slight wide-angle glare which suddenly zoomed in on the glass Froald was holding.

'What's that stuff you're drinking?'

'It's called French vermouth,' said Froald. 'They drink a lot of it in France, I'm told.'

Cambuslang was silent. Isham said, 'Mordle was telling me about his governess the other day. He must have had the same sort of time as you, only worse. She didn't have a haggis-type face, though. Rocky was what he called it.'

'So that's what's the matter with the laddie,' Cambuslang growled. 'When he switches off his eyes at you in that way of his he's thinking of his poor little white bottom being tanned in the long-ago.'

This was by way of a return blow for Mordle's behaviour the previous week, when he had been giving the reasons, in so far as he knew them, for certain difficulties he found with women, and had abruptly extended his denunciation from the female sex to the Scottish race, the governess having hailed from Aberdeen. Cambuslang had come up at this stage, already very slightly irritated by a tactless remark about the Luxor of the North from Froald, of all people, normally so tender of the other man's Scots susceptibilities that, alone among the members, he permitted him to use the adjective 'yon' without responding with a jeer or snarl.

The challenge-and-response system of upbringing, so evidently successful in Cambuslang's case, had panned out less well in that of Mordle, who seemed a little short on response. At least in the slight scene which had followed he had tended to falsetto apologies instead of the brisk and-the-same-to-you which would have appeased Cambuslang and, more to the point, made a better impression on the membership at large. Doubts about the wisdom of Mordle's admission, voiced at the time by the Secretary, had certainly not been checked.

When neither Isham nor Froald showed any inclination to pursue the matter of Mordle's bottom, Cambuslang returned to his earlier theme. 'The notion that these pyramid-piling pimps had a *civilization* has turned a lot of people on to the wrong track.

One wonders that they had enough sexual feeling left to go on reproducing themselves. Did you ever see anything more totally bloodless than the female figures on those reliefs and friezes of theirs? You have to look three times before you can see that they *are* female, for God's sake.'

Froald said deferentially, 'But that's better, isn't it? even so, than running round smeared with woad and . . . throwing spears at people, which is what –'

'Our ancestors may have been barbarians,' said Cambuslang, moving over to the drinks cupboard, 'but I'll warrant their lives weren't so gross as well as disinfected; I'm sure they lived among their refined cave paintings, enjoying a pure and vigorous sexual Arcadia, not like the notions you get from those heavy great limestone statues at Thebes and Memphis in Woldering's book, or those awful ones in Schimfen's illustrations.'

'The Venus of Willendorf, eh?'

This, for all its obscurity, was intended as a mild rebuke. Whatever the rights and wrongs of it, Isham felt it was a little demoralizing for Cambuslang to go on like this. Some application to Egyptology was after all necessary, and it was better for members not be worn down by this sort of theorizing. (The Secretary's sort was at least useful in suggesting a sense of purpose.)

The siphon snorted. Cambuslang regularly took soda with his Vaughan Jones and Angostura, on the theory that it got it to you quicker. He was about to reply when the low-pitched rattle of an idling taxi-engine drew him to the window, a reflex action that, like many such, bore no fruit. The porch of the building was unusually deep, which made it a useful vantage-point for surveying the street unseen, but which blocked off the upstairs view of that part of the roadway most likely to be occupied by vehicles setting down outside the premises. Chester had once recommended its demolition on this ground, a proposal promptly vetoed by the Secretary.

All three relaxed perceptibly when a key was heard in the front-door lock. Rapid footsteps heralded the arrival of the Treasurer. 'All quiet?' he asked as he hurried to pour himself a Manzanilla. 'Good. Look, you chaps, there's an Article 22 case coming up in about' – he glanced at his watch – 'God, is it that already? – about ten minutes. I've run it pretty fine, I'm afraid.'

'Anything you want us to do?' asked Cambuslang.

'No, all straightforward. Just the usual – nobody to leave the room and as little noise as possible, please. Oh, is Furze about?'

'I heard him crashing in the basement when I came in,' said Isham.

'I expect he'll be up in a minute. I just want to check one point with him. You all got the directive about him, did you?'

'Yes, thanks,' said Froald. 'Bit thick, isn't it? Christ knows how many times we've heard all that stuff before.'

'It's only until Ladies' Night,' said Isham. 'But I must say I think three of those a year is too many. We shall have the same sort of thing all over again in June.'

'You won't drive the Secretary off his point about that.' The Treasurer downed his sherry and poured himself another.

'He keeps at us too hard, you know,' said Froald querulously. 'He's got organizing mania.'

'I rather agree,' said Isham. 'You know, he confided to me once that he'd like to get us to *memorize* all directives and pamphlets and the rest of it and burn them. Admitted it would probably be too much of a strain on everybody though.'

'Decent of him,' said Cambuslang.

The Treasurer, though privately sharing the general view in large part, knew where his duty lay. 'It's very largely thanks to him,' he said, 'that the Society hasn't gone up in smoke years ago. When you think of what's at stake, the magnitude of the risks we run, you've simply got to have someone like that, who'll sit up all night thinking of ways of tightening up security and so on. And yes, he does like organizing, but think of what we get out of it. The Week-end Seminar, for instance.'

'If it ever comes off,' muttered Isham.

'Well, if it doesn't, it won't be his fault, I bet you.'

'That's true,' said Cambuslang. 'You're right, of course. He does have energy and we need it. If only he weren't so –'

There was a gentle knock at the door. 'Come in,' called the Treasurer.

Furze entered and stood at attention. 'Good evening, gentlemen.'

'Good evening, Mr Furze,' they all said with conscientious cordiality.

Turning to the Treasurer, Furze said, 'Everything laid on, sir. Chairs all away. Tea-chests in position. Box of shavings. When will you want me, sir?'

'Give it five minutes, I think.'

'You know, I can't help feeling that all this rigmarole is a bit unnecessary,' Froald cut in. 'Why not simply not answer the fellow's inquiry?'

'Because then he comes round here and plays hell, if he's the type,' said Cambuslang. 'At least two kinds of hell.'

'Couldn't you take him to a pub?'

'That was what the President did with Professor Armitage that time,' said the Treasurer.

'Oh, my God,' said Isham emotionally.

'Before your time, Froald. I don't care to let my mind dwell on what happened. Just consider that you can't control a man in a pub, you can't chuck him out and – most important of all as it turned out – you can't stop him coming with you when you leave yourself.'

'I see what you mean,' said Froald.

'Excuse me, sir,' Furze addressed the Treasurer. 'The electricity as usual, I take it, sir?'

'Yes, that's as good as anything I, think. The estate agent's too vague on its own.'

'Right, sir. When is stand-to, sir?'

'In about . . . three minutes, I should say.'

'Have a drink, Mr Furze,' offered Isham. 'You've just got time.'

'A small Scotch whisky if I may, sir, thank you very much.'

'How's Mrs Furze?' asked Froald.

Normally this would have had the sort of effect that asking Henry II what he felt about Becket might, but this evening Furze seemed actually to be considering the point. He sipped his drink before replying.

'Well, sir,' he said finally, 'it's not much use my going on in my usual way, is it, now? I mean, you're very sympathetic and all that, all you gentlemen are, I'm not saying that, but you don't really agree with me, do you? There's a fundamental difference in approach between all you gentlemen on one side and myself on the other. It came to me the other day. A fundamental difference of approach.'

'Oh, but there's a lot of agreement,' protested the Treasurer. 'We see eye to –'

'Not fundamentally, sir, if you'll pardon me. On the surface but not fundamentally.'

The impasse was solved by a ring at the front door. 'Few minutes early,' the Treasurer said. 'Right, Mr Furze, off we go.'

'Good luck, sir.'

They hurried down the stairs and then diverged, Furze to his basement, the Treasurer to the door.

3   A Breach of Security

CAESAR: Why have you stolen upon us thus?

A girl stood in the porch. She said, 'Good evening. My name is Lee Eddington Schwartz. I believe you're expecting me. I'm afraid I may be a little early.'

'Not at all, Miss Schwartz,' said the Treasurer at once. 'Will you come in? I'm afraid things are in a bit of a mess.'

'Wow! you certainly know how to play it cool,' said the girl pleasantly, stepping inside. 'Most people go right up in the air when they see I'm Miss and not Mister – or Esquire, the way you put it – you know, find out visually like this. I'm afraid I rather enjoy it. I guess it's the feminist in me having a little revenge on the male sex for never dreaming a person could know about something like Egyptology and be a woman.'

'I hope I've shown I'm not of that school,' said the Treasurer. 'This is our Lecture Hall – or was. As you see, we're in the middle of packing up.'

As a veteran lorry-driver will find his reflexes coming into action at the start of a skid, even when driving an unfamiliar vehicle under exceptional road-surface conditions, or – perhaps more appropriately – as even the stupidest of field-mice will react usefully to shadow cast from overhead, so the Treasurer's mouth spoke away at the requisite words and creased into the right sort of welcoming, apologetic smile. He was to bless the Secretary's inspired thoroughness in organizing a periodic course of training whereby members split up into pairs and acted out a kind of charade, one man improvising the part of an inquisitive policeman, journalist, don or maniac, the other trying to keep him at verbal bay. But that bit of blessing was to come much later. For the moment his brain was like a small computer in overload.

Recent data included: the girl's rather broad shoulders and upright carriage, a query whether she might after all be a spy, the blackness of her hair and eyebrows, concern about how Furze

28

would react when he made his planned entry and saw her, her long oval grey eyes, a premonition that much of his own carefully rehearsed patter would now prove useless, the utter straightness of the girl's nose, and above all the urgency of devising an effective leave-taking. Or nearly above all. The smooth planes of her face under slightly prominent cheekbones were that.

One item that had failed to register on the Treasurer's receptors was the presence of an anonymous-looking black car diagonally across the street from the Society's premises. Had he had less on his mind he might well have taken it in during the few seconds he had stood at the threshold. Its occupant, a closely shaven young man in a neat blue suit, was new to his job, or he might have parked less conspicuously. But at the moment, unseen by anybody, he looked efficient enough, speaking into a radio hand-microphone and making an entry on a printed form clipped to a mill-board.

Meanwhile the Treasurer had a moment's respite to concentrate on the more immediate of his problems. Miss Lee Eddington Schwartz was examining the Lecture Hall. It was of modest size for such a title, having doubtless served, in another age, as a large dining-room or very small ballroom. Hanging from the ceiling, a couple of naked bulbs gave a harsh but thin light. At the end opposite the windows a platform had been put up, sufficient to accommodate a couple of chairs and a small table but just now accommodating only a bucket half full of dirty water. Near by lay the fat grey cylinder of a rolled-up carpet.

Miss Schwartz moved to the heavy double shelf of books, mainly bound in red leather, that ran along the wall nearest the passage. These included *Das Aegyptische Verbum, Les Temples Immergés de la Nubie, Mostagedda and the Tasian Culture, Reallexicon der Altaegyptischen Religionsgeschichte, Studies Presented to F. Ll. Griffith, Les Maximes de Ptahhotep, Das Grabdenkmal des Koenigs Ne-user-Re, Egypt* by J. Manchip White, *The Book of Ptath* by A. E. van Vogt. (This last was not really an Egyptological book at all, but a fantasy by that leading science-fiction writer. Isham had provided it. It sounded all right and, as he had pointed out, added bulk.)

Before she could have taken in more than a tithe of all this, Miss Schwartz turned towards the Treasurer, unbuttoning her pale-yellow mohair coat and sighing deeply. All three actions showed that her physical assets extended well below the neck. She wore a

29

brown velvet dress. She said in her clear voice, 'I'm sorry, I'm afraid I wasn't listening too closely. It's so nice to just run your eye over some of this old stuff again. A lot of what you have is way beyond me, though. Did you say something about packing up?'

'Yes – actually the books should have gone this afternoon.' The Treasurer indicated two empty tea-chests and a large box of shavings. 'I'm afraid I can't so much as offer you a chair. The Society's had to close down suddenly. We're all rather cut up about it.'

Miss Schwartz moved over to the platform, glancing swiftly over her shoulder to make sure the Treasurer was accompanying her. It was an attractively youthful gesture, as might have been expected from one so attractive and youthful – still on the right side of twenty-five, evidently. 'Oh, that is a shame,' she said. 'What was the trouble?'

The Treasurer grimaced. 'The usual. Money. We've always run a rather heavy lecturing programme for our size, and I just haven't been able to square things up – I handle the finances, for my sins – and ... well, none of us have the private means to take us far enough out of the red.'

Showing a pair of knees that were not far off as good as knees get, Miss Schwartz sat herself down on the edge of the platform. She seemed dejected. The Treasurer remained standing, his head moving quietly about as he manoeuvred for an advantageous downward glance.

'One thing I can do for you,' he said, 'is to give the Anglo-Egyptian Archaeological Institute a ring – you know, the big boys – and introduce you there. I know their Deputy Secretary reasonably well.'

This was standard Article 22 procedure. Before the Society had even been formed, Chester had had the good fortune to become acquainted with the official referred to at the Savile Club, to which both belonged. The acquaintance had remained one-sided, in the sense that the other man, a martyr to alcoholic amnesia, clearly never remembered Chester's name or anything about him. 'But he always pretends he knows who you are,' Chester had explained. 'I "reminded" him I was an accountant called Kalb-ffrench one lunch-time and a whisky-taster called Mitchell Courtenay the same evening and he was delighted to see me again both times.' Twice in the last year the Treasurer had unloaded difficult Article 22 cases by this route, telling them to go and see the chap and say who had sent them. No further action was required. One of the cases, an elderly American, had rung the Treasurer up the following week to deliver effusive thanks, plus the information that mentioning the Treasurer's name had 'sure done the trick'.

'Thank you very much.' Miss Schwartz's response to the Treasurer's offer lacked animation. 'But . . .'

'You'd find them far better value, you know. We're nothing more than a bunch of amateurs.'

'Oh, but that's the whole point. I took a look at the Institute and it was far too grand and stuffy for me. I'm an amateur myself. I like to dabble. This kind of thing' – she indicated the unimposing, half-bare room – 'would have been right down my alley. But what the hell, it's no use . . .'

Furze's knock sounded. On entering, he faced the Treasurer at attention and said, 'My apologies for intruding, sir, miss, but I did as you ordered this afternoon, sir, and the Electricity Board have laid down that the supply of power to these premises be terminated with effect from eleven hundred hours tomorrow. Have you any further instructions, sir?'

'I don't think so, Mr Furze, thank you. Any word from the estate agent?'

'No sir.'

'Right then, carry on, will you?'

'Yes sir.'

'Invaluable fellow, that,' said the Treasurer when Furze had gone. Only one who knew Furze's peculiarities, he supposed, could have seen in his demeanour just now that of a member of the League Against Cruel Sports 'being very good about' a sudden confrontation with the Master of the local hunt. To an uninstructed eye Furze must merely have appeared to have lost the use of his arm and neck muscles. Well, that miniature crisis had passed. Much trickier would be the task of fabricating what to say later upstairs if, as was likely, Furze should be among his listeners. There was an even more urgent problem, too.

'He looks . . .' Miss Schwartz was saying, pausing as it dawned on her what she was taking on in offering to apply an adjective to Furze, '. . . kind of efficient.'

'Remarkably. Look, Miss Schwartz, are you a reader at the British Museum?'

'No, I'm not.'

'How long are you going to be in England?'

'I'm not sure. Probably some months.'

'In that case I must insist that you allow me to arrange that for you.'

And insist he successfully did, adding that he would telephone her shortly. Preparing to depart, she suddenly asked, 'What's your particular field?'

If the Treasurer had not been slightly elated, he would not have said in a careless tone, 'Oh, I fool around a bit with the eighteenth Dynasty. Tombs and royal sculpture at Thebes and Amarna and one or two other places.'

'Deir?'

'I beg your pardon?'

'Deir el-Bahari?'

'Oh. No.'

'That temple of Hatshepsut must have been really something.'

'Yes.'

'But this is fascinating. I did my senior thesis on that period.'

'Really? Well, I'm afraid you'll have to excuse –'

She stood by the front door in a position that prevented him opening it, unless indeed he should choose to give her a buffet across the shoulder-blades with its upper panel. And he did not want to do that to her. She stepped aside suddenly in a way that indicated she had had abrupt and premature and over-explicit intimation of what he did want to do.

The Treasurer's brain accelerated. Opening the door carefully, he said, 'How's your ear?'

'Pardon me?'

'Or is it your nose?'

'I'm afraid I don't –'

'Then it must be your throat. I must say they all look all right to me, though.'

'Oh, Ear, Nose and Throat.' Standing by him in the open doorway, she laughed in a relieved as well as mirthful way. 'That was about my room-mate. The girl I share an apartment with. Just a little polyp on her septum.'

'Oh, that's all right, then.'

Her glance was bright and friendly now. 'It's been great meeting you. You've been very kind.'

Refusing his offer of helping her find a cab, she strode out into the chilly street. Moving on to the step, the Treasurer became aware of a crouching figure, some superterranean Morlock, near him in the gloom of the porch. It was Furze, pretending to unscrew the Society's name-plaque in implementation of one of the terminating clauses of Article 22 – a waste of effort in the present case, for the girl had not glanced at him. Actually the Treasurer had forgotten all about Article 22 for the moment.

'Gone then, has she, sir?'

'Yes, Mr Furze,' said the Treasurer heartily. 'She's gone all right. That's the end of her. Everything went according to plan.'

'I'm glad to hear it, sir.' Was there faint menace in Furze's tone? Had the amiability of Miss Schwartz's farewell communicated itself to him as suspect? Thank God, at any rate, that in parting she had not thought to mention the promised telephone-call.

'I could do with a drink,' the Treasurer said.

'I'll finish up here if that's all right, sir, and then come and see if there's anything further.'

Upstairs, the others crowded round the Treasurer.

'You were a hell of a time.'

'How did it go?'

'It was a little complicated,' said the Treasurer, 'but I managed it. We shan't be hearing any more from that quarter.'

'Are you sure?'

The Treasurer went over to the drinks cupboard before replying. He wanted to delay matters until Furze appeared. Pouring himself a Bell's and water, he said, 'Quite sure. But there was one totally unexpected feature.'

'What was it? Stop being so bloody mysterious.'

'You'll laugh your heads off.'

'Well, give us a chance to, for Christ's sake.'

Furze arrived at that moment, having lost no time in giving the screws on the plaque the required couple of clockwise turns and belting up to the Club Room for his free liquor-issue. He traditionally got a couple on Article 22 evenings.

The Treasurer's demeanour stiffened. 'Well, what do you

33

think of *that*, Mr Furze?' he asked, trying to 'rap' or 'snap' it.

'Disgusting, sir.'

'Lee Eddington Schwartz,' said the Treasurer impressively, 'our visitor – an ambiguous name, I think you'll agree – turned out to be a *girl*.'

His inflection made Cambuslang look at him in mild surprise. 'What was she like?' asked Froald.

'She was quite pleasant in so far as she knew how,' said the Treasurer, 'but that wasn't very far, since she didn't appear to know anything about anything. Not even Egyptology.'

The general mild tension, which had almost subsided at the Treasurer's initial pronouncement, now dissipated finally.

'Good-looking?' asked Froald.

'I simply couldn't say. She was so plastered with make-up it was impossible to tell what her face was really like.'

'A painted harlot, gentlemen,' said Furze.

'What about her figure?' asked Froald.

'Plump? Chubby? Portly? What would you say, Mr Furze?'

'Definitely on the stout side, sir.'

'Not badly dressed, I suppose,' said the Treasurer, looking judicial. 'Bit tasteless, though.'

'A typical Yank bint, gentlemen. More money than sense and more cheek than either.'

'That just about describes her. It really does.'

Furze rocked up and down on heel and toe for a moment or two, his eyes on the floor. Then, in a tone more animated than he had been heard to use for weeks, he said, 'Well, everything has passed off satisfactorily, it appears, gentlemen. Now I'll just set the Lecture Hall to rights and then I'll be off, if I may.'

When Furze had gone, aurally bowed out with an effusive chorus of good nights, Isham said to the Treasurer, 'Was that girl as bad as you said?'

The Treasurer was thinking that to have perceptibly cheered Furze up was a service to the Society that might be held to mitigate slightly his breach, imminent if not already committed, of Article 3: *No member shall have voluntary contact with any person known to possess any genuine Egyptological knowledge.* But now he roused himself to screw up his face and shrug his shoulders. 'Well . . . I suppose not *quite*,' he said.

4   Uninvited Guests

CLEOPATRA: How do you, women?
                    What, what, good cheer!

On the eve of Ladies' Night the Secretary convened a short
informal briefing session in the Club Room. No doubt cheered by
the news of Furze's improved morale and of the successful choking-
off (as he and all but the Treasurer supposed it to have been) of
Lee Eddington Schwartz, the Secretary was in excellent form, and
even joined in the laughter when the President took it upon himself
to offer a few practical demonstrations, including the 'scholarly
stoop', the 'excuse me while I check that reference' and, as reply
to being offered a drink, the 'good heavens no'.

Half an hour or so before the event was due to begin, the
Secretary and the Treasurer converged on the Society's premises
for a last minute check-up. Everything, of course, was in order,
thanks to Furze. The Secretary marked off items on his list while
the Treasurer verified each in turn. *Stove:* smoking. *Tablecloth:*
freshly laundered, but with old coffee-stains and undarned tears.
Glasses: cloudy. *Ashtrays:* removed. *Chairs:* dusty. *Broken chair:*
in position. And so on.

By seven o'clock eight members and five wives had assembled
in the Lecture Hall. The unaccompanied three were Mordle,
Cambuslang and the President. Not an advantageous selection,
thought Isham to himself as the Rich Golden South African sherry
went round, carefully slopped by Furze out of dirty-necked
decanters. The President's wife stayed in the memory as young and
well made, with an air of indiscipline that attracted even while it
boded faintly ill. Mordle's wife nagged him fairly unremittingly
in public, but was civil to other men. And Mrs Cambuslang was
somebody Isham positively wanted to see, to substantiate his
impression that she approximated fairly closely to her husband's
haggis-faced sister, described for the first time the other week – an
interesting sidelight on Cambuslang's objections to Egyptian
dynastic marriage. Whereas Mrs Froald . . .

That lady now appeared in front of Isham, who had been pretending to examine with fascination and delight the model of some primitive ship, crewed by a couple of dozen really rather horrifying little earthenware figures, that was one of the showpieces of the Lecture Hall. 'Still peering at your ridiculous lumber, I see,' she said by way of greeting, using the Polish accent she invariably used in his company, and no doubt in everyone else's too. She had been born and brought up in Poland.

He now peered at her instead. 'Good evening, Mrs uh . . .'

'Froald. We've met several times, though you probably don't remember.'

'Of course . . . of course . . .'

'Tell me, Mr Isham, how old are you?'

Isham, who had been wondering whether he dared throw in a 'bless my soul' or so, was startled back into his usual demeanour. 'Thirty-eight. Why?'

'And you are old already. Tell me, have you become old by always thinking of your mummies and your tombs, or do you think of these because you're old already?'

'Bit of both, I expect.'

'And you don't seem to mind.'

'Not much use minding, is there, what?'

'Urgh!' said Mrs Froald. 'So typical.'

'Yes, it is, very.'

They were now joined by Mrs Isham, who had given up Cambuslang as a bad job. Isham was usually quite glad on the whole to see his wife, but wished she could have held off a couple of minutes longer this time. He might then have been able to provoke Mrs Froald into one of her famous denunciations of the English, even, possibly, into the legendary 'You English, you are so cold!' which Chester had sworn blind to having heard her mutter last year. But Chester was a wild fellow, over-addicted to exaggeration.

'Well, here we are again,' observed Mrs Isham.

'Yes, and why do we come?' asked Mrs Froald.

'Well, I imagine we all like to take a little interest in what our men-folk do in their spare time, don't we?'

'Myself I hate these assemblings, I abominate them. They are so dead, so –'

'In that case, my dear, I might put your question back to you.

Why do you come? Because you do come, don't you? very regularly. As far as I know you haven't missed a single one of these gatherings for eighteen months or more. Why not?'

'Oh,' roared Mrs Froald, 'he gives me no peace, he keeps on at me until I promise to come, I can't get to sleep till he persuades me.'

Isham reflected that, whatever her shortcomings, the woman was quite shrewd enough to see through her husband's protestations to his very real hope that she would stay away from the do. Froald himself had said that when the roll was called up yonder he would at least get credit for having given a formerly rootless, drifting person an aim in life: doing the opposite of what he wanted at all times. He must have a word with Froald and tell him to play it a bit cooler.

'You mustn't let him tyrannize over you,' Mrs Isham was saying with a smile. 'Persist in having your own way occasionally. After all, there should be some give-and-take in every marriage. Shouldn't there, darling?'

'Of course,' said Isham.

'Really Irina – I may call you Irina, mayn't I? – I hate to see you being trampled underfoot like this. And it's not difficult to turn the tide. Just say quite firmly, "I'm afraid I'd rather go to the pictures, darling" – or whatever it may be – and stick to it. Don't argue; just don't give an inch. He'll respect you for it in the end, my dear, I know he will. And the second time it'll all be much easier.'

Isham pretended to return a signal from across the room and slipped away. He felt he could safely leave his wife to it – more than that, the less time he spent in her company this evening the better. She was an inquisitive woman with an instinct for situations in which it would be hard to shut her up. He himself might suffer when he got home for having 'shunned her like the plague' all the evening, but his duty to the Society was clear.

He found Mordle and Cambuslang in the midst of an argument – Egyptians again, thank God, not Scotsmen – and Mrs Chester and the Treasurer's wife looking on. Cambuslang was throwing himself into it with such a will that Mordle, it was pretty clear to Isham, was wondering how much of it, if any, was a mere Ladies'-Night act. His voice was moving up into the treble much in the way it had during their for-real dispute two or three weeks earlier. Even Isham needed some little reassurance, to be found in the depth of Cambuslang's 'scholarly stoop' and his occasional use of the 'trembling explicatory forefinger', another Presidential routine. Without his wife there he could afford to let himself go.

'In any true civilization,' said Cambuslang, munching his lips together as he paused, 'in any civilization *worthy of the name*, what do we find as its distinguishing characteristic? Not the rearing of vast and vulgar monuments such as our friend here seems to find so impressive, so much so indeed that the contemplation of them appears to have, uh, mm, eh – *robbed him of the power of connected thought* . . .'

'But *I* didn't bring them up, *you* did,' brayed Mordle. 'I'm a *miniaturist*, I like what's *small* and *exquisite*, I'd give *all* the damned pyramids for a couple of Rembrandt drawings, say, or a vase from –'

'Are you denying the worth of what was undoubtedly the mightiest engineering feat of modern times having due regard for the facilities available and understanding by "modern" the last half-dozen millennia? Shocking irreverence, sir!'

'*No*,' said Mordle, sliding up a major second, 'it was *you* who –'

'Enough, enough, enough,' thundered Cambuslang. 'Back to the *point*, man! What distinguishes a true civilization?'

He turned to the two women. This movement adhered strictly to the Secretary's prescription for stimulating donnishness by affecting to assume that all the world was about as well up in your subject as you were, besides according with Cambuslang's natural inclinations, but it was unwise. The prettier of the two, the Treasurer's wife, giggled slightly and said, 'You tell us ' – she was merely being irreverent. But Mrs Chester, a dark blonde with a peachy skin, looked coolly at the Scotsman. Isham saw her eyes narrow. Cambuslang, after five large pink gins upstairs to fortify himself for the occasion, was certainly hamming it up. Worse, he had lost regard for continuity, so that his voice, pursuing contrary motion to Mordle's, had gone down by nearly an octave since first mooting the distinguishing mark of a true civilization. If Mrs Chester was really observant and got talking to Isham's wife, a dangerous team might quite conceivably achieve formation. Time to intervene.

'I wonder how you'd apply that to the Ptolemaic period, Cambuslang,' said Isham. 'Wouldn't you agree that the later kings were far less – ?'

'Ay, that does put rather a different complexion upon it,' said Cambuslang consideringly. 'I'm afraid you'll have to excuse me while I check that reference.' And he ambled off.

'That always shuts him up,' said Isham laughingly; 'it's his weak spot and he knows it.' This was a misleading explanation. Any reference to the Ptolemaic period was to be taken as tonight's code-word – there was a fresh one for every Ladies' Night – meaning *Get lost instantly: explanations afterwards.*

'He's a funny old chap, isn't he?' said the Treasurer's wife.

'I know,' said Isham, still laughingly, looking at Mrs Chester; 'he's like a caricature of a university don. Of course he was one for some years, you know, up in Scotland.' This was wholly untrue: Cambuslang had come to London at the age of twenty-two and had remained south of the Tweed ever since. 'He's a bit touchy about it, as a matter of fact. He'd probably deny it fiercely if you taxed him with it.' You could say that again and again, Isham thought to himself.

'He sounds a bit of a case,' said the Treasurer's wife. 'But then I suppose you've got to remember he's Scotch. They're different to us, aren't they? I mean, I don't mean they're not as good as us, nothing like that, but, well, let's face it, they're different, aren't they?' she finished confidently.

'That's perfectly true,' said Isham in tones of weighty approval. It was doubly charming to hear such sentiments issuing from such a mouth, from someone whose prettiness in general was so markedly, almost tangibly, non-virginal.

Mrs Chester's watchful air, he was glad to see, had tapered off. She said mildly, 'I thought he was putting it on.'

'Quite between ourselves, I think he does. A lot of the time, anyway.'

'Funny chap,' said Mordle. 'Funny chap.' He shook his long-haired head.

'Academics aren't normal men,' said Mrs Chester.

'Are you kidding?' asked the Treasurer's wife.

There was a pause. A few feet away, Chester and the Treasurer passed by on their up-and-down promenade, talking volubly but indistinguishably, hands clasped behind back. They were performing the 'Balliol quad peripatetic duologue' the President had demonstrated earlier with Froald, somewhat miscast, called forward to act as his partner. At the moment, actually, Chester was doing the talking, with all the appearance of one propounding defects in portrayal to be found in certain statues of Amenophis, son of Hapu. In fact, Isham learnt not long afterwards, Chester was telling a long dialect story about manifold immorality in a Welsh village. Farther off, Isham could see Froald, the President and the Secretary grouped in a listening triangle round the Secretary's fat rich wife. She appeared to be in full monologue, celebrating, if previous experience was any guide, the virtues of television quiz-shows or of frozen foods.

Mrs Chester looked slowly round the Lecture Hall. 'It's not that I'm carping,' she said, 'but wouldn't you agree that the decor in here leaves something to be desired?'

'I think,' said Isham, 'I *think* I would. If challenged.'

'You all seem so sold on Ancient Egypt, I can't believe that with just a little imagination you couldn't run up something more or less in keeping, something with a bit of atmosphere about it. A large aerial photograph of a pyramid or a sphinx, even, filling the whole of one wall – that would be a start, surely.'

'Ah,' said Mordle, 'what resources we have go into our lectures, I'm afraid. We haven't anything left over for the . . . niceties, unfortunately.'

'I'll say you haven't,' said the Treasurer's wife.

'I think if the things of the mind really appeal to one,' Mordle went on, 'what happens to be around one hardly impinges on one. What the inner eye sees is so much more absorbing and, uh, durable, don't you think?'

This was good boring stuff, but Isham saw no reason why Mordle should set about boring him as well as the women. Furthermore, the man seemed to believe what he was saying. And yet, Isham considered, he could hardly send him packing with a second reference to the Ptolemaic period. What was to be done?

Froald, looking slightly punch-drunk after half an hour with the Secretary's wife, arrived at his side. Just then, the Treasurer's wife, beating at a wisp of the brownish fog that emanated from the stove, said,

'Awfully stuffy in here, isn't it?'

Isham at once set in motion the procedure it had been agreed should follow any such remark. 'Mr Furze!' he called.

Furze looked up smartly. 'Sir?' He was using his handkerchief to clean the neck of a newly opened bottle of Rich Golden.

'Can we have some air in here, please?'

'Sir!'

With the eager stride he might once have used when marching defaulters in front of his company commander, Furze proceeded to the main window and threw the catch with a flourish. Then, by moving the top half down and the bottom half up until they exactly overlapped, thus ensuring the optimum circulation of air, he began admitting the damp March night by the cubic yard. Two side windows added converging streams. The door followed, but within a few seconds the draught took it and hurled it back into its frame with a noise like thunder, only much shorter and not so loud.

During the various reactions to this, Froald said, 'Could I have a word with you, Isham? In the Club Room, I think.'

First taking from the shelves Breasted's *History of Egypt* as cover, Isham followed Froald upstairs. When each had poured himself a drink and signed a chit, Froald said, 'You know I'm a meteorologist? In the Ministry?'

'So I'd always understood.'

'My job is correlating the reports from our various stations, marking up the map and so on. It's not quite so dull as it sounds. The chap at our Bass Rock post turns in some very odd stuff. I always look forward to his contribution. Only the other day he . . .'

Froald went on to talk about last month's rain of blood and – on January 3rd of that year, after two days of complete silence – the spirit of God moving upon the face of the waters at lat. 56° 6′ 44″ N., long. 2° 26′ 3″ W.

'How do you mark that in on your map?' asked Isham.

'You can't really. No, what I do, I just infer what's really going on from what the fellows either side of him say. But I just told you that because I thought it might interest you. What I really wanted to talk to you about is quite different.'

Isham glanced up. He had assumed that Froald had approached him merely to gain moral support for seeking out a larger and stronger and nicer drink than that available downstairs. But the chap sounded worried. He even looked it, which was unheard of. Shortly after meeting Mrs Froald for the first time, the Treasurer had suggested that her husband's habitual serenity of countenance must testify to a great inner strength, perhaps even a beauty of spirit, denied to more complex personalities. However that might be, Isham felt he ought to have noticed earlier the dark tan colour of the wineglass of Teacher's and water Froald was demolishing – and he normally temperate to a fault. Isham said with some concern, 'What's up?'

'I didn't like to bother any of the Society's officers at a time like this, so I . . . There's somebody called Maggs works in my office, very much a, you know, genial sort of –'

'Man-to-man man?'

'Well, yes. Anyway, we got chatting over a cup of coffee, and he said he thought it was a pity we didn't see as much of each other as we used to. He said that a year ago he could usually count on seeing me in the Nag's Head in Whitehall after work on Thursdays, but I never seemed to turn up now. I said vaguely I'd got into the way of dropping in at a club about that time. Then he shook me. "Would that be the Egyptological Society?" he wanted to know.'

'What did you tell him?'

'I didn't dare deny it. I just gave him Article 19 pretty well in full – surprised he'd heard of it, just a little bunch of hobbyists, expect he'd find it rather dull and so forth. *Then* he said, "I think I should tell you that the Security people have got some doubts about this Society of yours." What do you think of that?'

For a moment Isham was shaken, as Froald had doubtless been, by a feeling common among members of secret groups – that their opponents are equally well organized, but on a much vaster scale, and have just set in motion against them the whole apparatus of the State. 'My God,' he said with feeling.

'I told him that was nonsense,' Froald went on, 'and he said everyone was satisfied *I* was perfectly okay, but there could be things going on within the Society I didn't know about, and had I noticed anything that might point in that direction? That bothered me, I can tell you. Tell me, Isham: there's the Society as you and I and the rest of us know it and there's the Society as the outside world sees it – d'you think it's possible there's some sort of inner ring with a different purpose that's using the Society as a blind or a front or whatever it is? I know I can trust you, but – what about Mordle, for instance? And Chester – we've seen almost nothing of him for months, and he turns up tonight and brings his wife along too. Why? Honestly, I'm . . .'

'And the President. He founded the thing.'

Froald nodded gravely. 'He did.'

'I'll have to think about it. Anyway, was that all?'

'All Maggs said? Far from it. The next thing he did was to hand me one of the typescript copies of our programme for the season, with an "X" against one of the events – what we've got laid on for May 21st. What it boiled down to was this. The programme had been found left out on a desk in some other Ministry among some restricted documents. The whole bundle was taken to the Security man on duty as a matter of routine. As it happens, this chap is a cryptological wizard and had nothing better to do at the time, so he started working on our programme more or less out of curiosity. And came up with an anagram. Under May 21st it said, *Prof. L. Stone Caton*: Set (*D.V.*) – you know, just in case –'

'I know. And?'

'If you juggle with the letters, that gives you *Send p-l-t Rostov at once. F.* I've checked it myself.'

'What's *F* supposed to be, for a start?'

'I think I can give you what Maggs said more or less verbatim. I've got pretty good at that in the last year or so.'

Isham nodded. 'One has to.'

'I'll have a shot, anyway. "Our people use the sixth letter of our alphabet to designate the Sixth Division of the Soviet Military Intelligence – they do the same, only it's the letter 'zh' in their case. The point is that it's the section dealing with our positions in the Middle East. Rostov is a fairly obvious centre for operations directed southwards into that area – you've probably heard they don't like to put their D.S.S. stations too close to the part of the world they cover – and the whole thing makes an Egyptological front sound like a piece of sardonic humour."'

'Is the bit about humour you or Maggs?'

'Maggs. I told him it didn't sound quite in the Russian style.'

'Mm. What did he say to that?'

'Reckoned a Georgian might have thought it up, or an Armenian. Got an answer for everything, these boys, haven't they? Then he wanted to know how much contact we have with Cairo. I soon straightened him out there. Even then that wasn't the lot. He pointed out . . . there must be a copy of the – here we are. There.'

Isham read aloud, '*Metal Statuettes of Set in the Delta and at Thebes*. Well? If that's another anagram it must be a pretty powerful one.'

'No, Maggs just asked me what the Roman equivalent of Set was.'

'God of the Underworld? I suppose Pluto would be the closest you'd get – '

'That's what I said, anyway. And Maggs said yes, and what metal did I associate with Pluto, and before I could answer he said "plutonium", and didn't that connect up with the "p-l-t" bit in the anagram?, and then he told me it might all be coincidence and I was to keep my eyes and ears open and if I didn't come up with anything suspicious there *probably* wouldn't be an investigation. And then I sort of found myself outside the canteen again without remembering how I got there.'

'I know how you felt,' said Isham. 'But look, all this is pretty far-fetched, isn't it? I thought Swift had taken the piss out of the anagrammatic method for good and all.'

'Maggs kept agreeing it was far-fetched, but he said these things often are. Neither of us mentioned Swift.'

'Let's go back a bit. What about this business about the copy of the programme being found on someone's desk in another Ministry? I've been trying to run through the membership in my mind. As far as I can see the only chap it can be is . . .'

Froald nodded grimly. 'Chester.'

'This takes us round again to where we were a few minutes ago. Look, Froald, do you think perhaps there's something in this after all?'

'How do you mean?'

'Well, we know, that's to say you and I know that the Society doesn't exist to provide cover for a ring of spies, but I suppose it is conceivable that it might contain one. Who drafted the yearly programme, by the way?'

44

'The President – he's always been keen on it since he discovered the queer professor in Brighton.'

'Oh. Talking of queers, what about Mordle?'

'He certainly talks like one,' said Froald thoughtfully.

'And he said tonight he liked exquisite things.'

'And you did know he earns his living by advising some building firm on interior decoration?'

'Christ, and what about the President – who introduced him, you remember?'

'You mean this actor business of his? A lot of them are pooves, aren't they? As I was saying, there may be rings within rings, even if they aren't spy ones. I wonder if there are any concealed cupboards and things in here.' Froald got up and started tapping the walls.

'What do you expect to find? – a secret store of pictures of blokes dressed up as the Queen of Sheba? Anyway, no time for any of that now, we've been away long enough as it is. Let's go down and make the party go with a swing.'

Downstairs there was a tremendous splintering crash, followed by shouting and screaming and heavy footfalls.

'Sounds as if things are going with a swing already,' said Isham.

'Sounds like my wife,' said Froald.

'We'd better get there and have a look.'

As they drained their drinks, one or more sets of the heavy footfalls started up the stairs, and before they could reach the door it was flung open. A policeman in uniform, and another and horribly ugly man who soon turned out to be a policeman but was not in uniform, came in.

'Right, stay where you are, please.'

'What's this all about?'

'I'll do the talking.'

This announcement proved to be more the reservation of a right than the notice of an intention, for the speaker and his colleague said nothing as they looked Nefertiti up and down, turned over the piles of magazines (setting aside some of these for removal), looked hopefully into the cupboards and, more expertly but no more fruitfully than Froald had just done, tapped the walls. Then, at a nod from the plain-clothes man, the uniformed man started for the inner room. 'There's nothing in there,' said Isham mechanically, 'it's just an office,' but he was already certain that all was lost: all the records of the Society – the Constitution, the pamphlets and directives, the log books and minute books – lay on or in the Secretary's desk.

There was the sound of a drawer being forced open. Isham wanted to say to Froald that Maggs must have worked fast, that all good things come to an end, that whatever happened it had been worth it, but he kept silent. He felt as if he were already on trial.

5 State of Emergency

EROS: There's strange news come, sir.

No arrests were made that night, and after answering a few questions, too few for any overall drift to become discernible, members and wives were allowed to go to their homes. The Secretary called an emergency meeting at the Society's premises for 1 p.m. the next day.

The Treasurer, as his taxi circumnavigated Marble Arch shortly before that hour, was gloomy to a degree he seldom allowed himself. His wife's wonderment about what was going on, what was behind it all, who the police thought they were and related questions had remained unimpaired by time and sleep. She had gone on voicing it until he stepped into the lift outside their World's End flat. He had spent most of the later morning arguing with a drunken buyer who had bulk-ordered seventeen hundredweight of flood-damaged hairpins, sufficient to satisfy demand – provided public taste did not alter and the corrosion of the metal proceeded only slowly – for the next quarter of a century. All this had exhausted the Treasurer's energy, sapped as it was by apprehension. He tried to cheer himself up by reflecting on what was in a way the oddest circumstance of the previous evening: the Inspector in charge of the raid squad had seemed puzzled and slightly angry, as if, possibly, he had not found what he was looking for. But he had done no more than glance at the various documents taken from the office before giving orders for them to be parcelled up and removed. So . . .? Gazing abstractedly out of the window, the Treasurer suddenly caught the eye of a pretty girl in a bus. She raised her eyebrows and pouted. He shoved himself back into the corner of the seat as if she had pulled a gun on him.

Two workmen were replacing the lower pane of the Lecture Hall window through which the police had made their entry. Five minutes earlier they could have stepped into the room without fuss or damage, but Mrs Froald had soon countered Furze's ventilation measures.

When the Treasurer reached the Club Room, Froald was just finishing an account of the Maggs business for the benefit of Mordle and the Secretary. They listened as closely when he recapitulated it to the Treasurer.

After a moment's silence the Secretary, paler even than usual, said loudly, 'I blame myself entirely for what has happened. But at the moment blame seems a waste of time. The police are telephoning me here at two o'clock. We shall presumably know then what action they are proposing to take, and can begin to devise counter-action. Meanwhile we must reach certain decisions.'

'Who else is coming?' asked the Treasurer.

'Cambuslang is presumably on his way here. Isham and the President are tied up. I couldn't reach Chester at all. In fact the girl on the switchboard at his office seemed never to have heard of him.'

'The swine,' said Mordle. 'Left the programme on his desk, did he? By an oversight, no doubt. Ha ha ha. Traitor. All that geniality was a mask, you see. Filthy spy.'

The Secretary did a vigorous headshake. 'Out of the question,' he declared. 'A spy would never have allowed his identity to become known to one of us. A spy would have been among us all the time, whereas Chester has hardly been seen since Christmas. A spy would have been infiltrated into the group after its existence had become known to the authorities, whereas Chester was one of us from the very beginning. A spy would . . .'

Aware at last of the silence that surrounded his words, the Secretary broke off. Froald was glaring and the Treasurer staring at Mordle, who lifted one ham off the seat of his chair as if about to make a run for it. The Secretary intervened, saying firmly,

'That's enough of that. A movement like ours is peculiarly subject to internal suspicions. These are lethal. Let me reiterate once again the vital truth that what the outside world, what every element hostile to us *desires above all*, is domestic disagreement, internecine enmity. If we yield to these, we perish far more certainly and irrevocably than by any external force. Let's see that clearly. Let's keep our heads, shall we? Agreed?'

There was no dissension.

'Very well then. Chester appears to have committed a very grave breach of security, for which he deserves a reprimand, probably a fine, perhaps even expulsion, but not –'

'If there's anything left by tomorrow to expel him from,' said Froald.

During the ensuing depressed silence Cambuslang arrived. When he had mixed himself a pink gin and been put in the picture, he said,

'There's something here that doesn't fit. Surely to God it's obvious? If the Security boys had wanted to find out what we were up to they'd have got a warrant and simply seized all our documents. The whole thing would have been done far more discreetly. No need to have gone in for all that kerfuffle, smashing windows and waving truncheons. And they wouldn't have let us out of their sight, either. And why pick a night when the place is full of women? Unless . . .'

'The Vice Squad,' said the Secretary flatly.

'Exactly.'

'Well, that shouldn't bother us, should it?' said Mordle.

The Secretary made an exasperated face and noise. 'How often must I point out that *any* investigation into the affairs of the Society is dangerous? And I see no cause for cheer in the presumption that there are now *two* bodies whose curiosity we've aroused, instead of one. It may be better to take it that this is so. Very well. I propose that the Committee concoct a long circumstantial story, all about our total and proven innocuousness, designed to lull the suspicions of the man Maggs and his friends, and that Froald be coached in it until he's word-perfect. Plus some phony documentations. Is that agreed? Right.

'Now to the more immediate matter. We can do nothing for the moment towards framing a tactical policy, but we can determine what our overall attitude is to be. As I see it, if we go down, we go down fighting. No surrender, no confessions, no appeals for mercy, no disbandment, no flight. Total resistance. Are you with me? No, I insist on a show of hands.'

Cambuslang and the Treasurer signified instantly, Froald a moment later, Mordle after glancing round at the others.

'Thank you, that's most encouraging. One last small point. Work on the Isis Room was due to start next Monday. I take it you wish me to have this deferred for the time being?'

This was agreed amid some laughter. As during previous crises (though none of these had approached the intensity of the present one), the Secretary's air of clarity and resource had a calming effect on other members. They were heartened, too, by the short speech Furze made when he brought in ham and tongue sandwiches and bottles of Whitbread light ale and Guinness.

'Well, gentlemen,' he said, 'I needn't tell you how sorry I am at this unfortunate turn of events. But this I do want to say. I'm as much your man as ever I was. Nothing will ever shake my allegiance to all you gentlemen. I'd go into the box this minute and swear blind black was white if I thought it would be of service, *and* I'd regard it as a very small return for all your kindness and moral support.'

The faithful fellow was warmly thanked and rewarded with a small whisky, with which he drank to the continuing prosperity of the Society. When he had gone, Froald said,

'I have had an extremely significant dream.'

This, spoken in a serious tone, caused some stir. Under Article 29 no spiritualist, oneiromancer, Ouspenskyite, theosophist, astrologer, Gurdjieff-fan or otherworlder of any kind was eligible for membership of the Society. Apart from anything else, it was felt that such persons might fall into pyramidology, and what then? But for the prevailing lowered morale on this occasion, Froald would probably not have been allowed to continue. As it was, he went on to stress the vividness of this dream, so marked that he was almost tempted to call it an experience rather than a dream, a *proleptic* experience.

Like most imaginative people, he continued, he had a rather literal mind. And so, as they knew, he was a keen reader of science fiction. Last night, her malefic powers tuned to concert pitch by the raid, his wife had brought him to the stage of locking himself in the spare room, where he had presumably fallen into an uneasy doze. In the middle of the room there had appeared a blank and colourless oval which he had at once recognized, from his reading of Mr Robert A. Heinlein's works, as a Time Gate projected from the future. Through it had emerged two men who plainly intended him to accompany them back whence they came. He had been in a stubborn mood, and was on the point of refusing to go when a girl joined the men. She was dressed in tight tights of a silvery colour. The men had had the sense to let her do the persuading.

'How tight?' asked Cambuslang casually.

'Very tight. Or rather,' said Froald in a thoughtful tone, 'they seemed to lie close to the skin without the bulging effect that usually goes with tightness.'

The Treasurer said, 'From the point of view of textile technique that's –'

'Let him tell it,' said Cambuslang.

'They took me to some sort of party,' said Froald, jumping ahead a little, 'and I had two quick long strong funny-tasting drinks. It was in the middle of a park.'

'Whereabouts?' asked the Treasurer.

'London, I suppose. Not on Mars or anywhere like that. There were plenty of girls around, I can be quite definite as far as that goes.'

'From the way you're talking,' said Mordle, 'the *girl* aspect of this supposed visit to the future or whatever you like to call it appears to have made a profound impression upon you. Have you any useful *general* observations to offer on the way the whole problem had evidently worked itself out in the years that lie, presumptively, ahead?'

Froald stood for a space considering, half a ham sandwich delicately held near his face like some aristocratic poison pill. 'There seemed to be perfect freedom. It looked as if marriage had become disused. I think I remember putting down two credits fifty for a book that dealt with the whole question, but after those drinks I'm afraid I can't tell you what it was on about.'

'That is very understandable,' said Cambuslang. 'But look; Froald; my dear boy; now; please; a simple query. Was the standard of feminine beauty higher in this . . . place you apparently think you got to?'

'Oh yes. They were all beautiful. And,' Froald spoke with unusual readiness, 'don't give me that line about beauty only existing in comparison to ugliness. I like all sorts of chocolate, don't I? So why couldn't people just be beautiful and more beautiful?'

'This rather reflects on the authenticity of your tale,' said Cambuslang. 'Sheer blatant wish-fulfilment.'

'Wet blanket,' muttered the Treasurer.

'What were their voices like?' the Secretary suddenly asked.

'Fine,' said Froald indifferently.

'Were there any real innovations at all?' asked Mordle.

Froald abruptly took fire. 'I'll say. Girls could change the shape of their body more or less from day to day if they wanted to. I never made out whether this was done by some sort of super-surgical business, or whether they used a self-hypnotizing technique that produced physical effects, like stigmata only more fun. But anyway they could do it as easily as present-day girls fiddle about with their make-up and hair-style. Nothing to it.'

'It just occurs to me,' said the Treasurer, 'that if you'd got this system of changing your physique – I mean if they'd got it – plus ways of changing your personality via drugs – that's already been established, surely – then, Christ, monogamy would become possible.'

An awed silence fell. Then Cambuslang said, 'Tell me, if you will, did you, in this dream of yours or whatever, did you have any sexual experiences?'

'No. But I did find out a certain amount. There was a girl standing about when a kind of jazz started being played. Not unlike Stan Getz but with a range of tonal variation you couldn't imagine.'

There was a bustle of uninterest. Mordle in particular was heard to offer observations in a querulous but well-modulated voice. 'Get on if you must,' murmured the Secretary.

'Well, people were just *different*. For instance, I asked this girl about her boy-friend. I asked her what he did. These days she'd say he worked in a bank or drove a lorry. D'you know what she said? "Everything."'

'I wouldn't set too much store by that if I were you,' said Mordle. 'There are plenty of little trollops about today who'd say much the same thing if they thought it would shock an older person.'

'I'm not as much as an older person as that, surely to God,' said Froald anxiously. 'Am I? I'm only –'

Cambuslang took the last sandwich. 'Oh, use your head, laddie, you were the Man from the Past. If Godwin or Havelock Ellis could be resurrected we'd think them pretty damned antique, eh?'

'It doesn't seem to amount to very much,' said the Secretary.

'Apart from this last rather nebulous matter, it strikes me that the advances, if to be properly so called, were not much above the cosmetic level.'

It was later agreed that, by telling his story, Froald had provided valuable distraction, sustaining the morale of the membership at what had a strong claim to be considered its darkest hour (so far). A resolution commending him on behaviour consonant with the finest traditions of the Society was to suggest itself to the Treasurer as a proper agendum for the next General Meeting (should there be one). But at the moment Froald seemed to think he had been rounded on rather. Blushing slightly, he said,

'What more do you want? Beauty, freedom – more than one kind of freedom, too. One girl at the party was dressed in nothing but long black stockings and long black gloves. And nobody looked on it as at all out of the way.'

'Well, they bloody well should have done,' growled Cambuslang. 'Any time you see me confronted by a naked female torso and not looking on it as at all out of the way you'll know the end is near.'

'In any case, are you sure you didn't synthesize that from one of those photographs outside Raymond's Revue Bar?' asked the Treasurer.

Froald opened his mouth to reply, but whether in agreement or rebuttal was fated to remain unknown, for at that moment the telephone rang. The Treasurer never forgot or ceased to admire the way in which the Secretary stubbed out his cigarette, rose easily from his chair, walked at a moderate pace over to the instrument and settled himself on a hard chair beside it before picking up the receiver. It connected with something he had once heard General Horrocks say in a television programme: that during battle the hardest task of his day had been to walk, not run, across from his tent to the command post for the morning situation reports.

The Secretary said, 'Yes? Right,' and rang off.

They all looked at him.

'That was the President,' said the Secretary, adjusting his glasses. 'He's dodged out of his meeting and is on his way here.'

Mordle threw his head aside in a pettish gesture. 'I can't stand the suspense,' he told them, but none of them had more than another half-minute of it.

When the telephone rang again the Secretary's response was more immediate. 'Yes? Yes, speaking. Good afternoon, Superintendent. Yes, I do. Yes, I would. Yes, it would. I see. Just the other two members of our Committee, if I may. No, I don't think so. Yes. Good-bye.'

He put down the receiver. 'Somebody claiming to be a Superintendent will see the President, the Treasurer and myself as soon as we care to go round to Scotland Yard. He asked if I was going to bring a solicitor along and you heard me say no. His tone was non-committal, of course, but quite polite. There was nothing else worth mentioning.'

'More suspense,' said Mordle.

'Suspense is our condition,' said the Secretary.

6 Interview at the Yard

The President, Secretary and Treasurer duly presented themselves at Scotland Yard and were at once shown up to a small but dignified office where the Superintendent, rising from his chair, welcomed them courteously. The Inspector who had led the raid, all jaw and no forehead, stood scowling slightly. No doubt he had been briefing his superior. On a table in the corner the Treasurer noticed a small record-player plugged into the wall. The seized documents and files were heaped on the Superintendent's desk.

The Superintendent made a rather favourable impression, in spite of a very long and slanting sort of nose. He had something of the dignified air of a young Irish senator who has, very recently indeed, decided to abandon the slap-happy political methods of youth for the role of junior elder statesman. A slight touch of grey round his temples pointed up this effect, as did the twin nebulas of burst capillaries on his cheeks. All this was particularly welcome in contrast to the Inspector, whose jaw, now viewed by the Treasurer for the first time under relatively peaceful conditions, was so heavily under-slung that strong grounds were given for considering it a fake, like the one attached to the Piltdown skull.

The Superintendent said, 'All right, Inspector, you can leave me with these gentlemen.'

'Sure you wouldn't rather I stayed, sir?'

'Quite sure.'

'There are one or two points, sir, which I might –'

The Superintendent looked up as if astonished. He said briefly, 'No. I've got all the points.'

With a clumsy reluctance the Inspector left them, nodding very curtly.

Without a word the Superintendent rose again, went to the record-player and lowered the head on to a record already placed on the turntable.

A human voice issued from the loudspeaker, evidently speaking at considerable volume, but situated so far from the microphone that all that could be determined of it with any certainty was its pontifical tone and its marked Central European accent. (It was one of the President's most assured performances.) Occasionally a word or phrase struggled across the threshold of audibility: '... Sesostris II ... se Book of se Dead ... obelisks ... in se Delta ... ointment-cones ... Mut ... Nut ... Wreszinski's *Atlas* ... se high priest of Sos ... Sis ...' The foreground of the recording was a tissue of coughs, feet-shufflings, nose-blowings, match-strikings and the odd snort or chair-scrape.

After a couple of minutes the Superintendent removed the needle and switched off the machine. Returning to his chair, he said, 'I had the curiosity to play through both sides of that record. It's all like that, as you know, except for a few minutes on side two when a couple of chaps ask questions and you can't hear the answers. A most remarkable disc, I thought.'

'You mustn't make fun of us, Superintendent,' said the Secretary. 'We wanted to preserve that lecture by some means or other because Professor Asimov publishes so little – out of modesty: he's a world authority. The idea came to us very late on and this was the best we could do at short notice. As you can hear, the microphone was in pretty well the worst position possible. We're just a bunch of amateurs, I'm afraid.'

'Oh, I don't agree at all, sir,' said the Superintendent, bringing his hand down with a smack on the pile of documents. 'All this is highly professional. Tell me, have any of you gentlemen ever had any security training?'

'I was in Field Security during the war, yes,' said the Secretary.

'I see, sir ... I suppose it didn't occur to you to hire a shorthand bloke to take down your Professor's speech?'

'Not until it was too late.'

'Of course. And in the same sort of way no doubt you couldn't get hold of a tape-recorder?'

'As I say, we didn't think of doing anything at all until the last minute, by which time all the shops were shut. None of us happens to have a tape-recorder of his own.'

'Just so,' said the Superintendent. 'But one of you happens to have a record-recording machine, so to speak.'

'Yes. A very old-fashioned one, as perhaps you can tell.'

'I'm afraid my ears aren't good enough for that, sir. However, that's not the only, shall we say?, interesting thing about this record. Here's the cover it was in. Rather inappropriate, isn't it?'

The cover said, in green crayon on plain cardboard, *Ancient Egyptian Music and Musical Instruments in the New Kingdom/London Pro Musica Antiqua Ensemble.*

'It was in the wrong cover,' said the Secretary. 'I'm afraid I don't find that at all significant. Do you?'

'No. No, I don't. But it's a great pity that the record that belongs to this cover isn't in its right place. I'd very much have liked to hear it. Because, according to all the authorities I've been able to consult – Sachs, Farmer and one or two others – nothing is known about what Ancient Egyptian music sounded like, New Kingdom or Old Kingdom or any other kind of Kingdom. Nothing whatsoever.'

'This is really my department,' said the Treasurer. 'I'm the guilty party for having wished this ... white elephant on the Society.'

'White crocodile,' laughed the President.

The other three looked at him for a moment.

'It was a private recording,' went on the Treasurer, 'and very expensive. I got a copy out of curiosity. It started off not too badly, with a number of notes being blown on various temple instruments of the horn or trumpet family, so that however little we may know for certain about the melodies and rhythms of the Pharaohs' music, we can at any rate enjoy some of its characteristic timbres.'

The Superintendent had placed his hand over his mouth. 'Go on, please, sir,' he said in a muffled voice.

'That part, as I say, was respectable enough, if not very informative. But there followed a so-called recital of short pieces in which an attempt was made to suggest what Egyptian music *might* have sounded like. There was a spoken introduction by some musicologist, claiming that something could be deduced from the position of the musicians' hands in the various friezes and paintings – only as applied to stringed instruments, of course. But, honestly, it sounded to me as if they were just strumming and blowing as the mood took them. Yes, we'd been taken down for three guineas. I threw the damned thing into the dustbin.'

'I wonder you didn't do the same with your Professor's record.'

'Oh, no,' said the Treasurer in shocked tones. 'We kept it out of sentiment. It recalled the occasion to us.'

'I see, sir. Just one last tiny point on that, if I may. I notice there aren't any labels on the record itself. Why's that?'

'Well, really, we could hardly say proudly, *Professor Asimov: Cultural Life under the Ramessids*, could we? When we'd travestied a brilliant lecture and a great man.'

At this, the Superintendent chuckled admiringly. 'Well, you're a cool one, sir, meaning no disrespect, I assure you. You and the other gentleman there.' He indicated the Secretary. 'But let's get down to brass tacks shall we? This business of the record, it's a side-issue, really. It just appealed to my ... curiosity, let's say. When we get to this' – he smacked the documents again – 'we're in very different country. Now whoever kept these records, written records that is, and whoever composed these pamphlets – I'm not asking who it was, but he gave away as little as he possibly could.' He looked amiably at the Secretary. 'I'd say that he showed a well-trained sense of security. But one thing leaked through – not even Machiavelli or someone could have prevented it. Supposedly you're Egyptologists. Yet your rules are full of ways of dealing with other Egyptologists, getting rid of them, preventing then from joining your Society. There's even a whole pamphlet – I'm sure I put it with the ... Yes, here we are, Pamphlet 2, *Methods of Avoiding Involvement in Egyptological Conversations*. What about that, gentlemen?'

'From your manner, Superintendent,' said the Secretary, 'you seem to be under the impression that we're some sort of secret society. Let me enlighten you. We are.'

The President jerked in his chair. The Treasurer waited calmly for the Secretary to continue. In such situations as this he trusted him absolutely.

'In any subject, in almost every field of human activity,' pursued the Secretary, 'the amateur is at the mercy of the expert. All of us have had some experience of the world of what I might call, borrowing an analogy from the theatre, legitimate Egyptology. It does a great deal of fine work and of course we depend on it for almost everything we know. But ... it's systematic and scholarly, it's expert – indispensable qualities, but, to our way of thinking at

58

any rate, best appreciated at long range. All of us are hobbyists, amateurs doing our reading, our looking at works of art, merely for pleasure's sake, not as part of an academic discipline. Any respectable Egyptologists would laugh at us – and many of them have. Any respectable Egyptologists would assume leadership of our little band in five minutes – and a couple of them have tried. We had to expel them on technicalities, which made us feel pretty mean, so much so that we took steps to see that nothing of the sort happened again. Hence our rules and pamphlets. We enjoy our empire, and the fact that it's a minuscule empire in a backwater doesn't mean that we're any less proud of it or less concerned to defend it.

'Yes, we're a secret society, Superintendent, and our secret is our own ignorance, our own laziness and, if you like, our own attachment to a tiny bit of power. It's fun to be king of any size of castle if you've built the whole thing yourself.'

Here the Superintendent frankly exploded. 'Marvellous, sir,' he said when he was able to, 'bloody marvellous! We could do with a few chaps in the Force with a quarter of your unflappability and quick thinking and sheer old-fashioned cheek. Accept my heartiest congratulations, all three of you.' This was generous of him, in view of the President's minimal contribution. 'It would fool anyone who hasn't learnt, as I have, to make deductions from evidence. I know beyond all doubt that whatever your Society really exists for it isn't Egyptology. May I ask you what it is?'

Without hesitation the Secretary said, 'I'll answer your question, Superintendent, if you'll answer one for me. Is there going to be a prosecution in this case?'

'Let's just assume that there is for the moment, shall we, sir? For purposes of argument, if you like. Now, what about my own question? What does your Society really do?' The Superintendent's bearing indicated that much hung upon the answer.

'You didn't ask me that originally, you asked if you might ask that. Perhaps that's a quibble. Anyway, I refuse to tell you what you want to know. I shall reveal the truth only if and when directly faced with a term of imprisonment, nothing less.'

The Superintendent got up abruptly and stood with his back to the window. To some observers, this might have appeared a stagey move; to the Treasurer it bespoke simple relief from tension.

'I see, sir. I'm afraid I have an apology to make to the three of you. I've subjected you to a sort of charade. For my own purposes I had to find out just how you would all behave under pressure. You'll see why in a minute. But I have deceived you. It has been clear to me since ten o'clock this morning, not only what your Society doesn't do – that's to say take a bona fide interest in Egyptology – but also exactly what it does do.'

With what was more indisputably a sense of the dramatic, he replaced the record in its cover and handed it to the Treasurer, re-tied a length of coarse string round the documentary material and passed it to the Secretary.

'I should like to apply for membership,' said the Superintendent.

Five minutes later, all four were toasting the Society in Johnny Walker brought from a private cupboard. Now that the situation had resolved itself, the President was able to preside, outdoing them all in expansiveness.

'One point you might clear up for us,' he said, sprawling luxuriously in his chair, 'is why this raid ever took place.'

The policeman's festive look changed to one of professional capability. 'Liaison isn't as good as you might expect,' he said. 'We had an inquiry from another branch about you – nothing in it – and told them we had no information. I must say this did put it in my mind to raid you.'

He pulled his nose, unwisely in view of its already excessive length, and continued, 'As you can imagine, I have to produce results of some sort from time to time, however much it may go against the grain in certain cases. In yours, I felt I'd found a cover story that was too good. I got started on you mainly *because* of the apparent stuffiness of the Society. And I thought it would be good for a laugh, at least. I was wrong there, wasn't I?' He paused to refill glasses, then went on again, 'Of course, the Inspector was convinced there was some nameless-orgy type of thing going on, and I fixed it so that he'd carry the can if there was nothing in it. And so he will. I haven't made up my mind yet where he'll be going, but wherever it is he won't like it.'

A thought seeming to strike him, he went back to his desk and picked up a framed photograph, which he proceeded to display to them. 'You remember how in the war the lads used to show each other pictures of their nearest and dearest as a sort of sealing of friendship? Of course you do. Gentlemen, this is my wife.'

7 A Private Investigator

ANTONY: She is cunning past man's thought.

A couple of weeks later, Isham was sitting in an armchair in a corner of the otherwise deserted Lecture Hall, reading with admiring boredom a typescript of the Secretary's latest 'open' handout. It ran,

Society Text 64/11 ∗ The Book of the Opening of the Mouth, *extract 2*
Hail, Osiris, the royal scribe, Horus hath opened for thee thy mouth, and he hath unclosed for thee thy two eyes with the instruments SEBUR and TUNA, wherewith were opened the mouths of all the gods of the South.

And the AMI ASI shall say:
'My father, my father!
'My father, my father!
'My father, my father!
'My father, my father!
'My father, my father!'

And the SETEM shall take the instrument URHEKAU, and shall open the mouth of Osiris, the royal scribe, four times, and shall say:

'The mouth hath been made firm for thee, and I have made to balance for thee thy mouth conformably to thy teeth, O Osiris, the royal scribe.'

And the AMI-KHENT shall say to the SETEM:
'Horus is a *Sah*; is not thy father a *Sah*?'

And the SETEM shall say to the AMI-KHENT:
'Horus laid a snare [or, net] and "He whose face was covered by a snare" [or, net] layeth a snare [or, net] on him [i.e. thy father].'

And the AMI-KHENT shall say to the SETEM:
'Going round about [as] a bee [or, hornet] thou seest all the goings round about of thy father.'

And the SETEM shall say to the AMI-KHENT:
'The bees [or, hornets] giving protection, they make him to exist.'

And the AMI-KHENT shall say to the SETEM:
'There is [his] shadow, [and] there is no impurity [?] therein.'

This, according to standard procedure, would be duplicated

and sent out to members with an unwritten directive that as much of it as possible be read aloud at the domestic breakfast-table. In cases where husband and wife breakfasted separately, it was to be left behind 'by mistake' in a conspicuous position.

Laying the typescript aside, Isham strolled across the room and took the only readable book from the shelves. It was *Sex Life in Ancient Egypt*. He still wondered now and then why, on the occasion of the recent raid, this work had been suffered to remain while Steindorff's *Die Blütezeit des Pharaonenreiches* had been at once impounded.

Before he had reached his seat again, the telephone rang. He went to the record-player, which stood on a low table by his chair with its amplifier already switched on and the lecture-noises record revolving on its turntable. Having lowered the head on a random point in the outer inch, he answered the telephone.

'Hallo, yes?'

'Oh, is that the Metropolitan Egyptological Society?' Un-expectedly, it was a man.

'Ruh-hobbledy bobbledy beezle se later myssology hum bull-bull-bull ibis a wow-wow,' said the President's voice in the distance.

'Yes it is – just a moment while I shut the door, if you don't mind.' Isham reached down and cut the volume sharply to about one-quarter, simultaneously turning the treble control fully anti-clockwise: this latter in accordance with the findings of a recent experiment arranged by the Secretary. 'Sorry about that. Now what can I do for you?'

'My name's Eric Lasker, B.B.C. Television?' said the man with an inflection that suggested he was not at all sure of the reliability of this information. 'I wondered if I could possibly have a word with your President.'

'Whoom swisser-swatter se Divine Wives of Amun a lluh elf, elf-nee,' said the President's voice in a tiny rumble.

'I'm frightfully sorry, but he's in the chair at our lecture at the moment. My name's Isham – could I take a message or something?'

'Well, Mr Isham, the position is that I work for a programme called "This Evening", which you may possibly have seen –'

'Oh yes,' said Isham warmly, 'I watch it fairly regularly. Most entertaining and instructive, if I may say so.' Although bewildered, even slightly alarmed, he was a good enough Egyptologist to remember to pronounce his last phrase with the 'learned tremulousness' so often and effectively demonstrated by the President.

'That's very kind of you, Mr Isham. Anyway, I was having a chat recently with your President's brother-in-law, and he seemed to think that your Society would be an absolute natural for us. I'd very much like to have a look at it – I gathered you meet on Thursdays, and it occurred to me that if you've no objection I might drop round straight away and see you in action.'

'Sounds a splendid idea,' said Isham, full of cordiality still, 'but I think I'd better just check first, if that's all right. I rather fancy the lecture's about to end, so perhaps –'

'Already? But it's only nine o'clock. And won't there be a question period or something afterwards?'

'How long will it take you to get here?'

'Let's see, you're in Little Venice, aren't you?'

'Round about there, yes. Where are you now?'

'Well, I've just got to finish up here, and – I can be with you in twenty minutes or so.'

'I'll go and see if I can get hold of the President, Mr Lasker. I'll be as quick as I can.'

'Thank you, I'll hang on.'

Grinning slightly despite himself, Isham raised the volume for a couple of seconds and lowered it again. Then, after a chunky swig of Teacher's Highland Cream and Malvern water from the glass at his side, he embarked on his reading.

Solid fact, perhaps inevitably, came a poor second to thinly disguised speculation in the pages before him. An Egyptian male must often, his female companion would doubtless, have done things which, as regards those few particulars that lay beyond Isham's personal ken, fell easily within his conversational experience. The decor was undeniably different, what lay before and after the main matter of interest very odd and probably unpleasant too, but the actual goings-on were presented as much like one's own, whatever the fellows in question might or might not have said to themselves about it. Did what you said to yourself about it make all the difference, as he had often suspected, or none, as he had equally often suspected?

Isham gave up the problem. He moved the gramophone-needle

quickly to a place marked with crayon near the centre of the disc. A round of applause began. Turning up the volume, as he now did, brought adventitiously into prominence the effect of a number of scratches on the playing surface, so that those supposedly present seemed to be dropping jumping fire-crackers round the place or shooting at one another with cap-pistols, while flutter, wow and general deterioration of recording quality made the clapping hands sound like bags of wet gravel. But, to an ear now no doubt almost irreducibly uncritical, it should pass.

'Are you there?' asked Isham after twisting the control anti-clockwise. 'So sorry to keep you waiting. Look, it seems that unfortunately Professor Asimov has got to get back to Oxford more or less straight away. Picked up some sort of bug, apparently, when he was excavating near Elephantine recently. Got to take care of himself for a bit.'

'The Professor teaches at Oxford, does he?'

'He's staying there. And – I say, I do feel mean about taking up your time for nothing, but the President feels he can't really get out of driving the Professor to Paddington, and he's got to start, well, more or less now, if he's to make the –'

'I quite understand, Mr Isham. Thank you for trying. Well, not to worry – if you could just ask him to give me a ring, perhaps in the morning . . .'

Isham took down Lasker's number, apologized again, rang off, exhaled heavily, replenished his glass and drank liberally from it. A close call, and not only that: one likely to bring in its train calls closer yet, almost touching, in fact. He made an entry in the Duty Officer's log and a resolution to communicate with the Secretary at an early opportunity.

He was settling down to a further dose of undocumented assertion about Pharaonic amour when the front-door bell rang. To begin with he thought it was the telephone again and stretched his hand out to it. But the second ring following hard upon the first, was unmistakable. Moving now several times as fast as when the telephone had in fact rung, Isham bounded across the room to a wall-cupboard from which he took a large biscuit-tin labelled *Emergency Stores*. It contained an assortment of empty cigarette-packets, jettisoned tobacco- and snuff-tins, cigar-bands, chewing-gum wrappers, spent matches and toothpicks, plus a hefty pepperpot full of ash. He used these to bespatter the appropriate parts of the floor, then distributed three specially packed ashtrays at strategic points. Into another cupboard went the record-player: the bell rang a third time just then, but he was ready.

On the threshold stood the President's wife, a girl in her late twenties with long straight brown hair and rather heavy-lidded brown eyes. Isham had met her first a couple of years previously, at one of the series of 'open' lectures which the Society had organized when it was originally founded and to which wives had been pressingly invited. The series had been such a triumph of consistent intolerable boredom that, by the time the fourth lecture came along, no wives at all could be persuaded to attend and two had reportedly screamed when the matter was raised. The fifth lecture had been summarily cancelled and no further such had been found necessary, though the Secretary had been talking recently of putting on a short refresher course in the autumn.

The President's wife now greeted Isham by name, which was flattering in view of their having met only once, and that at a Ladies' Night, since the lecture referred to.

'How nice to see you – do come in,' he responded heartily. He was not by nature a hearty man and the prospect of having to behave like one for the second time in five minutes added to the strains inherent in the situation. 'I'm afraid your husband's just this moment left,' he went on, ushering her into the Lecture Hall. 'Not more than two minutes ago at the outside. He had to drive the Professor to Paddington.'

'Packed up early, didn't it?'

'Yes. It was most unfortunate . . .' He went on to fill her in carefully on the Elephantine bug situation, conscious that she and Lasker might run into each other any day and happen to compare notes about this evening. There was another point, too. If the chronological picture he had offered both inquirers were to be taken as strictly accurate, membership and Professor must have hurtled out of the house like Charlie Chaplin and driven off like the Keystone Cops. So he must try to confuse her sense of time, keep her hanging about for a few minutes, throw in false mentions of what o'clock it was.

'I was just in the neighbourhood,' the girl explained, 'at least

I thought it was the neighbourhood till I started to try to walk to this place, which must be about the most unfindable house in London. Anyway, I was having drinks with some friends of mine, the Yarmouths: do you know them? They live – what? East of here? North? One of those – facing the canal. So I thought I'd come along here and hang about till my spouse was free and then twist his arm till he took me out to dinner somewhere. But then things *dragged on*' – she made a gesture rather like a favourite one of her husband's, but less fluid – 'and I got into this rabbit-warren effect, so . . .'

'Would you like a drink?' asked Isham. 'I'm going to have one for the road.'

'Well, actually, you know, I rather think I *would*.' Something in her face or manner suggested to Isham that she might be a trifle drunk. So much the better. 'But I don't want to put you to any trouble,' she said.

'No trouble. What would you like?'

'I suppose you've no vodka? Gin will do fine. Just plain.'

While he was upstairs at the Club Room cupboard she was doing her best to take a look inside the Lecture Hall cupboards: but all these had Yale locks. Then she hurriedly scrutinized the bookshelves: but there was nothing there but books. Then she picked up *Sex Life in Ancient Egypt*, grinned consideringly, and put it down again. On Isham's return she was in mid-floor preparing to light a cigarette.

When she took her gin from him, the glance she gave from under those heavy lids suggested to him that, as well as perhaps being a trifle drunk, she might just conceivably be feeling the tiniest bit amorous. So much the better yet – other things being equal. Their gross inequality in the present case, however, the claims of his duty to the Society and much else demanded that he should continue to behave with absolute decorum. He tried to reconcile himself to this prospect.

The moment had, in any case, passed. As if recollecting herself, the girl shook her head almost imperceptibly and turned away, glancing round the room. Her eyes, Isham noticed when he moved round to the front of her again, looked keen now.

'Everything's in a bit of a mess,' he said.

'So I notice. You must have got some of the most conscientious smokers in England on your books.' She stirred with her toe a rather hastily dropped handful of cigarette butts at the rear of the aisle. The ankle indirectly attached to the toe was delicate, encompassable, it seemed, by a joined thumb and middle finger. 'By the way, what are you doing here on your tod when everyone's gone home?'

This caught Isham slightly by surprise. 'I was on the telephone,' he said, coming back almost at once with the laid-down procedure. 'That's why I was so horribly long in coming to the door – I should have apologized for that.'

'Don't give it a thought. I see – calling Seattle on the Society?'

'I don't know anyone in Seattle.'

'Oh, you *don't*? That's the most unlikely story I've ever heard.' Her demeanour still held a question.

'I'm full of unlikely stories.'

'I bet you are.'

Was the micro-amorous look back in those half-shielded brown eyes? Compared, say, with the Secretary or even the Treasurer, Isham rarely and dimly felt pride in doing his duty to the Society, but he felt a little now as, manfully setting aside the matter of the President's wife's eyes, he turned brisk and said, 'Just to keep you fully informed, I was on to the Professor's wife in Oxford to get her to meet his train. She was in a bit of a dither. Kept asking me how he was.'

'And how was he?'

'Oh, a little tired, undoubtedly. Otherwise in fair shape, I'd say.'

'Good.' She looked at him. 'Well, I suppose I'd better be . . .'

'Have another drink. But look, let me take you somewhere and buy you one. This place is pretty squalid, I must admit.'

'Granted. And the, uh, academic atmosphere isn't in key for things like . . .'

'Drinks.'

'That's it.'

'Fine, well . . .'

'Before we go, I wonder if I could just . . .'

'Of course,' said Isham. 'On the half landing.'

Left alone, he debated whether to make the necessary telephone-call now, resolving finally that the interests of security called for its postponement. He unlocked the stores cupboard, hesitated, then shut it again. The log book and other papers should by protocol have been deposited in the office upstairs, but this too would have to be deferred.

At that moment the girl was trying to get into the office. Baulked of this, she made a quick round of the cupboards in the Club Room, turned over the magazines, glanced through a number of mimeographed sheets – but naturally these were all of 'open classification', and she left the room none the wiser. A few seconds later she slipped down the top flight of stairs and into the lavatory-cum-bathroom, moving quietly, though not quietly enough to fool Isham, who was listening intently in the shadowy hall. But when, having pulled the chain vigorously, she rejoined him by the front door, he made no reference to what he had heard.

8 The Female of the Species

CLEOPATRA: He words me, girls, he words me.

That very evening the Society wives were in session. The venue was the drawing-room of the Secretary's house in Edwardes Square. Here, every Thursday when there was a meeting, wives with nothing better to do – and these were frequently in a majority – had got into the habit of dropping in for a couple of hours to drink the Secretary's claret and engage in conversation. It was not good claret, for their absentee host's interest in drink hardly extended farther than a lukewarm desire to provide some sort of socially acceptable minimum; the question of supplying an appropriately nasty beverage for Ladies' Nights furnished an exceptional departure from this attitude. And his wife, warned by her doctor to take alcohol only in moderation, seemed to think that self-restraint about quality licensed mild indulgence in quantity, so that she was very happy with a bottle of Bordeaux Rouge N.V. heavily adulterated with sulphur dioxide, even if each of her companions had to drive herself a little to get through one-quarter as much. Not that, being women, they took much notice of what they drank – they came for the chatter.

This, of course, was what the Secretary most feared. *Any* collective inquisitiveness about the Society, he was always impressing on members, was more dangerous than *any* individual inquiry, however tenacious. He had even – until stopped by Cambuslang – proposed the devising of a curiosity-lethality formula with variables including N to represent the number of potential investigators, S their degree of solidarity, I their mean intelligence quotient and a number of others rather lamely eked out with K as an invariable cussedness-constant. Anyway, his response to this distaff mirror-image of the Society was so educated as to disarm even those who, like Froald, were inclined to put into words their vague feeling that the Committee should never have allowed matters to come to this pass. Better a visible threat, the Secretary would argue unopposed, than a secret underground. And people like Isham claimed to see a mystical appropriateness in the quirk of chance that had picked the wife of the Secretary as nucleus for the membership's grass widows.

It had, not of course, been in the Secretary's nature to allow these gatherings to proceed without counter-measures. On the contrary, they had yet to establish themselves as a matter of routine when he had issued a directive laying down the means individuals should take towards subverting and sabotaging them whenever opportunity offered. It had read, in part,

Member	Recommended reaction to wives' get-togethers
Secretary	SP celebration of the cultural, social, ethical etc. benefits to be reaped from association between wives of members
President	Laughing tolerance
Treasurer	Saying how much he likes the look of Mrs Chester in as much detail as may recommend itself to him
Cambuslang	Saying how strongly he objects to the Secretary's wife's objections (supposedly reported to him by Froald) to his own wife's taste in clothes
Chester	Saying without qualification or explanation that Mrs Isham is a dangerous woman
Froald	SP encouragement of his wife to attend
Isham	Asking his wife to give his love to Mrs Froald
Mordle	Saying, 'You're not *really*, surely, *going* to that *curious* house?'

('SP' was the standard Society abbreviation for 'savagely persistent', adopted when Isham pointed out that the phrase cropped up at least once in every confidential communication. Others such were HI, AOJ and TFSL, the first two of these also serving as useful code-groups for employment on the telephone. 'Laughing tolerance' might be thought to be a waste of the President's very real histrionic talents, but the lack of regular outlet for these – or something – had lately, as Cambuslang and the Secretary had independently noted, led him to place the satisfactions of playing a part as such above the need to carry conviction. His rendering of 'bewildered innocence' on the night of the police raid, for instance, would have aroused the suspicions of a public-relations officer or even a sociologist, let alone someone who knew his way about the world. The police had probably just

70

thought he was barmy. Anyway, no more challenging roles for the President until – there might be a long wait until – he should seem amenable to being taken aside and given an updated version of Hamlet's advice to the players.)

Perhaps it had been the Secretary's campaign which saw to it that, on the evening in question, only four women were assembled in the Secretary's drawing-room drinking, for a change, Australian burgundy-character red. Mrs Chester had not come, on the grounds (confided to her husband only) that knocking down diluted red ink in female company was not enough of a lure to fetch her all the way from Hampstead. The Treasurer's wife had not come, on the grounds (generally notified) that Thursday evening was the only one her favourite old-school chum, now a staff nurse at Middlesex County Hospital, had at her disposal. Mrs Froald had not come, on the grounds (presumed) that she was still angry with everybody about Poland, of which a mention – not a denigration, nor yet a word of inapposite praise, but a *mention* – had provoked her, on her last visit, to throw her wineglass overarm into the fireplace, utter a diatribe, well spiked with four-letter words, against 'you English women', and leave. These, we repeat were presumed grounds only, for little *contretemps* of this sort had not kept her away in the past; one such, indeed, arising out of a disagreement with Mrs Mordle about the significance of the Beatles, had the following week brought her to the Secretary's doorstep at a quarter to eight, all afire with eagerness to continue the discussion. And finally, as already shown, the President's wife had not come, on no grounds at all.

The Secretary's wife, however, was present in full force. She had already entered upon her second bottle of burgundy-character – wines originating outside metropolitan France always tended to provoke her to a spasm of self-directed generosity – and was saying,

'The thing *is*, one should learn to follow the line of least resistance. Half the trouble in life comes from people pushing and shoving against things they haven't a hope in hell of altering. And half of *them* are only doing it because some awful man like Bernard Shaw or D. H. Lawrence says they ought to. If you can't get away from it, lie down and let it roll over you. That's what I do with these perfectly ghastly pyramids and dynasties and hieroglyphics and what-have-you. Not that it isn't a strain, I grant you. I can't *convey* what it's been like this last week. I've been out of my *mind* with it, under the *table* with it, you know. That *bloody* Book of the Opening of the what-not, I tell you, I shall simply – '

The ensuing cries of sympathetic hatred and terror would have gladdened the heart of the Secretary had he been present. It is a characteristic of every élite corps – such as the Society, in its field, might fairly claim to be – that it not only gives a good account of itself at all times, but now and then, *without any special effort being called for*, comes near to working a miracle of disciplined destruction. Extract 1 from the Book referred to had provided such an occasion. Some psychological alchemy, some trigger buried deep in the collective unconscious, had seen to it that Isham's weary tenor, the President's vibrant baritone, Cambuslang's resonant bass and all the other voices of the membership had brayed or bawled or boomed this piece of hundred-proof Pharaonic mumbo-jumbo at their helpless consorts again and again and again, returning to the charge as often as three times during a single meal, keeping up the pressure from early-morning tea to the final switching-off of the bedside reading-lamp, the recourse of leaving the duplicated sheet about the place for prying eyes to scan having been dismissed in every instance as paltry. What, it is tempting to speculate, would have been the case of these women had they but known that the deadly Extract 2, Isham's reading-matter of earlier that evening, would soon be on its way to their hearts?

Eventually Mrs Mordle said, in a speculative tone, 'Funny how they all seemed to get interested about the same time.'

'Oh, don't I know it, honey, I'm afraid you've got my spouse to thank for that,' said the Secretary's wife. 'I was in on the *ground floor* of the whole thing. One day my husband was a perfectly normal human being – well, sort of averagely normal, if you know what I mean. Anyway, there he is, off to a lecture on Cheops or Thebes or somebody, fully expecting to be bored to tears, only going so as to oblige a friend, he says, and then, the next morning – *full* of it? He was transformed. Possessed. Nothing had ever meant so much to him before. Like some terrible infection.'

'And he lost no time in passing it on,' put in Mrs Cambuslang in her grimmest tone, which had before now shown connoisseurs of grimness that they were not so well up in their subject as they had formerly supposed. The haggis effect in her face consisted solely of an olive tinge of no great depth, though substantial enough to make her one of the million or so Scotswomen given to wondering from time to time whether they might not be descended from a Spanish mariner shipwrecked after the defeat of the Armada. The tinge certainly helped her to look grim. So did the excellent bone-structure of her cheeks and jaws. But, as Cambuslang always said, she was an amiable woman at heart.

The others now followed her lead. 'Very true,' said Mrs Isham. 'But if I may just go back for a minute, it is a little bit extraordinary, isn't it, the way the thing sprang up like that? Almost overnight? My husband claims he's always had a soft spot for Ancient Egypt because of its art and so on, just in a minor way. I expect he had, but all I know is he never mentioned it until he was getting ready to join the Society. I'm not often wrong about things like that.'

'Darling, I'm sure you're not, but good *God* I wish you wouldn't boast about it.' The Secretary's wife spoke with emphatic disgust. Her habit of rebuking what she called going out of one's way to be a shit, whoever it might be whom she saw as sinning in this fashion and whatever the occasion, was one of the things that bound her husband permanently to her. 'If nothing gets past you,' she went on, pouring a little more wine for herself, hesitating, and then pouring a lot more, 'then I'm a tiny bit sorry for you.'

Mrs Isham flushed, supplementing unnecessarily the natural redness of her cheeks. She had been one of the first of the post-war school that eschewed make-up on the grounds of its fundamental dishonesty, and still, at the age of thirty, disdained its aid, although by now there was little left of the childish look that had once, possibly, justified her. 'I didn't mean that at all,' she said humbly. 'It's just that I take an interest in what my husband does and take notice of what he says to me. Surely we all do that?'

'Well *I* don't,' said the Secretary's wife. 'Not more than half the time, anyway. I think people should live part of their lives on their own. Otherwise one's in someone's *pocket*, you see, or he's in one's. That's why I'm basically for these Egyptological cavortings in spite of what we all have to *go through* because of them. I don't grudge them any of it. It's cheap at the price.'

'Let's see,' said Mrs Isham, in the tone of slight wonderment which was one of her most effective weapons, though a touch of eyebrow-pencil would have sharpened it up no end – 'let's see, you bought them their house, didn't you? I hope you don't mind my –'

'Yes I jolly well *did*. They had to have a lecture-room and a library and what-not, otherwise they couldn't . . .' The Secretary's wife swigged at her wine. 'I mean they couldn't hold their meetings and what-have-you.'

Mrs Isham looked at her with a touch of genuine inquiry. Mrs Mordle, a lady some years older than her husband and, except when alone with him, of gentle mien, said, 'I wonder if we might just go back a little – we never really discussed this question of all our better halves becoming Egyptologists at the same time, did we? I think we got sidetracked or something.'

'Well, crazes do spread, you know,' said the Secretary's wife.

'This is rather a specialized craze, isn't it?' said Mrs Isham.

'There's one important characteristic shared in common,' said Mrs Cambuslang, 'between all the members of the Society.'

'Energy?' suggested the Secretary's wife.

'You're forgetting our esteemed President,' said Mrs Cambuslang.

'So I am. Well . . . extroversion or whatever it's called. You know – being ready to take an interest in the things outside one.'

'That rules out old Isham,' said Mrs Isham.

The others mutely approved this point.

'Youth?' said Mrs Mordle. 'Oh, I don't mean in years. Youngness. Juvenility. Adolescentness.'

Mrs Cambuslang, who was clearly enjoying herself, shook her incongruously well-shaped head. 'You'll have to do better than that.'

'I say, this is rather fun, isn't it?' said Mrs Mordle, accepting several ccs. of burgundy-character with some show of eagerness. 'Mm . . . no, I was going to say intellect or something like that, but that obviously wouldn't –'

'Neurosis?' said Mrs Isham, apparently at random.

After another short silence, Mrs Cambuslang said, 'Ah now, you're all of you getting far too fanciful. I'm thinking of something completely simple and elementary and obvious.'

'Well,' said the Secretary's wife, 'every man *jack* of them is a human being.'

'Oh, do you really think so?' asked Mrs Isham with slight-wonderment accompaniment.

'Yes. Anyway, I give up. What's the answer?'

Mrs Cambuslang did a gentle smile. 'They're all of them men.'

'Oh,' said Mrs Mordle abruptly.

'I don't mean in the sense of being great lovers or virility or any of that,' said Mrs Cambuslang, dotting and crossing any i's and t's respectively which Mrs Mordle might be thought to have left imperfect. 'It's just their biological description.'

'Oh, I *see*,' said Mrs Isham, looking at Mrs Mordle.

'What's your point?' the Secretary's wife asked Mrs Cambuslang.

'Oh, they're a pack of great big schoolboys, every one of them. Scratch a man and find a child.'

'You've obviously scratched a good deal harder than I've ever cared to,' said the Secretary's wife. 'And I thought someone had tried the adolescent thing and you said it wasn't right. And what's your *point*?'

'Just . . .'

'You mean men have crazes and children have crazes so men are children. Just *that*. Yes, I think I follow you.'

Mrs Mordle had had time to recover, if she needed it. 'I hope I'm not being pernickety,' she said, all dulcet again, 'but I don't believe we ever quite got to the stage of going into the way all our menfolk suddenly went Egyptological at once.'

'Didn't we?' said the Secretary's wife, sounding a little weary. 'Well now, if we must. To begin with, although it may not seem so to you, honey, the Society was going for quite a long time before your husband joined it or even knew it was *there*, I dare say. And Mr Froald has only been a member for a little more than a year – but on the other hand he's been interested for quite a long time. He was out there in the army, you know, when they were having that fuss about the Suez Canal. Only a few weeks, but long enough to *hook* the poor fellow.'

'His wife told me she'd never heard a word from him about Egyptology until he started going to the meetings,' said Mrs Mordle.

'I dare say she did,' said the Secretary's wife.

'And I dare say she hadn't,' muttered Mrs Isham.

'What about Mr Chester?' asked Mrs Cambuslang. 'You're not going to sit there and tell me that that laddie could care less about Ancient Egypt.'

'Indeed I'm not,' said the Secretary's wife. 'He seems just to find the premises useful as a sort of club. Evidently he doesn't turn up at the meetings very often. I believe he's behind with his subscription, too.'

Her husband would have been delighted to hear this classic defence of one of the Society's weakest sectors, complete with the invaluable lucky fact of Froald's Egyptian service. (Actually, Froald had explained, he had never got within leagues of a pyramid and the nearest approach to hieroglyphics he saw had been the letterpress in the local newspapers that had come so neatly to hand when, taxed by widespread bowel disorders, official supplies of lavatory-paper had run thin.) But the Secretary might have been less delighted by reflecting that his wife was not normally the sort of person to play the role of *advocatus dei* to the Society.

'Then there's this new member, Superintendent something,' she was continuing. 'So *riveted* when the Committee were explaining about the Society to prove it wasn't a brothel that he went down on his *knees* to them to let him join. There must be something about the Pharaohs and the rest of them that we weaker vessels haven't caught on to.'

'That was a funny business, wasn't it?' said Mrs Mordle. 'The raid and everything.'

'Yes it was,' stated the Secretary's wife. 'But please don't let's go into it all again. We had enough of it last week.'

'He sounds a charming man, that Superintendent,' said Mrs Mordle, 'going by that letter of his you passed round. He sounded really sorry about the mistake, I thought.'

'Sorry or not,' said Mrs Cambuslang, 'the man should be sued.'

'I told you they discussed all that,' said the Secretary's wife. 'He asked them to consider how we'd all feel if we were in the papers as involved in a Vice Squad thing, mistake or no mistake. I must say I see his point.'

Mrs Isham nodded absently. For the last minute or two she seemed to have been pursuing some line of thought of her own. She looked up, however, as they all did, when the Secretary came into the room. He glanced around at it with apparent perplexity, perhaps considering for the first time the justice of the line about the curiousness of his house that he and the Treasurer had put into Mordle's mouth. Many observers might well have applied some such word to the curtains in here, patterned as they were in irregular oblongs of stripes and large checks as if run together from a job lot of football-club jerseys, to the flower-bowl containing white-washed poppy-heads and pampas grasses, to the full-sized fully-strung harp that stood unexplained only a yard to one side of the centre of the woolly purple carpet. But then quite soon the Secretary went and kissed his wife, greeted the other ladies and accepted a glass of wine.

'Yes,' he said in answer to the charge that he was back early, 'Professor Asimov had to get back to Oxford as soon as he'd finished his lecture. He wasn't looking at all well. He made light of it but I'm afraid he's a very sick man. Such a pity. Such a fine mind. Imaginative leaps that can seem absurdly wild until you start reconsidering the evidence from the ground upwards, as it were. For instance, it's always been generally assumed, as you know, that Middle Kingdom sculptures were only painted as regards certain details – principally the eyes and hair, and sometimes items of jewellery as well. The sculptors certainly seem to have had a distinct sense for the naturalistic effect produced by the bare stone. Agreed. But – '

'Now then, darling, pull yourself together,' said his wife. 'You're not at the Society now, you know. These poor people can get all that kind of thing at home, and they probably will.'

After the three visitors had left for their homes, where they would certainly get all that kind of thing if their husbands knew their duty, the Secretary apologized to his wife for having 'let his enthusiasm run away with him' as it so often did. 'There's a fascination about the whole thing that I just can't explain,' he said.

'Darling, you mustn't feel you've got to try. I don't really mind it when you bore the pants off me. You've the right to, in a way. I simply *grin and bear it*. Funny how people always put the stress on the bearing rather than the grinning there, isn't it? I don't myself, you know. Anything you like to take up or mess about with or what-have-you is all right with me. Now just you keep that in mind.'

At this stage she was padding round their bedroom in her underclothes, doing her stuff with handbag and hair-brush and bedside book and glass of water. (No pills, though.) Seen like this she looked fat all right, but nowhere near cylindrical. The Secretary would not have wished that there should be any less of her. He said, 'Anything? That covers a pretty wide field, doesn't it?'

'I suppose so, but I mean it. Anything at all.'

9   A Case for the Superintendent

LEPIDUS: What manner of thing is your crocodile?

A brief informal cocktail party was held early the following week at the Society's premises to mark the induction of the Superintendent. Also expected to attend was a certain van Dorn, an associate member from the United States who had been admitted the previous autumn while on a three-month visit to London on behalf of the cosmetic firm he worked for and who now, back again for a shorter stay, hoped to 'pick up the threads', as he put it, and renew a mutually pleasurable acquaintance.

The Superintendent arrived escorted by the Treasurer, smiling jovially but perhaps not wholly at ease. On the face of it, it was not at all unlikely that he was unused to meeting strangers socially. His diffidence soon melted, however, under the twin impact of Cambuslang and a couple of Cambuslang-made pink gins and soda. Even Mordle seemed anxious to make him feel at home.

'One or two bits of shop, everybody,' said the Treasurer, 'to get out of the way. Apologies for absence from the Secretary and Isham. The Secretary asked me just to mention a few items which he'll report on in detail when the time comes. First, the Isis Room. As you can see, the major part of the work has been completed – just the furnishings and fittings to go in now. I was to remind members that they are only to consider it available in case of a real emergency, the kind we're all afraid of but which no amount of planning ahead can completely rule out.'

'He's made that point every time the Isis Room has been so much as mentioned,' said Froald peevishly. 'How many more – '

'And this is me making it for him this time,' said the Treasurer. 'Things of this sort do need to be said over and over again. Let's all remember that.

'Right, next item. Week-end Seminar. The date's been provisionally fixed for May 9th and 10th. That means we've got six weeks or so to talk about it at home. The programme will be circulated shortly. The venue is a Workers' Educational Association hostel near Catterick in Yorkshire, six miles from Richmond, the nearest town, which is full of troops at week-ends. Interesting remains on the moors near by, traces of a sun-cult with what are possibly more than coincidental resemblances to Ra-worship. Details later – just note for now that that's why we're going to Catterick. We intend to spend one whole day examining the remains *in situ*.

'Only one more thing, but this is something rather special. I think you'll agree.' The Treasurer smiled, teasing his audience by pausing. 'A ten-day trip to Egypt in the autumn. Thebes, Karnak, Memphis, the lot. Motor transport as far as Hierakonpolis . . .'

An uproar of enthusiasm overwhelmed him. Cambuslang and Mordle, their differences forgotten, were shouting and clapping each other on the back, while Froald, actually cheering, shook the President's hand violently. The Superintendent laughed, without very much conviction. Him apart, the Treasurer was reminded of the behaviour of World War II R.A.F. bomber crews on receipt of the announcement, 'It's Berlin tonight, chaps,' or at least of what always followed it in films. Was the comparison so wildly unapt? Berlin and Cairo were different kinds of objective, admittedly, but nobody had ever settled unarguably the relative status of loss of life and loss of liberty.

The Cairo trip was swiftly christened 'Project Nefertiti' and a toast drunk to it. The Treasurer then explained to the Superintendent what it would entail. The organizational problems were vast, and those raised by the Week-end Seminar too different for their solution to be of much help. However, the Secretary had already had a couple of useful ideas, one of which would involve the employment of a photographer whose expertise must be matched by his discretion. Perhaps the Superintendent's experience, on one side of the law or the other, might come in handy here?

The new member said he would look into the matter, though in the tradition of public servants he added that of course he could not promise anything. He entered this caveat in a mechanical tone, one which suggested to the Treasurer that there was something on his mind. After a forgettable interchange of 'I'll see what I can do' and 'I'd be grateful if you would' and so on, it came out. Pointing his lengthy nose in the general direction of the Treasurer and sniffing lightly through it, the Superintendent said,

'Can I ask you a straight question – old man?' He tacked on the endearment with a perceptible breaking of his vocal stride, as if he had substituted it for 'sir' in the nick of time.

'Certainly,' said the Treasurer.

'This expedition to Egypt, now. And to a lesser extent the Catterick, uh, effort. Are they really going to come off? In your honest opinion.'

'I see no reason why not. There's a risk, naturally, but that's true of all our activities. And the potential gain is enormous. Think what it would mean to our side if we could pull off the Cairo coup.'

'It's that "if" I'm worried about, old man, to be quite frank with you.'

'You say that because you've only just become a member of the Society. Until now you've been completely on your own – a solitary resistance worker deep inside enemy territory. Your morale couldn't have been lower, agreed?'

The Superintendent nodded slowly. 'With you so far,' he said.

'Then suddenly you're one of us and you hear operations being discussed that you yourself would scarcely have dared even to dream about. People are quite soberly putting points about ways and means to objectives that no sane man could so much as consider – *on his own*. Let me put it another way. No individual could take a submarine through a system of mines and nets and the latest thing in undersea detection devices – I'm sure you see the analogy with our actual –'

'All too clearly,' said the Superintendent, shivering slightly.

'What's needed is a skilled crew in a high state of training and morale. That the Society provides, as you'll come to appreciate when you've had a bit of experience with us. And if I may just caution you,' said the Treasurer, rather enjoying the experience of cautioning a member of the police force as a matter of duty, 'in the friendliest possible way, of course – it doesn't really do to voice any kind of doubt or defeatism in the presence of the membership. Despondency can be fatal.'

This was without doubt very Secretarial stuff which the Treasurer would privately not have endorsed to the hilt, but experience, going perhaps a little against the emotional grain, had taught him the practical usefulness of such ideological rallying-cries. The Superintendent, at any rate, seemed impressed to the point of embarrassed apology. 'Oh, I think I can say I see that,' he said, accepting another aerated Vaughan Jones and Angostura from Cambuslang. 'You do brood by yourself, don't you? Inclined to get a bit morbid. But I mean, I hope I haven't –'

It was left to Froald (someone it was easy to underestimate, the Treasurer reflected) to say the helpful thing. 'I've only been one of the gang for a bit,' he said, 'not so long that I can't remember what it was like to be on my own. When I first came here I thought they were all *mad* even to *contemplate* the weekly thrust. Which I now take as a matter of course . . . as nearly as one ever can.'

The relieved laughter at this was broken into by the entry of van Dorn, rather painfully elegant in the latest of the Savile Row suits that he took as a fringe benefit, in his phraseology, of his visits to England. With this exception he was a forward-looking mid twentieth-century man.

'So here's the bunch,' he roared, laughing and shaking hands all round, 'that good old *bunch*. How goes it, fellows? How does *it* go, if I may so express myself? Huh? And how's my old friend Nevertitty?' He tickled the statue under the left armpit. 'Thanks, Camby, Scotch and soda will do fine. Hey, where's our gallant Secretary? That's too bad. I trust he's in his habitual excellent condition, full of pep and handing it out to everybody?'

'He seems well enough,' said Mordle – rather coldly, the Treasurer thought.

'He's unchangeable,' said Cambuslang. 'When the rest of us have succumbed to nervous strain, old age, creeping paralysis of the will, he'll be there, right in there pitching, as I believe you fellows say . . .'

'We used to,' said van Dorn. 'We don't any more, but we haven't forgotten what it means. I'm sorry, I interrupted you.'

'I was just going to say that if – or when – society changes in the way we consider desirable, it's men like the Secretary who will have brought it about, and he will have contributed personally as much as anyone I know or can conceive of. He's . . . I hope I'm not making a prophecy, but he's the stuff of which martyrs are made.'

'Or madmen,' said Froald.

'If he's crazy I'm half-way crazy myself and every day in every way trying to get further,' said van Dorn. 'Let's drink to him.

Gentlemen, I give you our Secretary – an architect of the future.'

The toast was drunk with every sign of goodwill, but the Treasurer was deeply uneasy. It was not so much Froald's remark that had impressed him – it had been made lightly and by no means unaffectionately – as the response to it of other regular members present. Cambuslang had given a disgusted glare, but the President had half-smiled in evident approval, Mordle had even nodded his unshorn head. In the dark days that lay in store for the Society, this was a moment the Treasurer was often to recall.

For the time being, at least, cause for anxiety seemed a long way off. Van Dorn extracted the maximum laughter-potential from his discovery of what the Superintendent did for a living and became the party's social and alcoholic fugleman, a position to which he had often detailed himself the previous year. After a bit of this he said he had an announcement to make, something he was inclined to do with increasing frequency as the hour advanced, but this one proved more interesting – certainly more intelligible – than most.

'Perhaps it's the discovery that you fellows here have got the law on your side at last,' he said, throwing his arm round the Superintendent, 'or it may be that I just had a birthday with a very unpleasant number on it and I thought I better get my shoulder to the wheel while I can still push. Anyway, take note of the date, gentlemen: here comes a piece of history.

'Effective May 1st a North American Branch of the Metropolitan Egyptological Society will open in New York City. I can't give you any details because I only just took the decision, but I know two like-minded guys I can depend on and that's all you started from, wasn't it? Your example has inspired me and I acknowledge with gratitude yet another case of the wisdom and indeed the vigour of the Old World acting as a, as an inspiration to the New.'

There were more toasts, of course, Cambuslang giving the company the North American Branch and the Branch replying through its representative. During them, an idea struck the Treasurer and he lost no time in putting it first to the President, then, as soon as he was free of toast-giving, to Cambuslang as senior member present, a quorum thus being constituted. The President thereupon called for silence.

'I will be brief,' he startled them a little by beginning. 'This country is the cradle of parliamentary democracy. When, in imperial times, daughter parliaments were inaugurated in what were then the colonies, it was the custom for a mace, resembling the symbolic object in use at Westminster, to be dispatched with official blessing to the colony in question, to serve the same function there as at ceremonial openings of the parent assembly. We, in what must hereafter be known as the London Branch of the Society, feel that our historical role is in no way less glorious than that of our fathers who brought government by the people to the lands of the painted savage and the ignorant aboriginal . . .'

Competent stuff, thought the Treasurer, but the fact that the President had the heart and soul of an amateur did not mean he was incapable of bringing off a professional effect now and again. The tone and style of his discourse was, in any case, less surprising than its content, which was recognizably Secretarial to the nth degree, and this a bare twenty minutes after he had seemed to be nourishing doubts about the Secretary's sanity: an impressive tribute to the power of the latter's ideas and the devoted skill with which he had imposed them upon the membership. The Treasurer remembered his own attack on despondency to the Superintendent a little earlier. Were they all of them, in their different ways, subdued fanatics, secret Secretaries?

'. . . in visible token of which,' the President was concluding, 'I in your name am proud to donate to our brother van Dorn this memorial to our esteem, this sign of our fraternal confidence, this embodiment of our hopes, our friendship, our joint will to victory.' And, at his signal, Cambuslang passed him the stuffed baby crocodile which Isham had picked up at a junk-shop in the King's Road for twenty-two and six and which ever since had occupied a place of honour second only to Nefertiti.

Receiving this gift at the hands of the President, van Dorn appeared deeply moved. 'Fellows, I just don't know what to say,' he said. 'Hell, if there was anything needed to get the North American Branch on the road then this is it. We'll surely prove ourselves worthy of this marvellous gesture and your trust and everything or we'll perish in the attempt. I'll have this little darling mounted on rosewood and a silver plate stuck on in commemoration with all your signatures if you'll let me have them. Anybody got a piece of paper?'

Yet another toast, of uncertain origin and direction, was drunk while members signed their names. The Treasurer reflected that the party was coming more and more to follow the lines of those vodka-punishing do's at the Kremlin – a mild irony, for the least acquaintance with the Society's activities would have affronted Comrade Brezhnev and enraged his predecessor.

The session had almost run its course when Furze appeared. His demeanour on being presented to the Superintendent showed all his habitual civility, and ascended to somewhere near cordiality when van Dorn wrung his hand, though without emphasis it dissociated itself from the American's transports of friendliness. Furze disapproved of Americans, but he had once told the Treasurer that he considered van Dorn a not ungentlemanly gentleman. The Committee had gone to some lengths to see to it that he remained ignorant of the nature of van Dorn's employment.

'How's Mrs Furze?' asked van Dorn.

'Precisely the same as before, sir, thank you very much for inquiring. Oh, there is just one difference you might possibly remark. An external one, of course. She goes to the hairdresser now all the time. Said she had dry unmanageable hair, sir. When she comes back from one of her sets it's like a curious helmet. You get the feeling that if you were to give it a push it'd rock to and fro, sir, like a pudding-basin on top of a pole. I can't imagine what process they employ down at that hair shop, but whatever it is they've got her properly hooked on it, sir. Like a drug. But with that minor exception she's the same as she always was. Oh, thank you very much indeed, sir.'

The Treasurer had put a small Scotch into his hand.

'And now, sir, if I may, there's a rather serious matter I feel I should bring to the attention of all the gentlemen.'

'Can we have a bit of quiet, chaps?' called the Treasurer. 'Mr Furze has got something he thinks we all ought to hear.'

'What's wrong?' asked Mordle anxiously.

'U.A.R. Ambassador want to pay us a visit?' asked the President.

Furze drew himself up. 'I don't like bringing up a subject like this on a convivial occasion such as the present, gentlemen, but I'm afraid I must. Last night, shortly after eleven p.m., I was on my way home from the Red Lion public house when I decided to look in here and make myself a cup of tea in my basement. It's a habit I've got into of late – sort of putting off the evil hour of returning home. On approaching the front door I noticed that this window was lighted. Nothing very odd about that; I assumed that one or two gentlemen had let themselves in to take a late drink, rather in the manner I was proposing myself. So I made my entry in the normal way, not taking any precautions against making a noise, et cetera. This I had immediate cause to regret.

'No sooner had I shut the front door behind me than there was the sound of a hurried departure overhead. I heard the slamming of a door which must have been the outside door of the Isis Room, the one giving on Old Lane via the spiral staircase. Not perhaps thinking very quickly I made my best speed up the main stairs and into this room. Nobody here, of course. So off I went through the Isis Room and threw the door open in time to see the intruder moving off down the lane at the double. He was some yards away already and pursuit, with that staircase intervening, was obviously hopeless.

'There you are then, gentlemen. On that small table there was a used glass that I found to have contained sherry – the Isabelita, I soon established. The level of the fluid in that bottle was down by more than an inch. I keep an eye on these things. I wasn't Mess Sergeant in 'thirty-nine to 'forty for nothing.

'And that, gentlemen, is all.'

There was an appalled silence.

'Superintendent,' said the Treasurer, 'I think this is your department.'

The policeman came forward, his hands clasped behind his back, his chin on his chest, rather in the manner of a concert baritone waiting for the end of the piano introduction of 'Die Forelle'. Suddenly flinging up his head, so far that he had to look down his considerable nose to bring his eyes to bear on Furze, he said, 'Nothing was missing?'

'There was the sherry, sir.'

'Yes yes, I mean no object was taken?'

'Nothing, sir, I'll swear to that.'

'Any litter, cigarette-ends or anything of that sort?'

'No, sir. I searched particularly.'

'Mm-hm . . . How did this . . . intruder get in, do you know?'

'I found no trace of entry being effected, sir.'

'Are the door and windows secure?'

'Absolutely, sir. It would take an expert with a picklock or some such device to get in without doing a great deal of damage. And that wasn't so here.'

'No no, so you said. Could you describe the man?'

'I'm afraid not, sir. Not helpfully. Tallish. Medium build. No hat.'

'Mm. What did you do with the used glass?'

'Didn't touch it, of course, sir. Wrapped it in my handkerchief and conveyed it to my basement, where it's available for your inspection at any time.'

The Superintendent fell silent. His hands were still clasped posteriorly and his head still lifted, but his eyes were now shut. After a time his lips started pushing in and out, like those of Nero Wolfe at the first hint of the solution of a puzzling case, a stage ordinarily reached a good deal later than after two minutes of investigation.

When nobody had spoken or moved for a further half-minute, Froald whispered to Cambuslang, 'What's the matter with him?'

'He's thinking, you bloody fool.'

'Oh, I see. Sorry.'

It was only a few more seconds before the Superintendent spoke, though without in the least altering his stance. 'I . . . see . . . half,' he said in a blurred voice like a trancing medium's. 'Half of it's there perfectly plain. But I can't see all of it, not yet. And –'

'And until you know the whole answer you're not going to tell us anything,' said the Treasurer, who had read a great many detective stories.

'That's right, old man,' said the Superintendent, opening his eyes in slight astonishment. 'However did you know that?'

'Oh, I just guessed.'

'Well anyway, I can tell you that if I'm right so far there probably isn't any immediate cause for alarm.'

'*If* he's right,' moaned Froald. '*Probably* no *immediate* cause. I don't think I can stand much more of this kind of thing.'

'You can,' said the Treasurer in a steady-lads-steady tone. 'We'll survive this, whatever it is, as we've survived everything else. You must have faith.'

10   The Great Departure

ANTONY: Say, our pleasure.
     To such whose place's under us, requires
  Our quick remove from hence.

The morning of May 8th, on the evening of which the Society was
to depart for its Week-end Seminar, dawned chill and overcast.
This was more satisfying than any mere good omen. It had been
agreed that a cordial invitation to accompany the expedition be
extended to all wives, plus an apologetic footnote to the effect that,
in view of the inability of the W.E.A. hostel to accommodate
women, these would have to be put up separately at a small inn, of
which nothing was known for certain apart from its being four
miles away. Should any wife have accepted, the member concerned
would simply have had to drop out, on such excuse as he might
devise. But, faced with the uncertainties of the inn and now the
near-certainties about what the whole-day outing to the near-by
remains would be like, no wife did.

The Treasurer arrived at King's Cross station shortly after five
o'clock, accompanied by his wife, who had come to see him off.
While he was paying off his taxi Mrs Froald suddenly appeared
and got into it, jostling aside an elderly woman waiting patiently
at its door with two misshapen string bags in her hands.

'Good afternoon, Mrs Froald,' said the Treasurer politely.
'Sorry you've had to rush off.'

The other turned her head aside sharply enough to court the
risk of a ricked neck. No doubt somebody had mentioned
something to her: Poland, the Society, trains, the time of day.

The Treasurer glanced over at his wife, who was placidly
guarding his luggage near by. Lowering his voice, he said to the
taxi-driver, 'I happen to know this woman who's just got into
your cab. She's a patient of mine, as a matter of fact. Nothing
wrong with her really – just a bit neurotic. What she simply can't
stand is rapid motion of any kind, such as going above, say, twenty
miles an hour by road. If you could manage to avoid that you'd
be doing her and me a great service. Not that she'll thank you for it.

She'll probably yell at you to go faster. Might even get abusive, but you take no notice, eh?'

The cabby's scepticism vanished when the Treasurer passed him two pound notes. One might have meant a rich joker; two was a proper emergency. 'Not to worry, doctor,' he said dependably: 'I'll take care of her. Twenty mile an hour it is.'

As the taxi drove away, with Mrs Froald already to be seen banging on the glass partition with her fist, the Treasurer turned to the elderly woman. 'Never mind, mother,' he said with a sympathetically democratic air. 'There'll be another one along in a minute.'

'No thanks to you if there is, you Tory swine,' was the reply.

The train was already waiting. Half-way along it a small group had gathered by an open first-class door. The Secretary had naturally reserved the seats nearest the restaurant car. He was not yet to be seen in person. With his luggage stowed above a back-to-the-engine corner, the Treasurer returned to the platform.

Mordle's face, normally on the edge of petulance, looked tired, perhaps strained. It was likely that Mrs Mordle, who had not (so far) turned up at the station, had spent the available parts of the day haranguing him about the mingled absurd childishness and far from absurd masculine selfishness of his Egyptological pursuits, as so often described to colleagues in the Club Room: 'it's a husband's duty,' he had put it to them once, shrieking a little with the eloquence of it, 'never to have got interested in anything his wife is going to come along much later and decide is trivial one moment and more important to him than she is the next.' But just as likely he was hating the people around them. He had contested for some time the Committee's choice of Yorkshire as the Seminar area. Somewhere in the West of England, he had argued, would have been preferable, both as being more readily associated – via Stonehenge and Avebury and so on – with ancient remains, and as having for its railway terminus Paddington Station, where, he had gone on arguing, a better class of passenger was to be met with than the Northern troglodytes who called unintelligibly to each other and rammed one's knees with their suitcases at King's Cross.

Skulking at Mordle's side, Isham too seemed a little on edge. During the discussions preliminary to the Seminar he had shown a surprising indifference, weighing in with no comments or questions. He would have been quite ready, the Treasurer guessed, to have opted out of the whole scheme. At the moment he was manipulating an empty cigarette-packet with his feet, evidently trying to tear it in two by their exercise alone, while Froald explained to him something about cold fronts. Froald's demeanour was in swift transition between whatever havoc his wife had wrought in him and simple anticipation. He wore a short hairy overcoat ill suited, on even a moment's thought, to a prolonged session on the Yorkshire moors in bad weather. But he had never been one for that sort of detail.

The President, at any rate, showed no signs of tension. His overcoat was rather on the long side, patterned in squares of dark blue differing so subtly as to forbid assessment of the number of colours employed. Just now the scarlet silk lining of the garment was visible to advantage as its owner stood with arms 'akimbo' talking and laughing with the van Dorns. He lost no time in introducing the Treasurer and his wife.

When her name was pronounced, Mrs van Dorn shut her eyes firmly, though without actually screwing them up, leaving it open whether she was demonstrating sensitivity or simply blotting out the sight of the Treasurer. Her opening remark, 'So the whole team of you are away up to the frozen North on the big choo-choo with your buckets and spades,' gave no certain clue.

'While our little wifies sit all alone,' responded the Treasurer, 'reading pretty bookies on modern marriage that the kind Book of the Month Clubbie has sent them.'

Abruptly abandoning her earlier idiom, Mrs van Dorn said to her husband, 'I hope you realize that you won't come within miles of anything you could call a dry Martini up there? Outside the Hilton and the Carlton Tower and the Connaught you're camping out?'

'I know it, honey. I aim to quaff deeply of those good old Yorkshire ales. In such time as is available, that is.'

At the mention of Yorkshire ales Mrs van Dorn covered her eyes with her hands. She did this circumspectly, doubtless to guard against rubbing off any parts of her make-up in that area or, possibly, dislodging drier fragments by sheer impact. To cover her mouth would have been more appropriate to the case, but a glance showed the hazardousness of that. All in all, she must have done as much as any individual could do towards keeping her husband's firm in business. 'Warm mud,' she said.

'Excuse me?'

'British beer is warm mud.'

'If you mean by that that it isn't a conglomeration of carbonic acid gas and other chemicals including synthetic brightening agents chilled so deeply as to have lost any flavour it might once have had then I'm forced to agree with you. Back home the notion of natural beers drawn from the wood and served at room temperature is a lost...'

The Treasurer left them to it. He had just seen the Secretary and his wife coming through the barrier. Turning quickly to his own wife, he said,

'Just to make sure we've got everything straight before everybody's talking at once... I'll ring you at this Flaxman number – that's Brenda's place, is it? – Sunday morning, didn't we say?'

'The time's right, sweet, but it's not Brenda's place, it's this doctor from the hospital I was telling you about, the one with the artistic wife, and they're giving a party for Brenda's pal, the one who's marrying the Indian. I expect we shall have a bite at the flat, and then we'll probably look in at the Queen's Elm and have a drink with Sean, and get along to the party about half-ten. You're sure you don't mind me staying the night? I get so nervous in the house alone. They're awfully nice people. She's a –'

'Fine, dear. Now you've got my number in case you need it. But do remember you may have a bit of trouble getting hold of me straight away. I've no idea what this bloody hostel's like – pretty primitive by all accounts.'

'You'll survive though, sweet, I know you. Oh, I did tell you, didn't I?, we're taking Brenda's sister's kids to the Zoo on Sunday so it would be a big help if you could phone before ten, so we can make an early –'

'Sure, sure. Now you have a good time, dear,' said the Treasurer. 'Let's say good-bye now, shall we? Give my love to Brenda.'

'I'll do that little thing. Good-bye, pet. Have a lovely time, and mind you don't catch cold on those horrible moors.'

Near by, the Secretary was saying, 'Where's my brief-case? It's gone. I left it in the taxi.' He would have been fully as likely to leave his right arm in the taxi, but truth to likelihood was never a feature of the 'harassed professor' act which he was now working as hard as he dared.

'It's here, darling. Now you're looking frightfully fussed and you're *not to be*. It's all going to be the most tremendous success.'

'Such a lot on my mind. So many things to think of.'

'But you've thought of them all, I promise you. You're the most marvellous organizer in the world. And listen, I'm in charge this end. I'm going to be the mother hen and look after them all. If there's anything you need me for, never mind *what*, darling, just you bloody well *snatch* that telephone and get hold of me.'

'You're a tower of strength,' said the Secretary, unconsciously revivifying this worn metaphor by applying it to one of his wife's physique. 'I don't know what I'd do without you,' he added, with something of a side-step in the direction of literal truth.

'Now you're to enjoy yourself, because that's what you're going for. Darling, doesn't Mr Cambuslang look most terrifically grand?'

The genial Scotsman was striding up the platform towards them. With his short tweed cloak and deerstalker to match (more readily to be associated with a theatrical costumier's than with any conventional tailoring establishment), the stout ashplant in his hand and his general air of grizzled benignity, he resembled James Robertson Justice playing some conflation of Sherlock Holmes and Dr Watson off to the provinces to show a whole pack of calf-sized mastiffs who was master. The vague aura of Shetland travelling-rugs, stone footwarmers and hampers of pigeon pie and claret that clung to this persona would admittedly have better suited the gracious purlieus of Paddington favoured by Mordle than the noisome and utilitarian hell through which the robust Gael now made his way. Behind him looked Mrs Cambuslang, so over-shadowed in this context as actually to seem reduced in size. And behind her came two figures identifiable as the Superintendent and his wife.

With this couple, the order of psychic precedence set up by their harbingers was decisively reversed. Like Mrs Cambuslang's overall stature, the Superintendent's nose seemed today to be scaled down to the minimally outlandish, the eccentric but solidly workable. Although his gait recalled the bags-of-time stroll of a midnight-beat constable flashing his torch into doorways and checking padlocks rather than arrival at an Irish brawl after stop-tap, he was clearly anxious to be on board and away as soon as possible. His wife, however, appeared to have all the time in the world.

The Treasurer recalled a science-fiction novel in which the hero, meeting a girl who later proved to get all her substantial kicks out of sticking sharpened knitting-needles into men's ganglia, had looked into her eyes and screamed. Such a reaction would, on the whole, have been excessive in the present case, which called for at most a whimper of dread.

It was not so much the more extravagant ornaments of the face that were so striking. The cylindrical eyebrows like two halves of a mustachio, with the bonus – or rather malus – of a vigorously sprouting mole on the cheekbone, the pelt-like skewbald hair, the corrugations of the skin over by the ears – the likes of all these had been seen before by most of those present, if never in conjunction. The sheer size of the area on which they were displayed was the real novelty. That and its flatness. The overall shape of the skull was of a roughly truncated cone with the larger section facing forward. Behind it was a lot of space for brain: too much, in fact. That was the real trouble, probably. What were all those extra lobes doing with themselves? How had they got there? The Treasurer glimpsed another image from science fiction – the computer or robot that on its own prompting adds mysterious new circuits to itself. He hoped to be far hence when their ultimate purpose should be revealed.

All-aboard time came at last. The Treasurer hugged his wife: the Secretary's hugged the Secretary. The van Dorns did a token but just about unmistakable embrace, like two Englishmen compelled by example at a French ceremonial. Cambuslang, though clearly still under the afflatus of his newly devised appearance, unbent and bent down enough to let Mrs Cambuslang kiss his cheek. None cared to see what the Superintendent and his wife did to each other by way of farewell.

The railway's servants did their stuff with doors and whistles, the members theirs with waves and good-byes. The Treasurer's wife, earlier than the others, turned and made for the exit with what her husband thought was unusual relaxation. Perhaps she was not sorry, after all, to have got rid of him for a couple of days.

11 Sealed Orders

SCARUS: I have yet
      Room for six scotches more.

Five minutes later, while the train lurched slowly northward, the membership filed into the restaurant car. As each man was given his seat by the steward, the President asked him what he wanted to drink, finally reeling off the entire order without hesitation. Since seven of the company wanted large whiskies (plus a red Cinzano for Mordle and a glass of cider for Froald) this was a minor feat of memory only. The drinks arrived quickly, no doubt much accelerated by the quid handed out by the President on arrival in the car, before he had opened his mouth, in fact. He now lorded it over their distribution, very much with the air of one ready to insist on paying for them and for all others consumed on the journey. In the Treasurer's mind's ear, however, a little voice rather like the President's was trying over the sentence, 'Divide the total by nine – that's the most sensible way, isn't it, chaps?'

Across the aisle at a table for two, van Dorn was saying to Cambuslang: 'Interesting point. I was the first man to arrive whose wife had accompanied him to the station. Those who'd arrived before me were all unaccompanied. Those who came later, like yourself, were all accompanied.'

Cambuslang nodded and sighed. 'It's the old story,' he said. 'The counter, of course, would be that it's only men whose lives aren't enriched and filled out by marriage who can afford to fling away twenty minutes of their time in order to leave a comfortable margin before a journey. I mean they wouldn't call it a comfortable margin but that's what it is really.'

It was van Dorn's turn to nod, so he nodded, but less confidently than Cambuslang had done. 'I see what you mean. Hey, there was a good one just before we came out. A classic. I sat around in the hotel bedroom for forty minutes while she hung that stuff on her face. My bag was all packed and I was reading the new *Galaxy*. Well, after a couple of false starts over a clean handkerchief out of

94

the drawer and so on we finally took off. We got as far as the lobby, no further, when I remembered I left *Galaxy* behind on the dresser. Our room's on the first floor right by the stairhead. Total time for the round trip, maybe eighty seconds. Then – you've guessed it, I was the one who'd made us nearly late. Which incidentally we weren't, nowhere near nearly.'

This time the Scotsman shook his head. 'I know. Still and all, we oughtn't to cloud this day with recriminations. It's too glorious an occasion.'

Now that the Seminar was actually under way, the general mood of relaxation was such that the first couple of sips of drink worked like half a bottle. It was a minor babel that the Secretary had to cut through when he addressed the company from his corner.

'This won't take a minute, gentlemen. Just remember that we're in a security-risk environment, though a low-grade one. I'll pass round your written instructions, which you might glance through now, if you will, in case there are any queries. The general narrative of events is the main thing, of course. I strongly advise members to commit it to memory before the Seminar closes. I hesitate to recommend this, but I think you'll appreciate the importance of really letting it soak in. I've made it as short as I can. Van Dorn, you'll notice you've got a special Appendix on the manners and customs of Yorkshire. You needn't bother with it too seriously, but I expect you'll want to get a grasp of a few salient points.'

Isham turned over his sheaf of roneo'd papers. One, he noticed, was headed, *Discussion Group*, *Keir Hardie Room*, *7.30 p.m. approx.* (*after high tea*). *Members are advised to bring their own chairs.* Below this, rather in the manner of an ambitious play-reading society circulating scripts ahead of time, were subjoined some verses for discussion 'in relation to ritual developments of the Heliopolitan period'. They ran, in part,

... the KHER HEB shall say:
  'The Hetch shrine with the Urer covering is for thee.' *Shrine Hetch.*
  'Depart thou not having thine Urer.' *Urer Covering.*
  'Verily the sledge [*tem*] is for thee.' *Sledge Tem.*
  'The pair of jaw-bones is for thee.' *Jaw-bones of Set.*
  'Thoth hath delivered the Eye of Horus for him in its name [sealed] of

'*Brought by Thoth for Horus*;
'in its name of *Carried away by Thoth for Horus*;
'in its name of *Made to be at rest by Thoth for Horus*;
'in its name of *Made straight by Thoth for Horus*;
'in its name of *Counted by Thoth for Horus*;
'in its name of *Ant*;
'in its name of *Sheti*;
'in its name of *Hetep*;
'in its name of *Maa*;
'in its name of *Apep tut Tem*.
'[The above] shall be said over the shrine THES NEFERU of this god, which shineth with [its] covering, according to that which is . . .'

Heady stuff, Isham thought to himself. But he could not get a laugh out of himself by doing so. What he was about to do weighed on him too hard. Staring into his now empty glass, he tried feebly to determine whether his irresponsibility or his perfidy were the more culpable. The second alternative seemed to him, as he looked round at the merry faces of his colleagues, from the excitable extravert van Dorn to the gravely smiling Secretary, at any rate the more immediate and painful.

The Secretary was speaking about the very sheet Isham had just been dejectedly scanning. 'Members will of course want to take it home. I'd like to recommend annotations – nothing fancy, under-linings will do at a pinch – in more than one handwriting medium, pen and pencil, for example, ballpoint and fibreglass stylus and so on. Gives a valuable effect of repeated careful attention.'

Isham barely took this in. He was used to intimations of, rehearsals for, gestures towards self-destruction; what horrified him was the prospect – absolutely inevitable, as it seemed by now – of pulling them all down with him: sensitive Mordle, tough, stout-hearted Cambuslang, plucky little Froald . . . The thought of them had been with him all day as he sat in his office at the advertising agency for which he worked, rendering him utterly incapable of deciding which of two campaign approaches to submit to an important client in the soft-drinks industry. He fancied them turning towards him, staring, as in a bad dream, asking mutely *How could you?*

The circulated instructions aroused no significant queries. The Secretary assured himself that no outsiders had entered the restaurant car and that the steward was busy fetching a fresh round of drinks. 'One or two more points which I'll clear off as we're all together. The matter of Maggs.'

There were groans, which the Secretary quelled with a raised hand.

'Froald informs me there's been absolutely no activity for seven weeks now – is that confirmed?'

Froald nodded vigorously.

'Evidently the report we concocted for him has done the trick. I think we can regard the episode as closed. But let's all take it, please, as an object-lesson about security. Which leads me naturally to Chester. Has any member seen or heard anything of him since we last met? No? Then have I your authority to consider him lapsed?'

After a pause, the President said, 'I think we should consider the length of time the old sweetie has been with us. It seems a bit hard to scrub him just like that. I suggest we keep him on the books until we get something definite out of him. I mean . . .' He swayed deprecatingly about in his seat.

'Very well,' said the Secretary, making a note. 'That's all, I think . . . Oh yes: additions to the library. *Eternal Egypt*, by Pierre Montet, Weidenfeld & Nicolson, fifty shillings, to be published later this year. ". . . Natural and political conditions of Egyptian life . . . literature, science and art . . . birth and progress of Egyptology . . ." Hm, might even be useful. May I order this volume? I take it I needn't stress the importance of constantly adding new books to our collection? Thank you.'

'Anything on the intruder?' Froald asked a moment later. 'It was never cleared up as far as I remember.'

Called upon by the Secretary, the Superintendent swivelled in his chair to take in as many of the members as possible. He put the tips of his fingers together and looked into space for a time. Then he said, 'This is a relatively familiar type of incident. Impulse felonies, they're known as. Of a random or sporadic nature, undertaken out of impulse as their name suggests, very often – as in this case – no discernible element of gain or revenge or sexual satisfaction, recidivism potential very low in the same context.'

'What?' said Froald.

'He means if the chappie does it again he'll do it somewhere else,' said Cambuslang.

'Can't you add something to that, Super?' asked Mordle. 'It sounds a tiny bit – well, academic as it stands.'

'By all means, old man,' said the Superintendent, and proceeded to condescend somewhat. 'These fellows, you know, you're up against a disordered mind – oh, I don't mean a raving lunatic, just ... *disturbed*, as so many people are in these times we live in. He makes a bet with himself, so to speak: has he got the guts to pinch a motor-bike? – not that he wants it, you understand, just seeing if he's got the guts. In our case it's seeing if he's got the guts to get into an empty house. While he's there he doesn't see why he shouldn't take a drink. Sort of setting his mark on the environment, I suppose. Like the people who write their names on statues, *Kilroy Was Here* and all that. Mind you, I'm not saying you don't get some pretty nasty stuff coming up that way because you do. When a bloke decides he'll break into a house to prove something to himself, well, it's a nuisance, granted, but we can deal with it. We know where we are with it. But what about when he takes it into his head to put a bullet through the wife's gentleman friend to show he's a he-man or passionate or that sort of nonsense? Now that's a very different pair of shoes, I think you'll agree.'

There was a buzz of serious-minded assent. Cambuslang said to van Dorn,

'Talking of wives' gentleman friends getting bullets through them, I take it you're a native American?'

'You mean back home they get them through them all the time? Maybe they do. Anyway, I am. Five generations, if you must know.'

'To hell, I'm afraid I left out quite a deal. I was wondering if you were any connexion of the Civil War general of your name.'

'Christ, Camby, I never knew you were such a learned son of a bitch. You mean –'

'Just a wee hobby of mine.'

'Well, you're right. I'm a collateral descendant, if that's not a contradiction. General Van Dorn was some sort of a cousin of my ancestor.'

Cambuslang mutely shook the American's hand. 'I admire him very much.'

'You're thinking of his raid on Holly Springs? That was a hell of a –'

'I was thinking more of his raid on Mrs Peters. Which cost him his life. As you must know, he perished gallantly under a husband's bullets. I constantly think of that. What an example to us all.'

'I see what you mean. At least I think I do.'

'Cambuslang,' called the Secretary, 'could you come over here a minute?'

The Scotsman excused himself and joined the President, Secretary and Treasurer across the gangway, changing places with the Superintendent. The atmosphere at the larger table seemed a little grim.

'We didn't want to alarm the membership,' began the Secretary, 'but this television threat is becoming quite serious. We can't obviously go into it here – I just thought the four of us might fix a date for lunch next week and work something out. Can we arrange that now?'

Diaries were produced and a rendezvous agreed for the following Thursday at the Wheeler's in Old Compton Street.

'Right,' said the Secretary. 'We'll all have a think in the meantime, though the three of us here have pretty well exhausted our ideas, which is why we called you in, Cambuslang.'

'You'd better just outline the present position, then. The last I heard, this Lasker fellow had telephoned when Isham was Duty Officer and you'd all gone out to lunch with him to choke him off. It didn't take, I suppose.'

'I will say we gave him a terrific pasting.' The Secretary permitted himself a reminiscent smile. 'I don't think I've ever known us in better form. I took him very slowly through my "special field" – you know, magical sodding cults and beliefs in the pissing Late Period – while these two argued about certain verses in *The Book of the Opening of the Mouth* which they both happened to have brought along copies of. Every time Lasker tried to say something to me one or the other of them would interrupt him and ask him for his opinion of some crappy sentence or image or what-have-you.'

'If it doesn't sound too conceited,' – the President took up the tale – 'I think I did excel myself with the "don's delivery". Lasker was pretty well on his –'

'What is that?' asked Cambuslang. 'I don't think I've ever had a demonstration of anything by exactly that name.'

'There are two principles,' explained the President: 'taking a long time over a platitude and speaking a tiny bit above the other fellow's aural threshold. It's the second where you really need the practice and the flair, gauging how much volume will keep him straining his ears off to hear what he doesn't want to hear. I'll try one for you now, if you like. Of course, the noise of the train will complicate matters and it's best aimed at only one victim at a time, but I'll see what I can do.' The President smoothed back the dark waves of his hair and cleared his throat. 'Right, Cambuslang, ask me a question. Anything.'

'What's your opinion of Pubes? I mean the laddie who had that tomb at Thebes.'

Above the rattle of the wheels and the murmur of other conversations the three could just distinguish the President's voice saying, 'Uh . . . well, it, uh . . . it rather, uh . . . I imagine you'd have to say that it, uh, well, you may not agree but, uh . . . without saying that this is the last word on the subject I'd like to put up the notion that it, uh . . . that it depends on, uh . . . depends on your point of, uh . . . on your point of, uh . . . I wouldn't want to have you think that I'm laying down the law on this but I put it to you that it depends on your point of, uh . . .'

Cambuslang screamed and said, 'I've got the idea. And you mean God knows how long of that didn't choke off this Lasker?'

'Evidently not,' responded the Treasurer. 'Anyway, he didn't stay choked. Back on the telephone a couple of weeks later saying he'd put up the project to his superiors and they were dazzled by it. Exploring the byways of the contemporary consciousness, going off the track without snapping the link with the L.C.M. of the viewing public, opening up areas of the life of the mind that have hitherto remained uncharted – uncharted on perishing TV, that means. Anyway, the lot. You know, with all respect it strikes me that we misconceived our strategy.'

'How?' asked the Secretary in some irritation.

'Well, we bored him to buggery, sure, but that might have been what he was after. Don't underrate this Lasker. And don't forget what this sort of programme's up to. To him and it, we're flat-earthers, anti-fluorinated-water fanatics, flying-saucer buffs.

100

We're twee, you see. We know so well that what we're up to is the least twee of human activities that we've lost sight of what a reasonably intelligent outsider would make of the Society if he took it at its face value.'

The train roared unheeded through a cutting. The President said, 'He's right.'

'Whether he's right or not,' said Cambuslang, 'what's to prevent us simply telling this fellow to go and get stuffed?'

The Secretary gave a percussive sigh. 'Everything,' he said. 'That's just the trouble. Lasker got on to us not out of the blue but via our President's brother-in-law. Family connexion. There has to be a *reason* for our stopping this programme happening apart from the fact that we don't want it. That's what we've got to devise next Thursday.'

Cambuslang set another round of drinks going. 'Isn't there any *good* news?' he asked. 'I'm a wee bit brassed off with intimations of disaster.'

The Secretary now gave a pleased smile, as if the Scotsman had shown unusual acumen. 'Indeed. There's now a very good chance that Boon will apply for membership of the Society.'

'Boon?'

'Pinsent Boon, the M.P. Used to be Under-Secretary for Home Affairs.'

This was clearly as much news to the other two as to Cambuslang, who said wonderingly, 'But he's the most terrible prick, isn't he? Anyway he looks and sounds it from his photographs and speeches.'

'He looked and sounded it all at once when Muggeridge did him on the telly,' said the Treasurer.

'He certainly seems to lack eclat,' said the President.

The Secretary's smile had not diminished, even perhaps growing a millimetre broader. 'I'm glad you all confirm my view,' he said.

'Christ,' said the Treasurer animatedly, 'we don't want a prick in the Society. We've got . . .' He was about to go on, 'enough of them as it is,' but noticed just in time that Mordle, to whom he had been on the point of referring, even pointing out with an inclination of the head, seemed to be doing his best to eavesdrop from his disadvantageous position at the far side of the next table, so he wound up rather tritely, '. . . interests to protect.'

'You leave that to me,' said the Secretary. 'Mr Boon will keep his mouth shut if I tell him to.' When the others showed signs of mild wonderment but asked no question, he went on. 'He'll be the most valuable asset, in one way, that the Society's ever had.'

'What way's that?' asked Cambuslang.

From smiling like a gratified schoolmaster the Secretary was beginning to do it like a complacent master-criminal, Ernst Stavro Blofeld, perhaps, or Goldfinger. 'You probably know that in the last few years Boon's acquired something of a name for bringing in private member's Bills.'

'Yes, something not at all flattering in the way of a name,' said the Treasurer. '"Bloody fool" would be one of the least offensive forms of it.'

'Litter,' said Cambuslang gloomily. 'Noise abatement. Untreated sewage. Detergent waste. Consenting adults in private, of course.'

'What I have in mind for him will break quite new ground,' said the Secretary, still *misterioso*.

'I suppose it's no good asking you what it is,' said the President. 'No.'

'Because you're not going to breathe a word to anyone until you're sure,' said the Treasurer. 'Like the Superintendent a few weeks ago.'

On hearing his title mentioned the policeman glanced over at them from across the way, where van Dorn had evidently been subjecting him to some form of playful persecution. 'I can't tell him,' said the Superintendent. 'It's no use, I've done my best, but I can't tell him. Well, you see, he seems to think it's my job to wade through reams of literature tending to corrupt those persons into whose hands it might fall, photographs of persons in a state of partial or total undress in indecent poses or engaged in improper acts and all the rest of it. Seems to think it's all I ever do. I told him I wish he was right, but he won't take a blind bit of notice. I can't tell him.'

'But surely,' said Froald encouragingly, 'you must get some quite interesting stuff passing through your hands, the no-ugly-retouching school of thought and the Scandinavian magazines.'

'Very little, old man. Very little. For the most part it's –'

'Talking of retouching, I heard of an unusual occupation the other day,' interrupted van Dorn. 'In this country among others, as you know, it's against the law to publish photographs of girls without their vital area being sort of smoothed out so that it looks like the rest of them. I don't know who the hell they think they're protecting – I should imagine the shock for a kid brought up on those photographs the first time he gets a girl's clothes off must be, what do they call it ? – traumatic. But that's by the way.

'What I heard was that the Danes have this law that says you mustn't do this smoothing-over thing if you don't fancy going to jail. Now apparently the demand for girlie pics over there is such that they can't keep pace with it out of their own resources. Have to import. So the *status quo ante* has to be restored, and there are guys earning their living out of drawing back in what other guys are spending at least a good part of their time taking out. I can't help wondering what they describe their occupation as in their passports and everything.'

'It must get frightfully monotonous,' said Mordle.

All the others looked at him in silence, those whose position necessitated it swinging round in their chairs to do so.

'I mean – you know, just repetitive after a time. Rather narrow.'

'I suppose you would find yourself getting into a bit of a rut,' said the Treasurer.

'What did you say you were dealing with for the most part, Super ?' asked Froald.

'Perfectly proper art studies of young women, unclothed or partly clothed. Not that there's anything wrong with that as far as it goes, of course. And it is quite pleasant to have the stuff arriving on your desk without you having to do anything about it, often before publication too. Rather like what I understand happens in the case of literary critics. Saves you having to sally forth and wear out shoe-leather going round the Books and Magazines shops. Which is a bit embarrassing for a man in my position anyway. Oh now – one point that occurs to me is that every so often you get an early look at something you think there's going to be a run on. Two or three times I've got rid of stuff so as not to look as if I'm holding on to every other mag. that comes before me, only to find it was out of stock in Newport Court. There is that danger with exceptionally attractive material. So let me just advise members that I reckon there'll be a run on *Titter 6*.

It's got one of those hot little bad-tempered-looking blonde bits getting every ounce out of a pair of slacks. Eight poses, I think I'm right in saying. And there's some very-much-up-to-standard Margaret Middleton in the same issue, if you don't think she's too heavy. The best three-and-sixpence worth I've seen for a very long time, a very long time indeed.'

Several members made a note. Then Froald said, 'But you must have seen *some* things that wouldn't have come our way. What about these blue films people keep showing at their hundred-thousand-pound Sussex retreats?'

The Superintendent snorted. 'We hardly ever get to 'em. They're pretty fly, the gentry who operate them. They tend to have a bloke standing by to whip the reels into a furnace of some sort the moment the law appears on the horizon. The ones we do get have very little appeal. The fellows who make them have been reading books. Full of stuff like plot and wit and visual quality – you know, Fifi the French maid and young bodies silhouetted against the dawn. Artistic restraint, I believe it's called. The most I've seen – '

'Like the psychological Western,' Mordle got off before being fiercely shushed by Froald and Cambuslang.

'I was going to say they did get hold of something recently, but it was at kind of an early stage of processing. What I saw was what might have been quite a fair romp between a lot of platinum-blonde negresses with black teeth. Still in the negative stage, see, and the chaps in the lab hadn't thought it was worth the trouble of putting it the right way round. Thought I had enough to go on to decide if it was obscene or not. Somehow I didn't like to tell 'em.'

'What did you decide?' asked the Treasurer.

'I recommended that no charge be brought. It was the least I could do.'

There was a sympathetic murmur, which eventually became divided into three or four separate conversations. As the time for the first dinner approached, other people appeared in the car and seemed to expect to be served drinks. The President called for the bill and split it nine ways, not neglecting to add in the quid he had disbursed at the outset. The company moved away to their compartments.

A change in the pace of the train was perceptible. The Secretary looked out of the window and then at his watch. Drawing from his inside breast pocket an envelope sealed with wax, he leant forward to the Treasurer, who was sitting opposite.

'Here it is,' he said. 'All checked and double-checked.'

'Of course.'

'I needn't add anything to what's in there. Which indicates how glad I am that it's you who are doing this.' The Secretary lowered his voice. 'I shall always be grateful to you for volunteering when you did. There are some duties for which we can depend on a lot or rota system, but this isn't one of them. It's the most vital operation in the whole history of the Society. You're the man to carry it through.'

While the Treasurer expressed his gratification, a shouting voice became audible as its owner moved down the corridor. 'Peterborough,' it called. 'Peterborough.'

Members bustled about donning overcoats and getting their things together. Each of them found time to shake the Treasurer's hand and say a few words of encouragement: the President, whose usual effusiveness failed to disguise his genuine feeling; the Secretary, quietly confident; Cambuslang, with a grip of iron and a clap on the back; Isham, still strangely withdrawn; Froald, grinning like a schoolboy; Mordle, with nervous bonhomie; van Dorn, offering a characteristic jest but plainly aware of the significance of the occasion; the Superintendent, cordial and respectful, more sensitive than any of them, perhaps, to the difficulties and dangers of the Treasurer's mission.

As the train gathered speed out of Peterborough, the Secretary's behaviour during the Boon conversation recurred to the Treasurer. He tried to visualize the kind of private member's Bill the Secretary might be contemplating, and felt a familiar anxiety. And what about the implication that Boon would do whatever he was told? Blackmail? By the Secretary? In that case –

'First dinner,' came the cry along the corridor. 'Take your seats, please.'

The Treasurer came to: more important concerns than Boon's destiny lay in the very near future. Taking with him a copy of *The Year's Best in Fantasy and Science Fiction* he returned to the restaurant car, there to fortify himself against his long, lonely journey to the North.

12   A Voice on the Telephone

ANTONY: The world, and my great office, will sometimes
  Divide me from your bosom.

Twenty-four hours later the Treasurer was lounging in an armchair, sipping a warm but strong Bell's and water and carefully reading through that morning's copy of the *Yorkshire Post*. Once or twice he made a note on the pad at his side.

A clock struck. He moved to the window of the small downstairs room and looked out past the drawn curtains. The house was at the top end of a village street up which the wind blew with pointless persistence. Scraps of paper stirred in it feebly, glued to the ground by the afternoon's rain. An elderly trio hurried downhill, en route no doubt for horror double-feature or bingo sessions, but moving with the incompetent urgency of a refugee group – the parents and aunt, as it might be, of an abruptly discredited satellite politician – making for the frontier.

At the moment, such fancies held no appeal for the Treasurer. He returned to his chair and wrote on his pad. Before he had finished, the telephone, an incongruously up-to-date instrument with spiral flex and dots and arrow-heads on its dial, started ringing.

He experienced mild stage-fright. The President had drilled him carefully in the Yorkshire accent, with footnotes about 'salty Northern wit' and 'provincial unhurriedness', but Presidential drilling had a way of producing a more hilariously confident frame of mind at the time than was recoverable when, as now, the pupil was on stage and alone. Gritting his teeth, he picked up the receiver.

'Allaw,' he said. 'Scotton Workers' Educational Assawciation Hostel.'

A female voice said, 'Who is that speaking, please?'

'Luke, I tawld you. W.E.A. Hostel, Scotton, Yorksheer.'

'But who are you?'

'I'm the wan as answers the fawn. What can I do for you?'

'Oh, all right. May I speak to Mr Isham, please?'

'Sorry, I'm afraid there's no wan of that name here.'

'Are you sure? Name of *I-sham*.'

'Aw, wait a minute now, he wouldn't be wan of them fellows as are digging and suchlike, would he?'

'That's it, the Egyptological Society.'

'Just hang on a mawment, would you, missis?'

The Treasurer moved about the room for half a minute or so, making noises with his feet on the hearthstone and knocking against items of furniture. Then he returned to the telephone and gave his name in his normal voice.

'Who do you want to speak to? Oh, Mrs Isham, good evening to you.'

'No, this isn't Mrs Isham, this is a friend of Mr Isham's. Is he there?'

'Yes he is, just a moment.'

Another pause. The Treasurer ruminated. It did seem a little odd, but there was no reason why a bona fide friend of Isham's, wanting to get hold of him urgently, should not have got his week-end number from his wife. And yet . . . He picked up the telephone once more.

'I'm sorry, I'm afraid I was a little too optimistic just now. Mr Isham seems to have stepped outside for a moment. I can't imagine why, on a disagreeable evening like we're having up here, but anyway he's not in the hostel. I don't see how he can be very long, so if you'll just give me your number, I'll ask him to –'

'Thank you, it doesn't matter.' The unknown woman rang off.

Further thought. If it was not worth being rung back from Yorkshire, how had it been worth ringing up from London? The Treasurer sighed, added water to his drink, hesitated, added more Scotch, drank. Before he could sink back in his chair a sound from upstairs sent his hand diving into his clothing and emerging with the bundle of instructions the Secretary had handed him in the train. Yes, here was Isham's name, and opposite it a telephone number preceded by a trunk-dialling code. He dialled code and number, recalling as he did so the Secretary's words at the final briefing for the Seminar. 'This great step forward in the technique of communications,' he had said, 'means that one can now dial one's home direct from supposedly Land's End with no operator's

107

voice to butt in with the information, "John o' Groats calling you, hold on, please." The history of warfare and of espionage shows how often their methods have been advanced by apparently quite remote and unconnected innovations in technology.'

The line clicked and buzzed. 'Garden House Hotel,' said an East Anglian voice.

'Mr Isham, please . . . Isham? This is Mr York. Are you alone?'

'Yes, but make it quick.'

In the finest Egyptological style the Treasurer now compressed what had happened into a couple of dozen swift unambiguous words. 'I should just ring your home,' he suggested finally, 'and ask if everything's all right. Then your wife's bound to say who it was who –'

'I don't need any advice, thank you,' said Isham's voice. 'I suppose you didn't . . .' He broke off and said away from the telephone, 'Shan't be a moment. There's your drink;' then, to the Treasurer again, 'Any idea who it was?'

'No.'

'Oh well, it can't be at all urgent. Good of you to let me know, all the same, York. I'll look into the matter on Monday. Good-bye to you.'

'Good-bye, sir.'

The Treasurer took another sip of whisky. Something was definitely wrong here. But before he could start working on what it might be, the door opened and Lee Eddington Schwartz came in.

With her black hair drawn straight back from forehead and temples, her high-necked olive-green jacket with black piping and buttons, and her tight black trousers, she looked like a young and ambitious captain of the Royal Lesbian Rifles in mess dress. The Treasurer was well aware, however, that any such seconding would have had to be the result of an error at Base. He kissed her and gave her a drink.

Over the last couple of months she had shown herself an excellent companion, asking no questions, making no demands, never going near that vast multi-manual instrument for the pressuring of men on which every woman is a virtuoso. His suspicions that she might have been a spy of some sort, from an employee of the Society's wives to an agent of the C.I.A. or F.B.I. interested in van Dorn, had vanished for ever. When she asked him now who it had been on the telephone (an exceptional indulgence in curiosity), he answered without hesitation, though without much candour either,

'Oh, that was the wife of that friend of mine I was telling you about, the one I'm covering up for. She's always fussing. I think she was quite pleased to get hold of me instead of him, so that she could ask me if he was taking care not to get his feet wet and so on. She'll probably be through another time or two before she's finished.'

'I suppose you have to call him now, do you?'

'I already have.'

'Does your wife fuss?'

'No, you couldn't say that against her.'

'What could you? Say against her. It's no business of mine and you shut me up right away if you want, but I'm naturally interested. There must be something wrong between you or you wouldn't be here with me, would you?'

'I wouldn't say there's anything wrong between us, never has been anything serious beyond, you know, the monthly row, and everyone has those. No, if I had to find something to say against her, I imagine it would be along the lines of her never having said anything the least bit interesting or amusing or original.'

'I see. And you don't call that having something wrong between you?'

'Well, it isn't what you'd call very serious, is it? She doesn't say anything striking and I don't expect her to. I should have thought that was an ideal arrangement. We certainly don't have rows about that.'

'What do you have rows about? I can ask you all this? You don't mind?'

'Not when you do it. You can get away with anything. You are the most attractive specimen of your sex I feel I ought to be able to imagine. All hail, Biology, mistress of sciences, and for that matter . . . You're my little trigger, and I'm your response.'

The Treasurer put his arm round her shoulders and his mouth against the smooth longitudinal strands across her scalp, not a difficult manoeuvre with her sitting on the floor beside his chair. He kissed the top of her head feelingly but with due restraint. He had never been known to disarrange a girl's hair-do, much less tear her blouse, had unhesitatingly forfeited the quite valuable effect of

109

ungovernable passion attributable to such excesses, and often thought that his (to be frank) not unremarkable success with women was in some part due to his moderation in such matters, or more properly to the attitude of respect which they must sense lay behind this policy. He put his hand up under the back of her jacket and stroked her spine. 'Splendid stuff,' he said vaguely.

She nestled against him. 'What about these rows? Don't tell me if you don't want to.'

'What rows?'

'You know, the ones with your wife. You needn't –'

'Oh, those. Don't you worry about them, I can handle them. Just says I never take any notice of her. Would if there were anything to take notice of. Funny thing to say. Not a besetting sin of mine. Rather the other way round, wouldn't you agree? Pay too much attention?' He moved his hand round to her waist. 'Always on at you? Never leave you alone?'

'Between us it's different.'

'But who wouldn't, anyway? I can think of people who wouldn't but I wouldn't like to have to.' The Treasurer put his other hand on the other side of her waist and squeezed inwards gently. 'Oh, very finely made. Funny how it's always so narrow just there. Well, nearly always. Argument for a benevolent Creator. Good sound practical reasons why everything else should be roughly as it is.' He indicated manually a couple of examples of the everything else. 'But no good sound practical reason why there should be this marvellous in-and-out arrangement lower down.' He had put his arms round her and was kissing her zealously when the telephone rang. Picking it up with no zeal at all, he said in a throaty voice,

'Allaw, Scotton W.E.A. Hostel here.' He managed to give Miss Schwartz a wink.

'This is an obscene telephone call,' said a girl's voice, speaking, it seemed, with unnatural precision. 'Do you know what I should like to do to you? First of all I'd take hold of –'

'Ee, I think you must have wrong number, lass. This is the – '

'. . . and then I'd tie you to the bedposts and give you a first-class – '

'Luke here, miss, whoever you are, you've got hold of the wrong – '

110

'. . . and if there was anything left in you after that I'd –'

'Will you listen a minute? You've naw call to keep on and –'

'. . . until you begged for mercy. This is a recorded announcement.'

The line went dead. The Treasurer drank, trying to conceal his disquiet and think up an instant cover-story at the same time. The unknown caller's voice had been clear but not loud enough, probably, to have been verbally audible at more than a few feet from the receiver. Bank on that, then.

'That woman was really quite abusive. I wonder who she was.'

'What did she want?'

'Well, she'd misdialled or something, asking for someone I'd never heard of. Called me a liar and Christ knows what when I tried to tell her.'

'Maybe she was mad at that hick accent? Was that Yorkshire?'

'As near as I can manage, yes. It's an old joke between my friend's wife and myself. She always pretends to think I come from Yorkshire.'

Here for once, he reflected, the Secretary would have been less than best pleased with his ingenuity. The devising of an explanation for the necessary 'Allaw, Scotton W.E.A. Hostel' formula had been left to him, on the sensible grounds that no man could lay down what would fool another's girl. The Treasurer had considered the private-joke notion adequate on first thinking of it, but that had been five minutes before meeting Miss Schwartz at York station, when his critical faculty had no doubt not been at its sharpest. Oh well, he was stuck with it now. With luck he would not have to use it again, unless indeed he was in for one of those experiences out of Evelyn Waugh in which a series of telephone calls keeps the recipient from a bed he is particularly set on climbing into. They were a little late in the day for that one anyhow, he said to himself, recalling complacently the events of the previous eighteen hours or so.

Just temporarily, that last call had had its anaphrodisiac effect: Miss Schwartz, after a glance that told of a successful effort to ask no more questions, had moved to an adjacent sofa and was lighting a cigarette. The Treasurer told her he thought he would nip up and have a quick wash.

'All right, honey. Do you want me to start fixing dinner?'

'If you would, darling.'

He kissed her lightly and went up to the small, barely serviceable bathroom. Outside, he saw, night was falling in a thin drizzle and the lights of the village were burning. Not an attractive area. He supposed he would never visit it again. Oh well, the world was full of other areas he would be visiting, and there was little enough about this cottage, obtained by the Secretary God knew whence, to encourage sentimental regret, unless one happened to like ill-fitting doors and windows, smoke-generating fires and trough-shaped beds.

He washed with unintended thoroughness, thinking hard. The conclusion seemed inescapable that 'Isham's friend' of half an hour earlier and the anonymous caller of just now were one and the same. Was that sinister? Not necessarily. By far the likeliest explanation was that the woman was one of Isham's discards who – yes – had got wind of the Seminar and guessed its true nature, knew Mrs Isham on terms which made it possible to ring her up and ask how to get hold of him, had failed to do so with her first telephone call and made the second out of fury, desire for a bit of 'fun' or some inscrutable motive to be positively expected in one of Isham's bits. He had said more than once that he liked them to be perverse and difficult. There might be awkwardness in store for the Warden of the Scotton W.E.A. Hostel should the woman take it into her head to return to the charge, but this could be dealt with – 'that lunatic woman abusing me again' and so on. No, any sinister quality in the situation threatened not the Society, but Isham, who must be acquainted with the new turn of events as soon as possible. Mm. How soon was that going to be?

Pondering again, but much relieved in mind, he went downstairs and into the low-ceilinged kitchen, where a meal which he recognized as of remarkable elaboration was in the making. He stood with his back to the sink, flexing his right knee, squeezing parts of the thigh between finger and thumb and wincing softly. It soon got him the attention he wanted.

'Darling, what's the matter? Are you sick?'

'It's nothing,' gasped the Treasurer. 'Just a tiny shell-fragment I got in the Ardennes. Plays me up a bit sometimes when the weather's like this. Comes and goes in a few minutes, very often. Makes walking a bit . . . dodgy.'

'There must be something I can do?'

'No, I'll be all right. Perhaps, though . . . No, it wouldn't be fair to ask you.'

'Please honey, what is it? Let me help you.'

'Well, it's just that I'm very interested for business reasons in whether a certain announcement was or was not made this afternoon. An evening paper would tell me, and I was just going out for one when this damned –'

'You want me to go? I'll do it now before I get too far ahead with dinner.' She whirled a black mackintosh round her shoulders. 'What sort of paper? Oh, any? I'll find one. Be right back.' She was gone.

The Treasurer ran painlessly into the next room and seized the telephone. His readiness with the shell-splinter story testified to no native wit but, as so often, to the thoroughness of the Secretary's preparations. Nothing was more necessary than that the Seminar Duty Officer should remain within reach of his telephone at all times, and the Treasurer, having mastered his instructions in this regard, had been ready with a lengthy display of wound-trouble so severe as to confine him to a circuit between his armchair and his bed (where the adverse effects of the splinter would fortunately prove unnoticeable). He had even been prepared to show on demand a suitable scar, a nasty-looking folded-in affair where a childhood playmate had bayoneted him in the leg with a park railing. But in the event none of this rigmarole had been needed. At breakfast that morning, a single introductory sentence about not feeling much like stirring outside had won instant and delighted agreement, followed up by an hour's shopping for meat, vegetables, fruit, herbs, spices and condiments. He had stayed indoors to 'work at his papers'. Nobody, of course, had telephoned during that time, though there had been the chance of giving the Secretary the morning situation report (nil).

After some delay he reached Isham, who had had to be summoned from the bar. He heard the Treasurer out in silence, said there was nothing to worry about, and broke the connexion. Ten seconds later the telephone rang, which presumably, there being no sign yet of a returning Miss Schwartz, was some kind of belated reward for careful planning.

The caller was Mrs Mordle. As soon as the Treasurer had come

113

on in his own identity, with the usual tale of momentary inability to locate but ability to swear that not five minutes ago, etc., the good lady went into a monologue at horserace-commentary speed about having been rung up by the Anglo-Egyptian Archaeological Institute with a request that Mordle present himself there at 10.30 on Monday morning. She had accepted for him. Had she done right. Could she please be rung back and assured that she had done right? She felt badly about the matter because the call had come through ten minutes after her husband had left for King's Cross yesterday afternoon and she had only just remembered it.

The Treasurer said okay. He dialled Mordle's number like a man possessed, helping out the anti-clockwise rotation by shoving with his forefinger, but had time to grin admiringly at Mordle's conscientious following of Article 31 : *For coded telephone messages and the like, a discreet use of Egyptological terms is recommended.* The fellow was licking himself into shape after all.

A young man's voice answered. He was afraid Mr Mordle was not available at the moment, but would be very happy to take a message. Yes, he would see that Mr Mordle was given that information as soon as he became available.

The Treasurer mixed himself another drink, grinning again. He looked forward to discussing this bit of Mordleana with Cambuslang. It really did sound as if . . .

The outside door slammed. 'Sorry I took so long. I had to go to three places.'

'Oh darling, you shouldn't have bothered. Mm . . . sweet of you.'

'I liked to do it. Don't you want to see if that thing is in or not?'

'Oh yes.' Quickly, but with some show of thoroughness, he scanned the main news pages of the paper and the City page. 'Nothing.'

'Is that what you wanted?'

'Indeed it is.' He spoke heartily. He felt he should pay her back in what coin he had in his possession for having forced her out into the rain for twenty minutes or so. 'Marvellous news. Calls for a celebration.'

She bounced up and down a few times, like someone getting ready for a standing jump. He did the same before breaking off with a timely wince. 'Got to be careful for a bit, I'm afraid.' He kissed her and stroked the top of her head. 'Your hair's all wet. You should have put a scarf round or something,' he finished severely.

'It's all right, I'll just let it dry. Nothing can go wrong with it when I've got it done up like this. I'm so happy.'

Dinner consisted of vichyssoise with chives, lamb cutlets with young peas and new potatoes, and home-made apple pie with ice-cream. The main course was washed down with a bottle of Bragg's Aloxe Corton 1959 which had largely survived being carried 250-odd miles in the Treasurer's suitcase. Over excellent coffee and a glass of Hine, a Willem II panatella burning in his mouth, his arm round an almost recumbent Miss Schwartz, the Treasurer felt that the mysterious caller, Isham, Mordle, Mrs Mordle, Mordle's boy friend were of no moment at all. What was so good about the Seychelles?

After a long silence Miss Schwartz said, 'It's funny we never talk about Egypt. Oh, I wouldn't want to go into it deeply, but I would like to kind of chat about some of those old guys. For instance . . .' She stopped.

'One day we will. But for the moment it's all tied up in my mind with regrets about that Society of ours and all the bitterness over the thing packing up, the recriminations and tension and . . . It's a painful subject even now.' And the Treasurer went on to contrast favourably his present situation with that current at the time of their first meeting, Miss Schwartz's attractions with the dubious and unserviceable charms of Nefertiti, and things like that. They retired early.

The evening passed more than pleasantly. Shortly before midnight the Treasurer said he thought he should go down and telephone his wife just to make sure she was all right. He was speedily connected with the Secretary, who sounded a little abrupt.

'You're not AOJ, I hope?'

'No, though ten minutes ago would certainly have been a bad time. She's asleep now. Well, what news?'

The Treasurer made his report, omitting reference to the sex of Mordle's presumed companion.

'Mm . . . I agree with you that the Isham thing is probably no concern of ours. I only hope the same is true of Mordle's Monday appointment.'

'What do you mean?'

'I'll tell you later. What's the weather like up there?'

'Rainy and gusty. Rather miserable.'

'Quite pleasant here,' said the Secretary's voice. 'Well, you can give us your full meteorological report on the train home tomorrow. See you in the compartment – probably best not to hang about on the platform. Thank you and good night.'

The next morning seemed at first to have very few hours in it. The Treasurer, in the presence of Miss Schwartz, telephoned his wife as arranged, saying he would be home about midnight. Then there was the preparation and eating of lunch. Then it turned out that there was still some time to go before they must leave. They used it to advantage.

In the afternoon the weather cleared. A watery sun illumined the Treasurer's sturdy form as he stood at the threshold waiting for the station taxi. Spring had won a foothold at last. From the very beginning it had been an enjoyable week-end and, as far as he personally was concerned, a completely secure one. This was, after all, a matter of duty. That soldier is recklessly vigilant who protects his comrades at the sacrifice of himself, and that spy vainly gallant who suffers capture in order to accomplish the – temporary – escape of his colleagues. The Treasurer was certain that Lee Eddington Schwartz knew nothing of the Society. She had accepted at once the condition that the two of them travel both ways by different trains, and no less readily the background to it: Yorkshire's importance in the clothing industry, the positive likelihood that some business contact of his would be travelling down to London that evening. Finally, she seemed satisfied that, as far as his wife knew, he had come north on a business trip – at the week-end? Yes, the fellows he had come to see, proverbially given to driving themselves even harder than their employees, would be accessible only then. It was a pity about the waiting-around necessitated by separate travel, but he had shared this out with scrupulous fairness. She had had a chance to grab a half-eyeful of York's antiquities on Friday while he came up on the later train; tonight, after she had caught the earlier, he would have

116

time for a few drinks with a real business contact at the city's Conservative Club before setting off for London.

The taxi rounded the corner and came rattling up the street. He went in search of Miss Schwartz and found her in the kitchen, apparently just looking at it.

'Come on, darling, the taxi's here. What are you up to ?'

'Nothing. I was making sure I didn't leave anything behind.'

'Good . . . Well, we've got plenty of time.'

13   The Cover Slips

CAESAR: Let's grant it is not
         Amiss to tumble on the bed of Ptolemy.

About half-past six the following Thursday evening the President, as was his custom, sought out his wife to say good-bye to her before going off to meet the Society's speaker, entertain him to dinner and take the chair at the lecture and subsequent discussion. This week, according to the official programme, they were to be addressed by Signor Ettore Miramare, Professor of Egyptology at the University of Padua, on *Syncretism under the Bubastide Dynasty*.

The President's wife, as was her custom, or one of several such, was lying on her bed reading an illustrated magazine. At her side was a half-drunk drink: vodka on the rocks, most probably.

'I'm away to my revels, my old love. Back to the nest soon after eleven, I hope. Depends how long the discussion goes on. I'm going to try to cut it short this evening.'

'You do that. I expect you feel you had enough . . . let's call it chit-chat at the week-end. Who have you got tonight?'

He told her. 'Chap's got an international reputation,' he added.

'Has he, now? What's this sin-what-not he's talking about?'

'Syncretism? Well, in the Late Period it means roughly the way the attributes of the various deities started to overlap and become blurred. You know, as if James Bond got a medical degree and started reforming alcoholics like Dr Kildare and so on.' The President did a patronizing smile to go with the 'homely analogy' line he had adopted.

'Really? Sounds *fascinating*.' She put her magazine aside and swung her legs off the bed. 'I'd no idea it was that sort of thing. Would it be all right if I made one more for dinner? I'd like to hear what this man's got to say. It's a long time since I came to one of your lectures. Might even improve my mind, if it's not too late.'

There was a small interval. During it the President's mind went into overdrive, though for the moment not helpfully. He was stuck

118

with the memory of a burlesque once contrived by himself and a schoolfellow, a version of Browning's 'Incident of the French Camp' distorted by some characteristic turns of phrase out of Lewis Carroll. It had run, in part,

> So tight he kept his lips compressed
> Scarce any blood came through:
> And this was odd, because, you know,
> His breast was shot in two.

Afterwards, the President was to reflect ruefully on the narcissism he had shown by finding his own predicament comparable with that of Napoleon's young staff officer who, especially as presented in this modified form, had achieved a far more noteworthy level of steadiness under fire than any he might himself aspire to. (He cheered up a little at the thought that narcissism of a kind had often been judged indispensable to great actors.)

Anyway, so tight the President kept his lips compressed that not so much as a squeal of panic came through. 'Excellent idea,' he heard himself saying with intent cordiality. 'Splendid. Now, you throw on a glad rag or so while I telephone round the place and get hold of someone to meet old Miramare – we couldn't make it to him in time unless we left straight away. Then I'll just have a word with the restaurant and we needn't rush.'

She seemed to be considering. He was calming himself down by telling himself that this special type of emergency, though it had arisen in its full form only twice in the whole history of the Society, was nevertheless exhaustively catered for in its Article 6: *Members whose wives wish to attend a lecture must block this by counterfeiting one of the following* – and there followed a list of incapacitators with attendant symptoms. Of these, food-poisoning probably offered most scope, or perhaps slipped disc. Anyway, the period of total alarm was over.

He noticed that his wife was watching him. 'What's this chap like as a lecturer?' she asked.

'Oh, really very good, considering. His English is appalling and he does go on and on rather, and then he has this rather mad thing of refusing to explain what he thinks are elementary references, so one does have to keep one's poor old wits somewhat about one, but apart from that –'

'He sounds a dream. But . . . perhaps . . . well . . . somehow

119

I get the feeling I might be out of my depth.' She was still watching him. 'Would you think I was an utter moron if I changed my mind?'

'Not at all,' said the President. 'In point of brute fact I think you would have found tonight rather on the esoteric side. We'll see if we can't find something a little more popular for you later in the year. The Secretary's got something of the sort in mind. Well . . . I think I'd better be off right away if I'm not to keep that charming old wop waiting.'

His wife waited until she heard the front door shut. Then she said aloud, 'Phew! That was a near one for our hero,' and got up off the bed.

An hour later, looking pretty good in a dark-brown antelope coat and with upswept hair, she was talking earnestly to Eric Lasker in the Salisbury public house in St Martin's Lane. Or rather Lasker was talking earnestly to her; she never talked earnestly to anyone.

'What is this barrier?' he asked her. 'I can't understand it – they were as nice as pie the day I had lunch with them, all chattering away about their various bits of obsession – they'd be absolute naturals if only I could get them on to the screen – well, the other two would be, certainly, though I'm not so sure about your husband, who I must say I found a bit hard to follow at times, mumbling away in his beard as if –'

'Oh, was he?' she asked interestedly. 'That doesn't sound like him at all. How very odd. You must have caught him at an off time.'

'Of course, a lot of people who burble away in ordinary conversation sound off as clear as a bell when they get in front of the cameras. Anyway, this barrier. None of them strike me as shy or modest men, and yet every time I talk about the actual programme they say, oh, the subject's too boring, not suitable for my audiences, they don't know enough about it really – unless they simply go on about Rameses as if I hadn't spoken. Now I know what ordinary sort of long-distance telly-fright looks like. And this isn't it.'

The President's wife thought for a moment. 'What form would it take, this bit of your programme, if it went on?'

'Say twelve minutes, five or six going round these premises of theirs with the members saying what they get out of it all, and then the rest of the time the three of them discussing it with a serious, well, an academic Egyptologist. I've got a very good chap lined up, a Senior Lecturer in Ancient History at one of the London colleges who specializes in Egypt. Pretty tough egg, he is, not what you'd expect at all.'

'That sounds excellent, that part. In fact, if it were me I'd lay more emphasis on the discussion. Give them time to really sort out a few points. Our three lads would have a chance to show off how much they really know.'

'Mm, I don't know,' said Lasker, pulling at his beard, which, unlike the one he had attributed to the President earlier, really existed. 'It's a pretty esoteric subject.'

'Yes, but I've heard you say yourself that what makes good television is people really knowing their stuff and getting worked up about it. The subject as such is much less important.'

'That's true. Yes, a nine-minute discussion would get down to things more. I'll have a think about that one. Still, we're no nearer getting through this barrier.'

'That one I'll have a think about,' said the President's wife, looking as if she had started to have one already. 'Tell me, when would this thing go out? It would be live, I suppose?'

'Yes. Well, I had hoped to get it in tomorrow week, but we're much too near that now, from their point of view. We're nowhere with them yet.'

'I'm not so sure. I think it might be good psychology, the idea that they can go on more or less straight away and get it over ... Would it be too late if I rang you on Monday, say, and gave you the word then?'

'No, there's always plenty of stuff on the spike. Sometimes we've actually had to start arranging to shove in a bit of standby film after the transmission's started.'

'We won't let on you can, though, will we? Make it easier for them to duck out.'

Lasker laughed. 'You've no need to tell me that,' he said. 'We're up to all those little ploys. Look, do you really think you can do something?'

'Yes. Let's make sure I've got it right. It would be Friday next week about seven? Good, I'll be in touch with you.'

'You really are most kind. Can I get you another vodka?'

'No thanks very much, I must be on my way.'

'Right ... Of course, the Society's meeting tonight, isn't it? What do you do with yourself on these occasions? Do you ever go to the lectures?'

'Very rarely. I've got my own diversions.'

'I'm sure you have,' said Lasker politely.

When the TV operative had vanished towards Charing Cross Road to pick up a taxi, the President's wife crossed the street and went into the Green Man, where Isham was waiting for her. He sprang up and got her into her seat with that show of urgency which, to the uncommitted observer, suggests a fear that the new arrival would, for two pins, do a smart U-turn and rush for the door. His many glances over his shoulder, similarly, as he waited at the bar for her vodka, hinted that he was hoping, if not to prevent her from stealing away, then at any rate to catch her in the act. Rejoining her, he looked quite tired.

'Well, what are we going to do?' she asked. 'What's in store for me?'

'Well, I thought we might go out and have dinner somewhere ...'

'What a mind you have.'

'... and then there's a place we can go to for a bit.'

'Oh, good ... A place? You mean not the usual place, your pal's place in Wilton Place? Well, I'm not going to that converted building-site shelter or whatever it was in Dulwich again. I'd sooner a telephone box on Waterloo station, thank you.'

'No, we haven't been to this place before. I think it's all right.'

'Whereabouts is it?'

'St John's Wood kind of area,' said Isham.

That was a just possible way of putting it, misleading without being flagrantly so. It would do. His whole scheme for tonight would probably do, and if it fell down, what then? The end of the Society, he supposed, but his attitude to that prospect had hardened a lot in the past week, since his departure for the Seminar and the accompanying medium-sized crisis of guilt. He was getting used to knowing that, any time at all, this girl might ask her husband one question which would blow everything sky-high. At times the idea became a positive stimulant, as submarine

122

crews are said – perhaps with minimal truth – to have been toned up by long spells of danger.

The President's wife was saying that if they had that far to go they had better see about dinner straight away, so they did. They went up the street to Beoty's. There he plied her with drink so assiduously that the waiter, misreading the situation rather, winked at him when setting down her third large vodka. Her more than fair share of a bottle of Gevrey Chambertin and a quick double Armagnac surely improved matters further, and when he followed her into the street and found night in the later stages of falling he felt quite confident.

He planned the taxi journey with a care that the Committee would thoroughly have approved, whatever they would have said about its purpose. He kicked off by wandering momentarily into truth and telling the driver that the place was hard to find, so let them be taken up Edgware Road and he would give directions from there. Then he got stuck into a bout of serious necking. This seemed to go down all right, so much so that he for his part forgot momentarily what he was about and was late with his notification of the left turn. No harm done there, though.

A pattern soon developed. 'Sharp right here and then first left,' a minute or so of scuffle, 'bear left past the pub and over the bridge,' more scuffle. After a while, both halves of the system began to give mild trouble. The cabman complained of being ill used: a close-range mumble from Isham about wanting to use up time brought an understanding nod, or what looked like one from a three-quarter-rear view under poor lighting conditions – at any rate, objection ceased. More seriously, he noticed at one point in the scuffles that the President's wife's eye, which he might have expected to find closed in passion or at least in a fine frenzy rolling, was in fact fixed purposefully past his shoulder on the details of the neighbourhood they were moving through. Or so he thought at the time. He redoubled his ardours, as far as he could without driving the lady through the upholstery.

They were there. Paying off the cab-driver, Isham received from him the second ribald wink of the evening, a gesture which, now the journey was over, he felt safe in returning with a glare and a sub-ethical tip. Then he led his companion across the street, through a wall doorway, across a small yard, up a spiral staircase

123

and into an irregularly shaped room. On the way he was asked a couple of questions, but not in any spirit of real inquiry, and once they were indoors no more were put. In fact, after saying brightly a minute later, 'Clean sheets, eh? We are going up in the world,' the President's wife desisted from speech for half an hour or more. When she finally returned to its use, however, there was plenty of inquiry.

'Who did you say this place belongs to?'

'Chum of mine.'

'Whereabouts are we, exactly?'

'That's just it, I can never remember the name of the street,' said Isham, adhering strictly to the Society's new Article 50 (Isis Room). 'It's not easy to find, either, as you saw.'

'Yes, I did. Aren't we quite a long way west of St John's Wood?'

'Are we? I don't know. I've only been here once before.'

'For the same purpose, no doubt.'

'Not at all, my chum brought me along so I'd know where to find him.'

If Isham's field of vision had not been entirely bounded by the President's wife's cheek, neck, shoulder and so forth, he might easily have noticed the grin that reappeared on her face as he answered each question. 'Jolly sensible idea,' she said now. 'Let's see, I suppose he hasn't been moved in here very long?'

'Don't know – what makes you think so?'

'Well, it's a bit underfurnished, isn't it? Just these sort of basic-minimum bits of furniture and a few ornaments. Where does he keep his clothes and stuff?'

'This is only the spare bedroom, you see. I imagine he uses –'

'Oh, there's more through that door, of course. Can I have a look round later? I'm interested in flats.'

'I'm afraid not. My friend's a nice chap, but a bit stuffy. He'll let people like me borrow his spare room from time to time, but he doesn't want to have anything more to do with it than that. He's got a lock on the outside of that door to sort of cut himself off when this kind of thing's going on.'

She succeeded, with some effort, in not shaking with laughter at this. 'I see,' she said. 'Sounds an odd sort of chap. Seems to have queer tastes.'

'Oh, there's nothing like that about him.'

124

'No. I meant these ornaments. They're Egyptian, aren't they?'

'Yes, he goes in for that sort of thing rather.'

'He's not a member of that Society you used to belong to, is he?'

'. . . No.'

'But no doubt it was your common interest in pyramids and everything that drew you together originally. You know, it really was rather nice of you to give all that up for my sake, just like that. A dedicated Egyptologist one week, and the next – finish. No more pyramids for Isham. What luck, though, having a ready-made alibi like that. Every Thursday, it's "Cheerio, dear, see you at bedtime – I'm off to find out a bit more about the pyramids." Marvellous. Tell me, what happens if your wife asks you about the lecture you're supposed to have been to? I suppose one of the chaps who's really been gives you a sort of briefing?'

'Yes.' Isham moved one of his hands. 'I'd give up much more than a few old pyramids for you, darling. Who wouldn't? You're the most –'

'That's the spirit. Look, I don't want to be a nuisance, but there is absolutely no chance of me having a drink, is there? If you could –'

'Oh, he said he'd put some in here. I'll have a look.' He got out of bed and went to a cupboard. 'He's a very hospitable fellow, you know. Here we are – vodka. I told him you liked it.'

'Super.'

'No ice, I'm afraid.'

'Never mind, straight is fine.'

He settled himself on the edge of the bed and they drank.

'How did the week-end go off?' she asked.

'Well, you ought to know about that.'

'No, I mean at home. No awkward questions? I suppose you had a pretty terrific briefing on a thing lasting that long.'

'Yes.'

'But it could be managed . . . I wonder if anyone's thought of carrying that idea a stage further.'

'How do you mean?' asked Isham, belatedly alerting himself.

'Well, supposing something like the Society existed simply to give its members alibis for quiet non-domestic evenings and an occasional dirty week-end. One chap would have to be really there at the end of a telephone, and he'd have to have the telephone

125

numbers of all the others so that he could get hold of them fast if anyone's wife started poking her nose in. You'd have to enjoy organizing and intrigue a bit for their own sakes if you decided to set it up, but then—'

'It's possible, I suppose, but I hardly think—'

'And you'd devote a lot of time and thought to deciding on your cover. A Society for something absolutely frighteningly boring. The wives brought along to a couple of genuine meetings right at the start, to show them how authentically boring it is and to reassure them as well. Lectures on Thursdays. That's a good touch. Nobody would believe anything interesting could happen on a Thursday. Oh, lots of other details. With a decent amount of luck you could keep it up for quite a time. There's only one thing that would be quite certain to blow up the whole issue.'

Isham looked at her dully. Medically convincing simulation of death seemed his only recourse.

'Aren't I doing well? Yes, what would send it all sky-high would be if one member started using the Society as an alibi for his goings-on with the wife of another member. He'd have to tell her he'd given up the Society, but he couldn't tell that to his wife or anyone else because he still needed it as an alibi. Then any one of a number of things could be fatal. The most obvious one would be if the wife, the one who was being carried on with, simply happened to ask her husband who was at last night's meeting or lecture or what-not. "Oh yes," he says, "we had a full turn-out. Your pal Isham asked a couple of frightfully intelligent questions." Eh?'

'I admit nothing.'

'It gave me a fair turn, ringing up that Catterick number at the week-end and being told you'd just slipped out for a second when I'd left you upstairs a couple of minutes before. What is it, two hundred miles? That's jet travel for you. Anyway, I couldn't resist making a bit of a nuisance of myself by telephoning your pal a second time and telling him how much I admired him. That set the wires humming properly, didn't it?'

He nodded.

'Mind you, that's nothing to the fun I'm going to have if another little scheme of mine comes off. By the way, it is the Society's offices and so on on the other side of that door, isn't it?'

126

He nodded again.

'Jolly daring of you, I must say, bringing someone along here who'd already been inside the place through a different entrance. Rather flattering too. Most men who'd got to the point where it was going to be here or nothing tonight would have plumped for nothing right away. Especially after that week-end. Yes, sir.'

'What actually put you on to us in the first place?'

'I told you, you did. No, that's not quite fair. I was just generally suspicious. That evening I came along when you were on duty I had a quick snoop, but I didn't find anything.'

'I know.'

'You mean you knew I was snooping and you still took me out and dated me up? Wow. You really jumped with both feet, didn't you?'

She was right, Isham reflected. That had been his first, worst, irrecoverable, unforgivable mistake.

'I suppose you'll be court-martialled or arraigned at the bar of the Society or what-not for this, won't you? If it comes out. I must see if I can't dope up some story that won't incriminate you, just for old times' sake. Oh well. What's the time? Mm, not bad. Now you put that glass down and come here.'

'Hm? Uh?' He looked surprised and slightly embarrassed.

'Oh, I see, I'm being unemotional, cynical, just *using* sex. Like a man, in fact. What a sentimental little thing you are. Fancy minding getting what you put into it out of it. You must learn to be practical . . . That's more like it.'

14   Storm Warning

CLEOPATRA: With news the time's in labour, and throes forth
   Each minute some.

Monday, May 18th, 11.15 a.m.

'Get out!' bawled the Treasurer. 'Out, I say!'

'But you've got to give me another chance. You should see the bills my wife's been running up at her dressmaker's. Even with what I've been pulling in here –'

'Then a life of penury is just what you need. With luck she may consider leaving you. Now go away.'

The man went. The Treasurer locked his hands behind his head and put his heels on his desk. He had just succeeded in sacking the buyer who had landed the shop with all those hairpins earlier in the year. The interview had daunted him rather in prospect, but in the event he had conducted it with effortless mastery. He recognized the sensation of easily clearing what would normally be an awkward obstacle as part of the process of falling in love. What would Miss Schwartz be like to be married to?

The buzzer on his desk buzzed, rescuing him from this dangerous line of thought.

'Yes?'

'Somebody says he must speak to you, sir. Sounds a bit agitated. Won't say who he is.'

'Oh Christ. All right, put him on.'

After a moment a muffled voice said, 'Is that the Manager?'

'Yes, sir, what can I do for you?'

'Does the name Heliopolis mean anything to you?'

'It might,' said the Treasurer warily.

'Good. It means something to me, too. Eight years ago I was nearer to it than you've ever been, nearer than any –'

'Who the hell are you and what do you want?'

'You know me well, but please don't mention my name. This line may be tapped. Now – I work among cold fronts.'

'Among . . . God Almighty, Fr –'

128

'Don't *say* it. I've been trying to get you all morning. Been trying to get the boss and the other fellow too, but neither of them's available. Now listen. You know our brother who lives many miles away?'

'Oh, old van –'

'*Quiet*, for Christ's sake. You remember he left us recently?'

'It's a dim memory, but I do.' The Treasurer and Cambuslang had accompanied the van Dorns to the airport some thirty-six hours previously. There had been a three-hour postponement of take-off with nothing but drink available to tide them over. Mrs van Dorn had gone to sleep at an early stage. 'On a great big silver bird.'

'Well, something disagreeable happened the other end.'

'You mean they –'

'No, they didn't crash. Now. I see the *New* – the newspaper from there every day. It's clear that you don't.'

'Look, my precious cold-front expert, if you don't tell me what this is all about I shall spell out your name at dictation speed.' Normally Froald's love of mystery was to be encouraged, both from the laughs to be got from it and as representing the right sort of attitude for an Egyptologist, but this was too much. He even sounded as if he had stretched a handkerchief over the mouthpiece of his telephone. The foes of the Society were too real to be put off with such bookish fantasy.

'Very well. Our brother was arrested for being in possession of narcotics. Hashish, to be precise. It was contained in that keepsake we gave him. With the keepsake in his luggage was a sheet of paper with a number of signatures on it. Our brother refuses to say who they belong to or to give any other information. According to him he bought the keepsake in London at a place he can't remember. The relevant authorities here have been informed . . . Are you still there?'

'Just about, thank you,' said the Treasurer, opening with his foot the drawer that contained his personal bottle of Bell's. 'Anything else?'

'That's pretty well it.'

'And quite enough too. So our brother's wife hasn't made a statement.'

'Not yet. Will you be at, uh, Heliopolis after work this evening?'

'I'll try. Thanks for letting me know.'

When Froald had rung off, the Treasurer tried to get hold of the Secretary at the firm of chartered accountants in which he was a partner, but to no avail. Communication at the first opportunity was arranged. Then the Treasurer sank his head in his hands, but soon recollected himself and got busy with the Scotch.

Monday, May 18th, 6.10 p.m.
'What's this all about, does anyone know?' asked Cambuslang.

The other three present in the Club Room – Isham, Mordle and the President – made negative gestures.

'It sounded to me like a pretty fair panic,' said Isham, 'but speaking for myself I find I'm getting used to them.'

'Well I'm not,' said Mordle.

'You need a drink,' said Cambuslang. 'We all do,' and he began the task of mixing and distribution.

'Has anybody been to the Fragonard Exhibition at the Philip Gallery?' asked Isham. He was quite sure why the Secretary had called the emergency meeting, but had determined to bear himself bravely to the end. 'It's a depressing experience.'

There were cries of incredulity and dissent.

'I don't mean in general, of course. It's just that for the modern painter – well, it's just not possible these days to have those marvellous décolleté poses with shepherdesses or court ladies showing off their bosoms apparently by chance. They all wear brassieres now, as we know, so a Fragonard-type arrangement would either look artificial or you'd get a tangle of straps and bits of cloth. You'd pretty well be recovering a lost art if you designed a brassiere to undo at the front. Has anybody ever tried?'

'I can answer that, I think,' said the Treasurer, who had entered a moment earlier. He resolved to continue this discussion as long as possible in the interests of group morale. It had an intrinsic appeal, too. 'They've got to do up – or let's say undo – at the back because the only adequate way of putting the damn things on is to lean forward slightly' – here he leant forward slightly – 'and, uh, allow the breasts to sink into the receptacles provided. I can give you a professional assurance that models designed to your specifications have never proved a success. It's one of those maddening –'

130

'Look,' said Isham animatedly, 'why not have them unfasten at the front *and* the back? They could then be put *on* with the front fastened and the back unfastened, and then they could be *undone* from the front and Fragonard rides again.'

'They'd go *insane*, the poor little dears,' put in the President, 'fathoming the procedure afresh each time. It would mean having to count up to two.'

But the Treasurer was pinching his chin in thought. 'There might be unforeseen user snags, of course. Nothing impossible in the theory of it, though. I'll have one put together at the shop, just out of curiosity. I run a little sort of *ad hoc* experimental laboratory there. Shouldn't take them more than a day or two.'

'That's very public-spirited of you.'

The Secretary came into the room at this point, closely followed by the Superintendent. The pair had a conspiratorial as well as grim air about them, reminding Isham of gangster chiefs arriving to conduct a purge of the rank and file. Well, that was appropriate enough.

When the meeting had been called to order, the Secretary read aloud the relevant clipping from that day's *New York Times*.

There was a horrified silence, into which the Superintendent manfully stepped.

'Well, gentlemen,' he said, 'not much use pretending we haven't taken a nasty knock, is there? But let's try and use our heads about this thing. Let's sum up what we know.

'Since our Secretary telephoned me this noonday I've had time to institute one or two inquiries round the place. It's possible to piece together some sort of picture of what's going on over there. A team of zoologists assembled by the New York Police Department find unanimously that the crocodile in the case originated in the African continent, most probably on or around the river Nile. An interesting coincidence, but one which neither attracts nor diverts suspicion in regard to ourselves, so we can –'

'Why mention it, then?' interrupted Cambuslang.

'Completeness, old man. Purely for the sake of completeness. All right? To proceed, then: van Dorn has a completely clean record with everybody, F.B.I., C.I.A., Interpol, the lot. I think we'd all have assumed that, wouldn't we?, but it's nice to have it in black and white, so to speak. Our friend has obviously been used

131

as an innocent carrier. What we've got to bank on is that the Yankee police – and don't go by the way you see them portrayed on the films and so on: they're exceedingly efficient and very nice people to work with into the bargain – well, we've got to hope they'll realize van Dorn isn't the man they want before their opposite numbers over here have time to uncover his British activities in a manner and to an extent that would embarrass us of the Society. And as to that, well, it's in the lap of the gods, gentlemen. They may be deciding as we sit here that van Dorn's contacts in Great Britain are no concern of theirs. Or they may not. I hate to end on a pessimistic note, but I'm informed that a team of handwriting experts assembled by the New York Police Department is working on those signatures of ours at this very moment. Well, no, that isn't strictly accurate, I suppose; their time being behind ours will probably mean they'll have broken for lunch. But in general I'm sure you take my point.'

It was all too clear that they did. Froald said hesitantly, 'Isn't there anything you can do, Super? To choke them off in any way? After all, we're completely innocent.'

The Superintendent looked shocked. 'Oh no, old man,' he said. 'There's nothing I can do to hold up the course of justice. Nothing at all.'

Tuesday, May 19th, 12.45 p.m.
As often before in periods of crisis, members seemed anxious for one another's company. The following lunchtime a small group assembled in the Club Room to discuss the situation. No new facts had become available since the day before, however, and the old ones, though rich in horror, gave little firm ground for debate. With the second round of drinks there developed a praiseworthily light-hearted chat about personal security, led by Isham, who still felt doomed but not very actively so. His view was, or purported to be, that the greatest danger lay in the most obvious traps: letters thrown into the wastepaper-basket instead of the furnace or the lavatory, telephone calls at 'safe' times, even that old smudge of lipstick, which after all these years still took its daily toll.

'Nobody's improved on the tie method yet, have they?' asked Froald. When the others stared uncomprehendingly he went on,

'Wiping it off on the lining, the folded-over part you can't see. Sorry, I thought everyone did that.'

'Indeed they do not,' said the President. 'In your usual unassertive way, my dear boy, you've made a contribution whose originality is only matched by its outstanding usefulness.' And he gave the little Egyptologist one of his sincerest smiles.

'What about scent?' pursued Isham. 'Has anyone ever been caught by that? Or is it just an old wives' tale, so to speak?'

'Scents all smell the same, don't they?' asked Froald.

'Good *heavens* no,' said Mordle. 'Not to some of us, anyway.'

'I find I personally have an uncommonly keen olfactory sense,' said the President.

'Have you really?' said Mordle respectfully. 'Have you really?'

With a vague idea of improving the tone of the conversation, Isham went off into indelicate reminiscence about once having had to dispose of a far more substantial indication of guilt than any mere lipstick or scent. He was in the middle of it when the door opened and the Secretary came in with Pinsent Boon, the M.P.

'This is our Club Room,' said the Secretary.

Boon nodded weightily, as though at the enunciation of a profound but decreasingly regarded truth. Then he said to Isham, who had stopped speaking, 'Do please go on. I mustn't interrupt. Won't you please go on?'

'So I had to stuff the damn things into my overcoat pocket and throw them off Chelsea Bridge the next morning,' ended Isham rather abruptly.

'Now I wonder how you'd have coped if it had been summer,' said Froald, but the President stepped in front of him and presented the company to Boon.

Isham thought the new arrival – not a member yet, but due to be put up the following week – looked very nasty. The volume of his jowls made undesirable any movement of his head, let alone the weighty nods he was renewing at each introduction. While these lasted, however, his narrow green Thai-silk bow-tie was only intermittently visible. He had at least one ring on each hand. It was hard to imagine him being any use to the Society, certainly not on the grandiose scale the Secretary had more than once hinted at. It was as hard to see why today had been chosen for showing him round, though if the arrangement had been made earlier than yesterday he could hardly have been asked to wait until the membership knew whether or not it was going to be arrested *en bloc* on suspicion of dope-trafficking, and admittedly the business-as-usual aspect of his induction was bound to be good for morale.

Just as the last handshake was disjoined the telephone rang. Isham, who was nearest, answered it.

'This is your most recent recruit,' said a voice.

'Sup –'

'Yes yes. Now listen. Our friend's wife made a statement early this morning – our time, that is. She's mentioned a number of names; I wasn't able to find out whose. Our people are starting to trace them. They won't make a move, though, unless and until they hear something definite from the other side of the water. You'd better tell all our party to be on their guard.'

'That's a great help,' said Isham. 'What sort of on their guard?'

'I wish I knew, old man. If I did I'd tell you, make no mistake about that. I just thought I'd better pass on what I'd found out. I'll keep in touch. Good-bye now.'

'That was our pal the Super,' said Isham.

'Oh good,' said the Secretary. 'How is the old fellow?'

'Not quite so well.'

'I'm sorry to hear that. Not really bad news, I hope?'

'I didn't gather so. Those tests the American blokes are running haven't come up with anything definite yet.'

'I see. Grounds for cautious optimism, then. Well, what about something to eat? What's been laid on?'

'Furze is doing ham sandwiches for six,' said the President, 'and there'll be some cold beer.'

'Fine,' said the Secretary. 'Will sandwiches and beer be all right for you?' he added to Boon – a shade hectoringly, Isham thought.

The politician nodded with a dance of jowls. 'Very much so,' he said with fervour, no doubt sensing that any lesser emotion might result in his being told that in that case he could bloody well go out into the garden and eat worms.

Froald pressed the bell and very promptly Furze appeared with the refreshments. He was looking a little more crazed than usual today – though polite enough when presented to Boon – and

134

nobody (except perhaps Boon) was much surprised when he launched a tirade. After all, the next Ladies' Night was on the horizon.

'I'm taking advantage of my length of service with this establishment, gentlemen,' he began earnestly, 'to remind you all, speaking very much off parade of course, of what to my way of thinking is a fundamental error in your attitude. I refer to the fact that although you're all very properly opposed to the institution of marriage, you appear not to have glimpsed the undesirable factor common to all marriages. The trouble with them is that they're contracted with women.

'Now it's not my intention to attempt to break new ground. I just want to very briefly run over the main points. No use or ornament after they're forty. Unable to put together or to follow three consecutive statements. Total devotion to their own interests – and don't talk to me about your nurses and your teachers, they're just sly and nothing more. They end up as matrons and headmistresses if they can and I take it that none of us here need any reminding about what *they're* like. They'd be prison wardresses if they could, only there aren't enough jobs to go round in the clink. That'd be something like a world, though, that would – half the ladies in prison where they belong and the other half looking after 'em. That'd take some silly grins off a few faces and no mistake.

'The trouble with you gentlemen, and believe me I say this with all respect, is that you're obsessed with sex. And what's that? Playing with yourself in company. When Mrs Furze and I were united in matrimony I told her she was going to get it once a month as long as I continued competent, no more, no less. And I've stuck to that for nearly thirty-five years. It can't be very long now before I'll have worked out my service.'

'One point it seems to me you've overlooked,' said Boon, doing everything possible in the way of face-crinkling and shoulder-raising to show how totally equal with Furze he felt, 'is that if everybody adopted your attitude the human race would very soon die out.'

'Yes, it would, sir, wouldn't it? Now there's quite a bit of ham left down in my basement, so if any gentleman would like seconds he's only to say.'

There were no takers, and within a few minutes the remnants of the meal were removed.

'What's it like being a politician?' Froald asked Boon.

'Heaven,' said Boon, crinkling his face anew. 'And hell, of course.'

The front-door bell rang.

15 A Deception and an Unmasking

ANTONY: Now sirrah – you do wish yourself in Egypt?

Tuesday, May 19th, 2.05 p.m.

Everybody agreed afterwards that it was a case of simple bad luck. Furze could not have been allowed to answer the bell in his current manic state; Mordle was nearest the Club Room door and so was tacitly elected to do the job.

On the front doorstep he found himself confronting a woman whom he recognized as Mrs Cambuslang. She explained that she had been passing through the area and had decided to look in at the Society's premises, where she knew her husband sometimes appeared for a snack lunch. Mordle's ready enough counter that Cambuslang was not present today drew no response. In the few seconds available to him he tried his best to think.

Although he had proved quite capable of performing the duties of a member of the Society, even to the Secretary's partial satisfaction, he could hardly be said to carry them out *magna cum laude*. There had been the unfortunate occasion when, as Duty Officer, he had played the Club-noises record to a telephoning wife at 78 r.p.m. instead of 33⅓. Not exactly a weak link, even so, but certainly one of the weakest in the chain.

The trouble was now that Mrs Cambuslang was a powerful woman in every sense. Worse still (as Mordle later explained), she reminded him strongly in both accent and appearance of that Scottish governess he had previously denounced, a woman apparently carved out of some unusually refractory rock, and in fact known to him and his brothers as Old Granite. Mrs Cambuslang was smiling, but even her smile looked to the flustered Mordle like some fault in a Grampian cliff-face. Given time, he would no doubt have rallied from this left-right of boyhood memory and present actuality. But before this could happen she had rumbled past him like a rock-slide. The best he could do was to divert her into the Lecture Hall. The solemnity of the place appeared to quieten her down a little.

She looked a trifle gloomily at the magazines lying on top of the bookshelf, possibly expecting something like the display at station bookstalls: *Annales du Service des Antiquités de l'Égypte*, *Journal of Egyptian Archaeology*, *Recueil de Travaux Relatives à la Philologie et à l'Archéologie Égyptiennes et Assyriennes*, *Sphinx*, *Zeitschrift für die aegyptische Sprache*. If she had opened the last-named she would indeed, it was later discovered, have found a copy of *Titter 6*, insecurely left there by some Duty Officer, presumably Isham. (The consensus of the membership had been that, while perhaps not quite up to the Superintendent's rhapsodic account, it was an outstanding buy, the Margaret Middleton poses being particularly singled out for praise.)

She – Mrs Cambuslang, that is – turned and walked across to the display case, where she picked up one of the figurines from the boat and asked quite mildly what it represented. Mordle even began to reflect that her figure, though more unrelievedly convex than Miss Middleton's, confirmed a periodic impression of his that there was something to be said for women. He was soon recalled to his duty when she said,

'Will you excuse me while I go to the bathroom?'

This request, while throwing some reassuring light on the motive of the lady's visit, caught Mordle on the wrong foot. He remembered that the original lavatory, one flight up from the ground floor, was in process of redecoration by Furze and encumbered by buckets and a stepladder. Before he knew what he was doing he had directed Mrs Cambuslang to the recently installed facility next to the Isis Room. Then he dashed into the Club Room and explained the situation. He had hardly finished when a female voice came down the stair well,

'Oh, Mr Mordle, do come up and explain the things in this room to me.'

The President started, thereby throwing into prominence his slight resemblance to a neurotic borzoi. The rest of the company registered alarm in their less spectacular ways.

She had got into the Isis Room!

The Secretary took command. Wasting no time on asking how the vital door came to be unlocked, he said, 'Mordle. Up there and waffle, quick. We'll dig you out as soon as we can.'

Then he turned, walked unhurriedly over to the door of the office, unlocked it and went inside. A drawer could be heard opening.

In the Isis Room, Mordle was saying, 'We haven't got this properly organized yet, but we're trying to turn the place into some sort of replica of an Egyptian shrine. It's been delayed by argument among the members about which period we should aim at. Your husband, for instance, favoured the Ramessids . . .' And he went off into an account of the dynastic schisms which, to hear him talk, had all but brought the Society down in a welter of blood.

After a couple of minutes of this, Mrs Cambuslang suddenly asked, 'What's this bed?'

'I know, it does spoil the effect, doesn't it?' Mordle went quite smoothly into the relevant paragraph of Article 50. 'Our man Furze is redecorating his quarters in the basement and we've had to put him in here meanwhile. It's a nuisance, but it'll only be for a few days.'

At last, voices were heard on the stairs. And a moment later the door opened to admit the Secretary and a distinguished-looking bearded stranger wearing pince-nez with a black silk ribbon.

The Secretary was saying, 'And here, Professor, we have the little room I was speaking of – incomplete, alas . . . Oh, good afternoon, Mrs Cambuslang – how nice to see you. Let me present Signor Ettore Miramare, who as you probably know is Professor of Egyptology in the University of Padua. None of us will forget the magnificent lecture on syncretism he delivered last Thursday.'

The Professor, going perhaps a little too far, gallantly kissed Mrs Cambuslang's hand. He started to explain in voluble but heavily accented English how delighted he was to have been able to look in.

'. . . And this rooma. It is certainly very creditable to your enthusiasmo, but it looks a little curious to me, Mr Secretary. The frieze shows Twentieth Dynasty features, but this here, this faience bowl, a poor reproduction with all due respecta – surely this belongs rather earlier . . .'

Evidently too polite to censure further the very slight amateurishness he seemed to feel he had detected, he turned to Mrs

139

Cambuslang and asked, 'This subject which we all love so much, Signora – you love it too, or is it to you, ha ha, so much Greeka?'

Mrs Cambuslang ignored him. Sniffing the air, she demanded, 'What's this scent?'

The Professor also raised his nose. 'Ah, a very subtle touch! You have been burning the so-called Ra incense . . .' A roguish Latin twinkle appeared on his face. 'And this will interest the Signora! For it is, I believe, the proto-scent from which so many of our present perfumes are developed. Here too the civilization of Egypt must be given the credito. The base is the same, Vander-velde maintains, as several employed by Chanel and others, being derived from the musk-deer, which in dynastic times, as you know, frequented the Delta.'

The Secretary said, 'You shouldn't miss the opportunity of hearing the Professor expound his views on the influence of animal migration on the early cults, Mrs Cambuslang. We really need a blackboard for that, so if you'd like to come down to the Lecture Hall . . .'

Watching the Professor with admiring curiosity, Mordle saw him sniff the air again, more deeply, whereupon his expression, in so far as it could be read behind beard and pince-nez, seemed to become puzzled, or at any rate thoughtful. But he shepherded Mrs Cambuslang downstairs keenly enough, and five minutes later was pursuing her towards the front door, saying,

'Almost no royal activity was portrayed so frequently as hunting. The lion, the leopard, the antelope, the ibex, the gazelle, the giraffe, even the hippopotamusso . . .'

In the Club Room once more, the President removed beard and pince-nez and handed them to the Secretary, who put them back in their drawer among other items of similar purpose. The membership was given an account of what had taken place.

'Jolly quick-thinking of you to come up with that incense thing,' said Froald admiringly.

'Was the Isis Room in use last Thursday?' asked the Secretary.

'Yes, I had it,' said Isham. Always admit at once what can be found out anyway, he told himself.

'Better tell her to go easy on the scent-spray next time.'

Isham was light-heartedly agreeing when the President said

140

reflectively, 'I've smelt that scent somewhere before. She's not an actress by any chance, is she, your girl?'

'Article eleven,' said the Secretary, invoking the statutory interdiction on inquiry by one member into the sexual dealings of another.

Its mention gave Isham an instant's respite. He went into a pantomime of amazed, amused, rueful admission. '*Yes*,' he said. 'Who would have *thought* . . .? How simply –'

'That must be it, then.'

'Anyway,' said the Secretary, 'that was a creditably executed defensive operation against a formidable intrusive element. Your behaviour in the first phase, Mordle, was less than satisfactory, if I may say so, but you recovered well.'

Boon was glancing from face to face. He seemed a little bewildered. 'Does this sort of thing,' he asked, 'happen *often*?'

'All the bloody time these days,' said Froald peevishly.

'Agreed,' said Mordle.

'But it won't make you any less keen to join us, will it?' the Secretary asked Boon, smiling tightly.

The M.P.'s negative sent his jowls flying laterally.

The President still looked preoccupied.

Tuesday, May 19th, 11.25 p.m.

The Treasurer, doing nicely thank you with a glass of Glenlivet, a Shimmelpenninck Duet and Brian W. Aldiss's *The Dark Light-Years*, was sitting in his sitting-room when the telephone rang. He had acquired an aversion from this amenity in the last week or two, but this time picked up the instrument with moderate cheerfulness: at the other end would be his wife, hung up at Brenda's place in Barnet by a defaulting taxi or something.

'Furze here, sir. I'm afraid there's another emergency. I'm speaking from the public call-box at the end of the canal bridge about two hundred yards from headquarters. The Secretary's compliments, sir, and you're to report to me here as soon as possible. I'll be waiting in the immediate vicinity of the box. The Secretary said to say at the double, sir.'

'But look . . . what am I going to tell my wife? I can't just –'

'I'm authorized to tell you, sir, that you can state quite securely

141

that this is an emergency affecting the Society. I'll explain when you get here.'

The Treasurer said he was on his way, hung up, dashed off a note to his wife along the lines suggested and ran out into the street. A cruising taxi presented itself so readily that, as he flung himself into it, he half expected to be rushed off to some grisly interrogation by a Maltese revolutionary junta, say, or a group of Frenchmen. Yet no such translation occurred.

A thin tepid rain was falling as the Treasurer paid off the taxi and made his way towards the lighted parallelepiped of the telephone box. Three figures converged on him noiselessly out of the shadows, a collective feat set at naught by the presence on the opposite pavement of a small group of Negroes, held there for a moment by the simple fact of the converging, or possibly its noiselessness. As nothing more seemed likely to happen they moved disconsolately on.

'All right, old man,' said the Superintendent's voice. 'You come with me, if you will. I'll fill in the background for you as we go. Five minutes from now,' he said to the other two figures, identifiable in the strong light of a street-lamp as Furze and the Secretary. Then he led the Treasurer across the road and into a side-street.

'Not often you have to wait as long as this to confirm a hunch,' he went on. 'Though perhaps I'm being a bit unfair to myself by not calling it a deduction. Yes, check a deduction.'

'Do you mind telling me what the hell this is all about?'

'Sorry, old man, I quite thought Furze would have filled you in over the phone. Sensible of him not to have done, though, considering the time element. Not that that's going to be crucial in the present situation . . .

'Anyway, I can tell you're impatient. I want you to cast your mind back to ten days ago, eleven to be exact, when we were all on that train honking away like fools in the restaurant car. You can probably picture the scene quite easily. After a bit young Froald comes up with a question. "What about that intruder?" he wants to know. Then I dole out a load of old rubbish to do with impulse felonies and recidivism potential out of *The Criminal Investigator* – that's what I'd imagine you'd call the C.I.D. house magazine – and everybody's happy. Well, that was all a stratagem devised by the Secretary and myself to make a certain person think

142

he was safe and at liberty to try again. Come along, old man, we haven't got all night, you know.'

The Treasurer had slowed in his walk involuntarily as they passed a lighted window behind which a fair-haired young woman was in the act of unzipping her dress. 'Person?' he said, quickening up again. 'You mean a member of the Society? But anybody who – '

'Oh, I'm surprised at you. Not seeing that it had to be a member, I mean. There are only two ways of getting into a house without leaving indications of how you got in. One is by the highly expert employment of one of three sorts of highly specialized instrument. Now your expert criminal doesn't waste his time on places like our premises. He won't move for under five figures' worth and that junk we keep in there would hardly raise three. And whatever happened he wouldn't lower himself to drinking sherry, not with bottles of gin and Scotch handy. So whoever it was must have used the other method of entry, that's to say a latchkey.'

'When you say "whoever it was,"' said the Treasurer, 'I hope you don't mean you're pretty sure you know who this chap is but won't let on until your suspicions are confirmed. Because I'll just – '

The Superintendent laughed. 'I'm not as bad as that, am I, old man? You must have a low opinion of me. No, I'm *quite* sure I know who our friend is. I'm just giving you the chance of using your deductive faculties in the same way as I did. And it might be awkward my coming out and telling you, if by any chance he slips through our fingers tonight.'

'Deductive faculties?'

'Yes. Let me give you a clue to the clue. In the most old-fashioned manner possible, he gave himself away by something he said. Well, here we are. You've got . . . a good two minutes before he appears. Plenty of time to do all the deducing necessary.'

They had halted in Old Lane by the Isis Room exit. 'Before I get down to any of that,' said the Treasurer, 'I'd like to know the first thing about what's happening now.'

'Sorry, I thought that was obvious. Acting on my advice, the Secretary instructed Furze to watch for a light in the building as he walked home from the Red Lion each night. We had to wait some weeks, because our friend got a bad scare the first time.

143

But I knew he'd try again some time and tonight he has. So Furze complies with his standing orders by phoning me, and then while I call the Secretary Furze tries to get hold of another reliable member.'

'That's rather flattering.'

'Cambuslang was out,' said the Superintendent, perhaps in retaliation for the Treasurer's sarcasm about 'whoever it was'.

'Oh. Well, anyway, I presume Furze and the Secretary go in the front door and we grab the chap as he scoots out this way.'

'You can deduce after all, I see. Well, I don't expect you'll have time to do much with the other problem now. You'd better content yourself with drawing a name out of the hat, so to speak, and seeing if you're right.'

'Yes,' said the Treasurer. 'Okay, I've picked my candidate.'

'Who is it? I won't give anything away.'

'Chester.'

'Oh, yes, the man nobody ever sees. Why him?'

'I don't know, he's the most likely, in a way, because we know least about him. His motives seem mysterious.'

'That's just it. Oh dear oh dear. We don't know anything at all about the most important question of the lot.'

The Treasurer felt a fool, but had to say it. 'And that is?'

'What he's doing in there.'

'It may be something quite innocent.'

'So he runs away when he hears Furze come in the front door. Which piece of history should be repeating itself in ten seconds ... from now.'

In less time than that the door above their heads was flung open and a figure began to plunge down the spiral staircase. 'Don't make a move until I do,' muttered the Superintendent.

The figure shot into view through the doorway in the wall. Grabbing it somewhere about the upper arm, the Superintendent swung it round sideways, but imparted an equal and opposite motion to himself, so that the two flew asunder again. The Treasurer flung himself forward as the intruder started to run and was up with his man, who had not yet quite recovered his balance, in a few strides. He caught hold of a shoulder and hung on until the Superintendent had the other. 'All right, Mr Mordle,' said the

144

latter, 'you might as well come quietly. Your little game's over, whatever it is.'

'Didn't handle that too cleverly, did I?' he muttered to the Treasurer as the two of them followed a slouching, sagging Mordle up the spiral staircase. 'Had no idea I'd got so rusty. Fancy me going for a single arm like that. Well, just lack of practice.'

All five men assembled in the Club Room. Mordle sank into a chair and gave himself a fresh shot of sherry. The Treasurer went to the drinks cupboard in search of Scotch. The Superintendent and the Secretary began turning over the books, periodicals and pages of manuscript that were grouped around Mordle, on the table before him and on the floor at his feet. Furze said they would not be needing him further, accepted and downed in one a small Scotch, wished them good night and left.

'The soul of tact, that man,' said the Superintendent. 'Now, what have we here?' He picked up a typewritten sheet and read aloud, '"The verb in the earliest known form of Egyptian had displaced the Semitic imperfect and the perfect largely by new suffix-tenses derived from a participle with pronoun, such as *sdm-f* 'hearing he (is)' + 'he hears,' *sdm n-f* 'heard (is) to him' = he has heard. Coptic presents a remarkable contrast to" blah blah blah. Now I don't pretend to be able to follow all of that but if it isn't suggestive I don't know what is. What have you got to say to that, sir?'

Mordle might have quailed at this formalization of address had he had an equanimity left to quail from. As it was, he said with little inflection, 'It's out of the *Encyclopaedia Britannica*.'

'Perhaps it is and perhaps it isn't, sir. We'll be checking on it, naturally. Meanwhile, I think it'd be in your own interest if you made a statement.'

'Am I under arrest?'

'No,' said the Treasurer. 'And can we have a little less of this court-martial atmosphere? There's no reason to think he's guilty of any crime.'

'You shut up!' Mordle shouted at him. 'Yes, you! Shut up!'

'But I was only trying to –'

'What do you mean, court-martial, crime? How dare you! I haven't even done any harm to the Society, let alone break a law

145

of the land.' What had temporarily deflated Mordle had obviously been shock, not fear; he was now reflated and to spare. 'But why I should care about this . . . puny little concern I can't imagine. That's the mistake I made, caring what you thought of me . . .

'I've been sneaking in here like a wretched felon to write an article on the grammatical usages of the Middle Kingdom for the *Egyptological Bulletin*. I couldn't do it at home, or I'd have been ridiculed until I went out of my *mind*. A lot of the books and periodicals I needed were here and it was quiet. I ought to have come in openly, but people like Isham and that beastly Cambuslang would have jeered at me all the time. So here I am.

'I don't care what you do now. I'm hooked on Ancient Egypt and that's that. No doubt you'll simply split your sides when I tell you that on that Seminar week-end, when you lot were with your women, I was in the Cotswolds with a little informal reading-party of Oxford people studying the early inscriptions. I'll send you my resignation in the morning – you'll be glad to have it and I hope with luck to be admitted to the Anglo-Egyptian Archaeological Institute before very long. Then I shan't need you any more.'

After a short silence, the Superintendent said, 'Well, this beats cock-fighting. It certainly does. I knew it was you straight away, old man, as soon as you let on you were worried that time Furze turned up to tell us about the intruder business. The Treasurer here just said Furze had something we all ought to hear, which might have been anything from a bit of dry rot in the Isis Room to a row with the window-cleaner, but you wanted to know in a big way what was wrong. So I had no difficulty there, but it beat me fair and square what you were up to. There are limits to what the deductive process can achieve and I doubt if I'd ever have been able to work it out by the light of nature, so to speak.

'Just one question, old man, if you don't mind. Where does your wife think you are tonight?'

'I told her I was going out with a girl. We had a rumpus at dinner, and I just – '

Laughter arose. Mordle resisted it, but only for a space. After that, not very much effort on the part of the Secretary and Treasurer was needed to persuade him not to tender his resignation. They assured him in antiphon that a member with real Egyptological knowledge *and standing* would be a priceless asset to the

146

Society. The rest of the membership were to be sold the idea as a new and massive security measure. The Superintendent, humorously dilating on how silly the four would have looked if they had closed their net on Froald and Isham quietly playing chess, offered a hand and was accepted. A cover story for the episode, involving an unsuccessful and unapprehended burglar, was quickly run up. The Treasurer peeled the seal off a fresh bottle of Bell's.

Van Dorn, his toils, the danger he represented, seemed far away.

16   The Net Tightens

LEPIDUS: Noble friends,
        That which combined us was most great, and let not
    A leaner action rend us.

Wednesday, May 20th, 6.10 p.m.

The next evening the Treasurer turned up a few minutes early for
the usual pre-Thursday session to find Froald, Isham and Cambuslang deep in a discussion of marriage.

'Most women,' Cambuslang was saying, 'even if they don't
regard it as absolutely desirable in itself, sooner or later begin to
think of it as a test of whether a man really loves them. They say,
"If you loved me you'd marry me," in much the same way they
might say, "If you loved me you'd jump off that cliff for me." Only
the vainest and most egotistical woman would insist on the second
test, but the first, being one that vast numbers of apparently
reputable couples go in for without immediate injury becoming
evident, seems acceptable. In fact it is its very insidiousness that
makes it such a corrupter of character.'

Isham said, 'Like that girl throwing her glove into the lion's den,
with King Francis and all. Not love, he said, or rather quoth, but
vanity sets love a task like that.'

'*Exactly*,' said the Treasurer. 'And the hell of it is that no man of
any spirit can fail to accept the ordeal when he's crazy about a
girl and she insists – just as he'd fight a duel or take on a smallish
dragon.'

'So we're divided, then,' said Cambuslang, 'into the foolish
and the rash, who get married, and the wet and egotistical, who
stay single.'

'Well, perhaps that's as sound as the traditional three-fold
division into those who can't get women, those who can get them
but can't leave them, and those who can get them and leave them
but don't want them,' Isham replied.

Froald had been carefully pouring himself a French vermouth.
He now returned to the group to say, 'My wife's got the habit of

mumbling some song from a musical that everybody else has had the good taste to forget. It begins,

> 'Love and marriage,
> Love and marriage,
> Go together like a horse and carriage . . .'

'Perhaps if it occurred to you to point out what ten years of uninterrupted carriage-pulling does to a horse,' said Cambuslang, 'you might contrive to rid yourself of this little irritation.'

'Well done,' said the Treasurer absently. 'Can any of you think why a policeman should get into a punt?'

'I'll stop you if I've heard it,' said Isham.

'No, I mean my taxi had a red light at the bridge just now, so I looked down on to the canal, and there were a couple of chaps in a punt doing something I couldn't fathom. Something technical with a rope or something. One of the chaps looked a bit like that Inspector who led the raid that night, but I couldn't be certain. The other one was in uniform, I rather thought.'

'Police uniform?'

'I couldn't be certain. He wasn't wearing a helmet, but there was a thing that might have been a helmet on a gunwale or thwart or whatever.'

'Probably a baling-can,' said Cambuslang. 'Anyway, what of it? They couldn't have seen anything of this place from as far away as that.'

'If they'd had binoculars they might have been able to see who was arriving.'

'Did they have binoculars?'

'I don't know. I just got a glimpse of these two characters and then the lights changed and off we went.'

Cambuslang glowered and growled. 'All imagination, laddie,' he said. 'I'll warrant the water-level in that canal's pitifully low.'

'You mean they'll have run aground by now?'

'To hell, they'd be too far below street-level to get a view of here, even with binoculars. Dismiss it from your mind. You're havering. You can do better than that.'

'I suppose I can,' said the Treasurer. 'Oh well.' He looked about him and lowered his voice. 'See what I've got, chaps.' And he pulled from his pocket what proved to be an experimental model of the double-fastening brassiere they had been discussing on the Monday.

'I had quite a job getting this run up,' he went on. 'The woman in charge of Research was dead against it.'

'That's interesting,' said Froald. 'Why, do you think?'

'Well, her own bosom seems to be supported by a system of pulleys, weights and levers. It's probably so close to critical mass already that she feels she can't afford to weaken things any further.'

'What's she like otherwise?'

'No good. Teethy and bat-eared.'

'Oh.'

'Anyway,' said the Treasurer, 'what about a trial run now? No, you fool, I mean on old Nefertiti here.'

'That's a thought,' said Cambuslang.

The Treasurer considered. 'It's no use just strapping the thing on, that won't test anything. She'll have to be let down *into* the cups in the way I showed you.'

'Consider us under your orders,' said Isham.

'We'll have to get her off the pedestal first,' said the Treasurer. 'You and Cambuslang might care to have a crack at that . . . No, Froald, I think this is a job for two, thanks all the same.'

At the cost of some grunting and a deep graze at the edge of the pedestal the two designated finally manhandled the statue to the floor. Cambuslang surveyed it and finally said,

'This business of letting the breasts down into it – surely that wouldn't apply to stone? They'd stay rigid.'

'Well, it may apply to the way the brassiere itself hangs, not only the breasts . . . and anyhow let's do it properly,' said the Treasurer severely. 'Froald, would you hold the brassiere open by the straps? A trifle lower . . . that's about right. Now, you two, an inch at a time. Don't hurry it . . . steady as she goes . . .'

Cambuslang and Isham, breathing heavily, tilted the heavy object bit by bit and manoeuvred its breasts into the waiting cups with all the controlled care of a crane depositing a hundred-ton locomotive on a quayside. When contact seemed complete Froald, acting on his own initiative, pulled the straps round to the back and fastened them, thus completing the operation.

At this point the Secretary came in with Boon, who was actually

150

wearing black coat and sponge-bag trousers. It was probably this garb, with its hefty smack of officialdom, which produced the ensuing undignified flurry round the statue. The Treasurer found himself leaping forward and unclipping the brassiere, so hastily that he seemed to create an imbalance beyond the control of Cambuslang on his own, Isham having straightened up guiltily at the first sight of Boon. In any event, the statue at once fell heavily to the floor. Its weak point, the neck, held all right, but its left breast came into contact with the wainscoting and was knocked clean off. With a vague idea of keeping up appearances, the Treasurer pocketed it.

The Secretary had been glowering considerably since entering the room, but fortunately Cambuslang now pulled himself together and said,

'Our Treasurer here is in the clothing business, and we were trying to check one of his new developments, unsuccessfully I fear. I hope the result didn't look too absurd.'

'Not at all, not at all,' Boon assured him. 'One sees curious enough scenes in the House and its environs.'

'What, you mean blokes mucking about with brassieres and things?' asked Froald.

'I was alluding,' said Boon, still very tolerantly, 'to the element of, uh, high-spirited horseplay I thought I detected a moment ago. Quite harmless, of course. In fact very much to be encouraged. There's a schoolboy in all of us, what?'

Cambuslang gave him the kind of look that, a couple of generations earlier, might have been accompanied by a dirk being slid from its stocking. The Secretary caught the edge of this and said firmly, even repressively,

'Let's have a drink, shall we? We'll give the President another few minutes. I've had apologies for absence from Mordle and the Superintendent.'

If the Secretary had such a tight hold on Boon as he had claimed, the Treasurer asked himself, why this evident disapproval of the cavortings with Nefertiti? Presumably it could not matter less what Boon thought. Ah, but (the Treasurer suppressed a grin) maintaining the dignity of the Society was an end in itself. No outsider, and preferably no insider either, should see that dignity in disrepair.

151

Perhaps by way of assault on this view, Cambuslang said loudly, 'I've had one of those sexy dreams about the future we discussed the other week.'

'You mean like mine?' asked Froald eagerly.

'A bit like yours, laddie, but to my mind the differences are more important than the resemblances. To begin with, there was nothing that could have been called a Time Gate. I suppose I might have been carried through it while I was still asleep . . .'

The Treasurer, who considered himself something of an authority on the Time Gate (and had indeed presented the Society with an anthology containing the Heinlein story, 'By His Bootstraps', in which the concept had originally appeared), now put in thoughtfully, 'Or it is just possible . . . I imagine that once the first physical contact was established, the rest could be done by direct telekinesis. Naturally, they'd choose people whose existence they'd become aware of by attuning to Froald's mind. Sorry, Cambuslang, do go on.'

'Well, the first big difference was that I was obviously *not* on Earth. For one thing, the gravity was considerably less than one g. I may say that this had a significant effect on those parts of women's figures specially affected by weight.'

'Viz., so to speak, their breasts, I presume,' said Froald.

'Correct, my son,' said Cambuslang with an asperity he continued to show from time to time, as if his own dream constituted a critique not only of Froald's but of its dreamer. 'Furthermore, the shape of the trees was not that of any Earthly flora. Of course, they might have been trained that way by a biological engineering beyond our present powers. But if not' – here he dropped the asperity for a spell and sounded rueful instead – 'then some of their forms seemed to suggest only too persuasively that I was having a dream and not a vision. What they resembled were fantasies of the unconscious. And pretty crude ones too.'

Froald opened his mouth to ask a question and closed it again.

'But that's a side-issue. They seemed to know a good deal about our time and its marital barbarities. That sort of thing had been –'

Here the Secretary, who had been glossing 'telekinesis' and 'one g' and so on to Boon, broke in momentarily. 'I suppose they didn't mention, uh, the efforts of some of us to . . . improve the position?'

'Not that I remember,' said Cambuslang. 'The main point they made was that the efforts of virists all over the world had been successful, that people were no longer living in a sexual police state and so on. But the really revealing moment was when I was standing talking to one of the chaps on a hill overlooking the space-port. Nice type of fellow called Tsutsugimushi-Duncan or some such name. I thought he looked a bit gloomy. He said something like, "I find it quite a therapy to look at those rockets, all heading away and all phallic, when these bloody women get me down too much." He went on to explain in the most authoritative manner what a pest the women were.'

'In what way?' asked Isham.

'I can't remember. But it was clear that happiness had not been achieved.'

The expressions of the listeners changed considerably at this conclusion. Isham seemed completely stunned. Froald looked simultaneously lost and angry. The Secretary was black as thunder. The Treasurer frowned. Only Boon, glancing from face to face in his habitual way, was almost unaffected. It was Isham, who, after a pause, put the issue into words:

'Are you trying to tell us that women are the trouble, not marriage after all?'

Cambuslang, not looking up, as if to avoid catching anyone's eye, waved his right hand a little and muttered, 'It looks like it.'

The front-door bell rang.

Froald reacted as if a weapon from Cambuslang's future had caught him between the shoulder-blades. The Secretary glanced at him severely and said,

'I expect the President's forgotten his key. Let him in, would you, Cambuslang?'

The Scotsman departed. The silence prolonged itself.

'Whenever I am out of luck' remarked the Treasurer, 'I use a word that ends in "uck". I'm sorry I can't be more definite, but here's a clue: it has an –'

Cambuslang returned to the room preceded by a stranger, a tall, lean young man with strikingly luxuriant brown hair and a friendly yet incisive manner. He said,

'Excuse me for butting in, but I'm making a few inquiries on behalf of my bosses. Your . . . colleague here was kind enough to

153

ask me up so that I could consult all of you. I'm interested in a Mr Chester, who I understand is a member of your club.'

'Society,' said the Secretary rather coldly. 'The Metropolitan Egyptological Society. Do sit down, Mr . . .'

'Raymond's the name. I won't keep you more than a couple of minutes. You wouldn't be expecting Mr Chester along this evening, by any chance?'

'Oh, not really, I think he'd have turned up by now if he was coming.'

'Have you seen him recently?'

'Of course,' said the Secretary without hesitation, 'he was here last Thursday at a lecture we had.'

'Were these gentlemen here then?'

All except Boon said they had been.

'Have any of you seen him since?'

None had.

'But you'll confirm that he was here then?'

They would.

By now the Treasurer had become very uneasy, and he could tell that others had too, however smartly they had followed the leads given them. He had the utmost confidence in the Secretary and had before now agreed with him that inquirers of any sort should not immediately be asked to say who they were and what credentials they had, on the principle that innocence is slow to resent or suspect. But surely a point had now been reached at which *not* to ask Raymond what the hell he was up to would look odd? Surely the Secretary saw this?

Raymond had nodded in a pleased way at the ready response he had had. He went on, 'Thank you very much, all of you. I wonder, would you care to put that in writing? The matter is of some importance and I think it would look better like that. Or at least it might become necessary.'

This terrified the Treasurer so much that he blurted out, 'What sort of nonsense is this? You'd think Chester had committed some serious crime and had given us as an alibi.'

'It's nothing like that, I assure you,' said Raymond decisively.

With a minatory flash of spectacles at the Treasurer, the Secretary said, 'What you ask is certainly rather unusual, but I see nothing against it.'

And he wrote down a short statement giving the time and date of the supposed lecture, signed it, and passed it round. The others dumbly added their signatures in turn, though Froald seemed to have difficulty in remembering how to use a pen.

Handing the document to Raymond, Cambuslang said, 'What exactly do you want this for, if, as you say, there's no hanky-panky involved?'

'Well, I don't know about no hanky-panky,' said Raymond as he rose to his feet. 'I only said that Chester himself hasn't been up to anything as far as is known. But it's quite serious.

'He hasn't been seen last since Monday week. Last Thursday his wife came to us – oh, I ought to have explained. "Us" is the Metropolitan C.I.D., in which I serve as a humble detective-constable. Yes, Mrs Chester seemed to think her husband's been murdered. You've all been a great help, anyway, in helping us to trace him up to late Thursday evening. I shouldn't worry too much about it, if I were you. I doubt myself if there's anything in it – probably he's just run away from his wife! Well, thank you all very much indeed. No, please don't bother, I can see myself out.'

Nobody in the Club Room spoke or moved until the front door was heard to shut. Then there was noise and activity in abundance. The Secretary had to call loudly for calm.

'Calm!' yelled Froald. 'I like that! When you've just made us all perjure ourselves in a criminal case!'

In the last five minutes the Treasurer had, for once, been wondering if the Secretary really knew what he was about. A question put at the very outside about Raymond's purposes could have saved all this. Or could it? The shameful scintilla of doubt passed, but it was to recur.

The Secretary sat on, totally motionless, more idol-like than ever, until something like order prevailed. Then, in his most dehydrated tones, he said,

'Making an erroneous statement not on oath is not perjury, nor is this yet a criminal case, but let that pass. We had no alternative. In the absence of specific instructions the Society has always alibi'd its members for all purposes and will continue to do so. I admit that I was mistaken in concluding that the man Raymond was an inquiry agent or private detective or brother or some

155

such nark commissioned by Mrs Chester. But that was no more than a mistake in deduction. If Raymond had kicked off by telling us that he was a sodding C.I.D. man and Chester had been missing for over a week and was he here last Thursday, that would have been a different matter. But even supposing we'd known from the outset the bastard was a policeman, we couldn't have said anything different from what we did say *unless we'd also known Chester was missing*. And how were we to envisage that possibility?'

Speaking perhaps with some effort, Cambuslang said, 'He's right,' and went to the drinks cupboard.

Froald and Isham seemed unconvinced. 'He ought to have thought of something,' they said.

'You're talking like a couple of bloody women,' the Secretary said.

To hear this used as a reproach within these walls horrified the Treasurer.

The long night certainly seemed to be closing in.

Thursday, May 21st, 9.10 a.m.
The President and his wife sat at breakfast.

'The new *Egyptian Studies*,' he said, 'has got a fascinating article on the growth of superstition under the Hyksos. Religious beliefs –'

'They're having a White Week,' she said, 'at Robinson & Cleaver. As you know, they specialize in fine Irish linen. There are some tablecloths –'

'Oh, very well . . . Anything interesting in your post?'

'No. What about yours? Anything from Eric?'

'Eric?'

'Eric Lasker. Weren't you going to do some TV with him?'

The President was never at his best in the morning – he often said that he only awoke fully about six, the time when actors contemplate going down to the theatre to make up – but he switched on as much of himself as possible now. 'Oh, nothing was ever fixed,' he said. 'I think he's dropped the whole idea. He said he had to fit it into his schedule and presumably failed to do so.'

'But it was only on Monday he rang up and said there was a chance he could do it this Friday, tomorrow. I told you. He said he'd let you know.'

'Well, he hasn't, I'm happy to say.'

'*Why* are you happy to say? That strikes me as most mysterious. I should have thought that you of all men would have jumped at the chance of cavorting about on the old goggle-box. Why are you so dead set against the idea?'

Here they went again, and it was worse each time. Last Thursday's lunch, at which the Committee and Cambuslang had met to devise a valid way of choking Lasker off for good, had been a total failure. Not a social or gastronomic failure: so much the contrary, in fact, that when, after a dozen Portuguese oysters each and a lobster each and a couple of bottles of Krug each, they got down to their discussion, nobody had seemed to have anything very businesslike to say. They had frankly given up after a few minutes and, over coffee and Hennessy XO, pursued the far more alluring problem of devising a sexual utopia that should be agreeable to all four. (They had got nowhere with that one, either.)

The few minutes devoted to the official topic of the occasion had at any rate established one point: that the choking-off of Lasker now took second priority to the conciliation of wifely opinion and resistance to its pressure. In the last week or two 'the Society telly programme' had become a favourite wifely subject for questioning, teasing, speculating. No wife seemed to know quite how this had come about, least of all the president's.

That lady was watching her husband steadily now as, for the dozenth time, his brain closed feebly with the task of answering her convincingly and came out with the same hollow rigmarole as before. 'I'm not *dead set against* the idea, I just rather dislike it,' he said loftily. 'Television is a vulgar, shoddy medium with which no man of decent feeling would wish to be associated, a pistol pointed at the head of our culture, a poison capsule in our –'

'You ought to know. Who threw a tantrum if he missed a single "Maigret"?'

'That was an exception. Rupert's an old friend of mine and I –'

'Is Efrem an old friend of yours too?'

'Who?'

'Efrem Zimbalist Jr, the fellow who plays Stuart Baily in "77 Sunset Strip". That's another one you were glued to all last winter.'

'Oh yes. Zimbalist is an excellent actor of a rather limited range.

157

I found him worth studying. Acting is an interest of mine, as you know.'

'I'll say I know. Well, if people like that can go on TV without falling down dead with corruption and vulgarity why can't you?'

'They take their decision,' said the President, fighting tooth and nail not to overdo the dignity; 'I must be allowed to take mine. And besides, consumption and production are different. I read the *Daily Express*, but I wouldn't consider taking a job on it.'

Pleased with this new point, which obviously ought to be circulated to the membership at an early opportunity, he drained his coffee and rose to go, but his wife had not finished with him yet. She said, emphatically for her.

'All right, I'll wear it so far. But listen. If that programme ever does come up and you refuse to go in front of the cameras I'll know that you and that Society of yours are up to something fishy. One or two of the wives have got a vague sort of feeling about that already, you know – Mrs Isham, for instance.'

He was up to that last one. '*Oh* how gorgeous the human heart is! I had no idea you and that divine creature were all palsy-walsy.'

'You and he are friends, aren't you?'

'Yes yes yes. Perfectly proper, perfectly proper. I must be off.' He went on in a semi-mumble. 'Something fishy. Mm. Almost wish we were.'

'You haven't forgotten I shall be away tonight?'

'Of course not. Give Mother my love.'

She said casually, 'Will you be coming back here after the office? In case there are any messages or anything?'

'No, if you're not going to be here I shan't bother. I shall have a drink at Gow's and then go and pick up the speaker.'

'Who is it tonight?'

'Chap called L. Stone Caton. Brilliant fellow, evidently – I don't know him at all myself – but a bit unreliable by all accounts. Hope he turns up, or I shall have a miserable evening.'

'You'll get by, I expect. Well . . .'

They embraced affectionately.

'See you tomorrow evening.'

She watched him back his Jaguar out into the street. It was his story that a member of the Exchange had to demonstrate how well he was doing, but she knew he would have sold everything but his

158

clothes to be in possession of it. When he had driven off, she went to the telephone.

'Good morning, Mr Lasker's office, please . . . Never mind, if you'd just give him a message. It's about the Society – he'll know what I mean. Now. He's to send the packet round to me between six and seven this evening. And if you'd just remind him – plain envelope marked Personal. And tell him I'll be in front of my set tomorrow evening and the best of Egyptian luck.'

17 If Tomorrow Comes

ANTONY: Give me some wine, and let me speak a little.

Friday, May 22nd, 5.55 p.m.
The traffic seemed worse than ever. Kingsway was a solid block
from Holborn down to Aldwych, its components creeping forward
a meagre half-dozen yards at a time. It occurred to the Treasurer,
whose taxi was even slower off the mark than the surrounding
vehicles, that he might quite plausibly find himself taken past
Bragg's hemmed in too closely by buses and articulated lorries for
the taxi to turn across the Strand, drawn inexorably right round
Trafalgar Square and up to New Oxford Street once more, and
then taken east by a Right Turn Only sign as far as the Kingsway
junction, where . . .

Not only plausible, this fancy, but appropriate to his low
morale. He sank back on to the upholstery, though not, as in the
past, to daydream about the Seychelles. His mind reverted, not
for the first time, to a few spoken exchanges of the previous
evening.

Lee Eddington Schwartz had finished tidying herself and
accepted a drink before going off to her flat in Bayswater. Then she
had said informatively,

'I'm flying back to the States tomorrow.'

'How long for?'

'For good. I already stayed a month longer than I intended
because of you, but now I just have to go.'

'Why?'

'Because of you. I nearly told you I loved you that week-end we
were in Yorkshire, only I couldn't figure out what would have been
the right way to apologize. What made it hard was I knew I'd
broken your rule number one, but I just couldn't feel sorry, even
though I agree it's a good rule. I agree very sincerely that it's an
excellent rule.'

Nobody ever called the Treasurer a hard-hearted man. He had

gone over and knelt by Miss Schwartz's chair and put his head on her lap and said, 'I'll leave my wife tonight and come and live with you if you'll have me.'

'*Oh* no. That really would be jumping into the dark. Most people in my situation are supposed to be afraid the man'll go back to his wife in the end. I'm afraid you'd marry me in the end. And I'm not the marrying kind, not for your kind of marriage. The kind you talked about that week-end.'

'Ours would be different.'

'Oh yes, for a while. I'm not going to lecture you – that's what wives do, isn't it ? – but how long do you think it would be before you thought about rejoining that Egyptological Society of yours ?'

'But I told you – '

'Please, darling. You never talked with me about Egyptology. I don't miss that as such – I can pass up the pyramids any day. But listen. How would you like me to ask you three elementary questions about Ancient Egypt ?'

The Treasurer said nothing.

'You've a low opinion of either me or women if you think I'd swallow that junk about it all having such painful associations for you that you could never discuss it? Your poor disbanded Society? I called up the number last week and asked for the Treasurer and the chap said he was out right now but I could leave a message. There went rule number two.'

'I'm afraid,' he said without any irritation, 'that that does sound rather like wifely behaviour.'

'You see? You'd better call me a taxi before I break any more rules.'

As his own taxi nosed at last into the Strand it struck the Treasurer that the momentarily disappointed girl-chaser's slogan, 'There'll be another along in a minute,' need carry no jaunty overtones. Then he dismissed the matter.

The President was sitting alone in the alcove in Bragg's, the traditional claret and cheese and biscuits before him and the equally traditional Jones incompetently sweeping up the remains of a glass he had evidently just dropped, or possibly dashed, on to the floor.

A lock or so of the President's normally flawless hairdo had come adrift. He greeted the Treasurer with something less than his

161

usual warmth. After apologizing for being under par today, he added, 'I don't like the look of my wife.'

'I hate the sight of mine,' riposted the Treasurer in music-hall style. 'What seems to be the trouble?' He poured claret and drank.

'Nothing I can put my finger on, as they say. But there's a good deal of sort of grinning behind her hand. The last time I saw her like that I wound up at a dinner-party in Staines between two of my ex-mistresses, to my mere acquaintance with either of whom I could have sworn on the *book* she was not privy. I'm not at all happy about it.'

'Is that all you're not happy about?'

'I wish it were. What was this simply farcical business Wednesday lunch-time about Chester and the perjury? Froald rang me up in a great taking and told me what had happened. I can't help thinking our esteemed Secretary's losing his grip, poor thing.'

'I don't think he had a lot of choice,' said the Treasurer. 'Anyway, you can ask him about it yourself.'

The Secretary's approach march to their table showed buoyancy, even vivacity. He waited until Jones had grudgingly replaced the broken glass, then filled the new one and sipped carefully once. Finally he beamed at the two and said,

'Van Dorn's in the clear.'

'No!'

'Oh yes. I had the Superintendent on the telephone to me only half an hour ago. A team of analytical chemists assembled by the New York Police Department has established that the substance in the crocodile, while it no doubt was hashish at one time, had degenerated into a harmless allotrope years ago. No doubt the thing was brought into this country crammed with genuine hashish, and then the bloke who was supposed to pick it up didn't for some reason, and the stuff just mouldered away. Anyway, van Dorn's been released and they've dropped the whole thing.'

'Bit of an ordeal for him,' said the Treasurer. 'But it's marvellous news.' He noticed that he spoke without much conviction and glanced at the President, who was still looking a little out of humour.

The Secretary, obviously in what was for him a festive mood, scooped up half a handful of cheese and washed it down with wine. 'Interesting to speculate,' he said thickly. 'Van Dorn told me the one thing his wife can't stand is any kind of scandal, unfavourable public attention and such. If he plays this thing right he may get a divorce out of it.'

'Wouldn't help him if he did.' The Treasurer also took cheese. 'He told me that whatever might happen in that sort of way his secretary would stand by him and remarriage would be inevitable.'

Laughter possessed the Secretary, silently except for the regular steam-engine-like hissings as he drew in air between his teeth.

'Christ,' broke in the President with something more than petulance, 'how you two can sit there giggling and guzzling when we've got the C.I.D. round our necks knocks me silly. And *you*,' – he faced the Secretary – 'you must have been out of your tiny little *mind* to have got everyone whacking down their signatures to support a non-existent alibi. In a case like that you should have thrown Chester to the wolves. He never comes near us – we don't owe him anything.'

'It was you,' said the Secretary mildly, 'who wanted the "old sweetie" kept on the books when I proposed considering him lapsed. If we'd done that there wouldn't have been any trouble. And in the circumstances I did the only possible thing. Agreed?'

'Yes. Completely.' The Treasurer, feeling he was defending himself as well as the Secretary, spoke with more emphasis than inner conviction.

'And I spoke to the Superintendent about it while he was on,' put in the Secretary again, 'and he said that from the length of time that had elapsed between Mrs Chester going to the police and this inquiry being made it was clear they weren't putting any kind of priority on the case and were very probably just trying to keep her happy.'

At this show of strength the President retreated a little. 'Well, anyway, what was all this nonsense last night?'

The Secretary said to the Treasurer, 'I was Duty Officer last night, as you know. Two incidents occurred within fifteen minutes of each other, the first after seven o'clock. A woman rang up and said she was Professor Caton's secretary and could I confirm that somebody had been sent to meet him. I didn't know what the hell to say – I'd already admitted I was the Society. So I just told her yes and rang off. I realized at once it must be that female joker of Isham's who got on to Scotton during the Seminar. He needs a reprimand there, by the way. Letting girls in on things like that contravenes Article 8. Still, there's nothing seriously wrong, though I admit I was rather worried for a minute or two.'

'So worried,' said the President in a sneering tone, 'that he rang me and told me all about it. Though what use he thought I'd be, out at Putney, I can't imagine.'

'You weren't A O J when I telephoned, were you?'

'No, but . . .'

'And I merely mentioned that matter in passing.' The Secretary addressed himself to the Treasurer again. 'What caused me to telephone was the second incident. About 7.15 the bell rang and someone dropped this through the letter-box.'

He opened his brief-case and took out a sealed envelope addressed in long-hand to the President, c/o the Society. It was marked *Personal* and bore no stamp.

'I opened the door but there was no one there. A taxi was just driving off. Anyway, I thought the addressee should know about it straight away.'

'Yes, I always think drink bills are top priority. Certainly call for getting chaps out of bed.' The President drank fiercely.

In a different mood, or if it had been the Treasurer who had asked him, the President would probably have referred jestingly to his fans and opened with a will. But as things were he stuffed the letter away in his clothing and mumbled something about when he was good and ready.

The Secretary glanced at the Treasurer and shrugged. Then he went to his brief-case again and took out a file. 'Just one or two other matters,' he said. 'Boon. I suggest we admit him next week. Is that agreed?'

'I don't like the look of him *at all*,' said the President, glaring slightly. 'Do you? What did you think of him?'

'He struck me as a really massive shit,' the Treasurer had to confess.

'I know, I know,' said the Secretary, 'but his potential value to the Society overrides any of that. You've got to remember he'll do as we tell him.'

'I think I'd find it easier to keep that point fixed in my mind,' said the Treasurer, 'if someone explained to me just *why* Boon's going to be so obliging all the time.'

The Secretary pondered. 'Yes,' he said, 'now that he's up for admission it's only fair. Not an unamusing story, though simple. My current young lady has an even younger brother. One Thursday evening she told me she was worried about him. He'd been seeing rather a lot of a well-off older man called Boon.'

'How much of Boon would rather a lot be?'

'Well, I rather gathered all of him. Or so she thought. Anyway, I pricked up my ears. What was this Boon's Christian name? She didn't know, but she'd heard her brother telephoning someone called Pinny. Good enough. I got asked to a party where Boon was, dropped our young friend's name to him and he turned very courteous right away. I haven't put my main scheme to him yet, though. That'll probably mean quite a lot of name-dropping. The Superintendent's was one I thought might go down well.'

'What's the main scheme?' asked the President, more amiably. His affectation of uninterest in the Secretary's tale had quickly collapsed.

Almost with diffidence, the Secretary flashed his glasses. 'I want you to remember,' he began, 'that the Society isn't and has never been a mere instrument of its members' convenience. It has a role in the cause of virism. We've a responsibility to men unborn. This was brought home to me in the most striking way last night. I had the Dream.'

He paused impressively. 'I won't bother you with detail. The central feature was a rather formal visit to a huge statue set in the middle of a park. It was on the lines of the Colossus of Rhodes or that thing of Stalin, a sort of idealized representation of a man. A bit vulgar, actually, but undeniably powerful in its way. On the base' – he paused again and stared at each in turn – 'was a handsome plaque with gold lettering. The inscription read, "In loving and grateful memory of the Metropolitan Egyptological Society, London, Earth. They fought that we might conquer."'

'What happened then?' asked the Treasurer.

'What more do you want? I woke up, or was taken back through the Time Gate, whichever you prefer. Well, I took that experience as a sign. What Boon is going to do for us is this. He'll bring a private member's Bill into the House proposing certain revisions of the marriage ceremony. The parson or registrar will be required to ask each of the couple in turn whether they have any reservations, whether they propose to deny each other certain

165

basic freedoms and so on. I thought of cocking up parts of the actual service – "forsaking nearly all others" and "with most of my worldly goods I thee endow" – but I decided that would be disproportionately unpopular. Anyway, if either party says yes to any of the questions it forthwith becomes illegal to continue the ceremony.'

'That'll make a fat lot of difference,' said the President. 'It'll just be treated as another bit of mumbo-jumbo and people will say no without thinking.'

'That's where the lie-detectors come in. The best man will have strapped one on to the groom's wrist and whoever gives the bride away will have done the same to her. One buzz and the marriage is off.'

The President was gazing at the Secretary with tolerant amusement. 'Genius, my dear boy. We'd be living in a technological age then all right. But I sense an element of farce here, if I may so express myself.'

The Treasurer was gazing at the Secretary too, but with horrified alarm. He remembered Cambuslang remarking recently that the laddie reminded him from time to time of Napoleon making up his mind to set off for Moscow. 'You don't imagine such a measure would survive a single reading, do you?'

'Of course not,' said the Secretary. 'It probably wouldn't even get on to the order paper. But that doesn't matter. Boon calls a Press conference and we're away.'

'Away where? What good would that do?'

'It's a start, a showing of the flag, a gesture.'

'I don't care much for gestures,' said the President, making a particularly flamboyant manual one.

The Secretary ground his teeth. His forehead and cheeks shone as if wrapped in polythene. 'All freedom movements begin with a handful of impotent fanatics.'

'Powerless fanatics, I trust you mean,' said the President.

'I'll leave you to think it over,' said the Secretary impassively. He glanced at the typewritten sheet he held. 'Project Nefertiti. I've given some thought to the problem of links with home and I think I have the answer. In fact I've taken some preliminary steps already. On Tuesday I went to the U.A.R. Embassy and after a bit got hold of a very decent minor official there who's going back to Cairo on leave next month. I told him I collected picture post-cards of antiquities and that Egypt was the biggest hole in my collection. I didn't have to go on – he suggested himself that he should send me some when he got home. I asked for an assortment of five hundred. Wouldn't hear of taking any money, either; I could give him something when he gets back to London if I feel like it. Really most charming. Educated over here, of course.

'When they arrive, there'll have to be a very serious and thorough session at which members complete them under our supervision and in accordance with the prepared fictional narrative of the supposed trip.

'Now as to postal arrangements. The Society's representative will send them off on the appropriate dates in accordance with the official itinerary. Who that representative will be needs considera-tion. I think perhaps Mordle might care to volunteer. Failing that, Furze says he'll go, but he hates Arabs so much it might be dan-gerous. We don't want him knifed in some brush with the locals on the first day. Still, plenty of time for that one.

'Travel arrangements. The Peterborough technique, of course. Book through to Cairo and leave the plane at Paris, returning in the same way. I'll see that the Egyptian representative writes out his local-colour report with as many carbons as possible, so that we can study it at Orly and on the way to London, where I think we can expect to be met in force – and inquisitively.

'Visible proof.' The Secretary produced a photograph of himself evidently standing in front of St David's Cathedral. 'Just a specimen. Very clever use of back-projection technique, you'll agree. The man says he can prepare enough convincing Egyptian backgrounds for our purposes and he'll do group shots, individuals, anything we like. It'll simplify matters if only two or three of us supposedly take the photographs on the trip. Any other member who possesses a camera will have forgotten to bring it, left it in a taxi, had it stolen from his hotel and so on. Details later.

'That completes my report on the project.'

This recital, so full of inspired common sense, completely restored the morale of the other two, who exchanged admiring glances. Another bottle was ordered from Jones, who went off almost as if he meant to fetch it at once.

'Lastly,' said the Secretary, 'Lasker. I have nothing new. Anyone else?'

'He was supposed to have it set up for about half an hour from now,' said the President. 'He'll have to get a move on if he thinks he's going to get us on the air, won't he?'

There was laughter. During it, Jones reappeared, though he bore no bottle. 'Telephone, sir,' he said to the President. 'Said to say it was urgent.'

'Urgent for someone is very seldom urgent for one, as Somerset Maugham remarked less neatly,' said the President before he sauntered off.

The Treasurer felt relaxed. 'Any other ideas for Boon's Bills? While his political career lasts?'

'Well, you know there was that perfectly serious idea of Leon Blum's, a measure for prohibiting marriage for anyone under thirty.'

'Really? What happened about it?'

'Oh, someone got pregnant, I expect. It never came up as far as I know.'

'Mm. Very conventional chap, your Johnny Crapaud.'

'There's another thing one would like to encourage,' said the Secretary. 'I was astonished, and very cheered, to read somewhere recently that over one-half of one per cent of ostensibly married couples look like it because the woman's changed her name to the man's by deed poll. Now that seems to me to show the right attitude.'

'As you say, it's a start.'

'What's missing so far is the element of social acceptance, or even of ordinary enjoyment. I'd like to get the Society to add an Article making it obligatory upon members remarrying not only to do it by deed poll but to throw some sort of champagne party the day the thing came through. A deed-poll reception, in fact. That would be a blow struck towards the abolition of the term "Mrs". I've often daydreamed about that. Long way off, of course. Won't come in our time.'

The President was returning to their table faster than he had left it, and evidently in an inferior state of health. The other two jumped up.

'I was wrong about urgency in this case,' said the President.

'That was good old Furze. Two van-loads of B.B.C. Television men and equipment have arrived at the Society under the command of Lasker.'

The Secretary stood still for five seconds. Then he said to the Treasurer, 'Telephone. Dial 999 and ask for an ambulance. A man has collapsed.'

'What man?'

'There'll be one. Move.'

The Treasurer did as he was told.

18 Their Finest Hour

MAECENAS: This in the public eye?

Friday, May 22nd, 6.35 p.m.

Stretched out on the ambulance bunk, the President alternated between bouts of immobility accompanied by light snoring and moments when he looked up at the Secretary and seemed to be trying to communicate with him.

'You'll be all right,' said the Secretary. 'Just rest.'

'How is he, doctor?' asked the ambulance attendant.

'He's over the worst now, but of course these conditions fluctuate. The first attack was undoubtedly the most severe – when I got to him I thought he'd gone. But then he came right round and told me who he was and where he lived and this story about these pills of his.'

'They're special, are they?'

'Stuff called BC 30. There can't be more than ten patients in England on it. It's the best thing we've got for this type of condition, but unfortunately it's turned out to be what we call somatically addictive: that's to say an ordinary heart stimulant like – well, any ordinary stimulant would do him no more good than aspirin. So we've got to get BC 30 into him fast.'

'I wish you'd let us take him to hospital. They're bound to have this BC thing there and they can fix him up nice and comfortable afterwards.'

'How many times must I tell you? – there's almost certainly none in London outside my surgery and perhaps a couple of others. It hasn't been produced commercially at all yet.'

'All right, but what I can't see is this. According to you this BC stuff is the only thing that does him any good and here he is walking round London without any of it on him. Doesn't that sound a bit screwy to you?'

The President gave a deep groan.

'We'll worry about that later. Just now there are more important

170

matters on hand.' The Secretary set about taking the patient's pulse, interposing himself to hide his ignorance of how to do this. 'Just a little stronger, I think. What do you say?'

'Oh, thank you, doctor . . . Yes, I think just a touch in the right direction. He had almost no pulse at all when I got to him in that pub.'

'Just so. What's your diagnosis, old chap?'

'Uh . . . valvular, perhaps?'

'Mm . . . it's possible. That would explain his colour, which has been surprisingly good throughout.' No way of turning his face blue or green had suggested itself to the President. 'Yes, indeed, quite possible. Yes.'

After that the attendant sat in contented silence while the ambulance tore along Bayswater, took the right turn like a close-hauled yacht in a gust and belted northwards. A very short time later, guided by the Treasurer in the passenger's seat, they drew up in Old Lane, by the Society's side entrance. The President was obviously a little better still and was able to get out on the Secretary's arm.

'This is my temporary place,' said the Secretary. 'I've had the builders in my new Harley Street premises two months already. However, I shan't need you any more, old chap – we can walk him up the stairs if we take it easy. You've been most helpful. Split this with your mate, would you?'

'Thanks a lot, doctor. Hope all goes well.' The attendant tucked the pound note quickly away, then got up beside the driver.

The Committee assembled in the Isis Room. The President took from his armpit the balled handkerchief he had put there, a device culled from a film seen in boyhood: pressure of arm against side cut off most of the blood supply and so attenuated the pulse. He looked at his watch. 'Seventeen minutes from Bragg's in the Friday rush-hour,' he said. 'I must come this way more often. I must also have a drink.'

'You've earned one.' The Secretary turned to the Treasurer. 'Go and see who's about. If Cambuslang's there send him in. Find out what time they propose going on the air but don't let Lasker in here.'

The Treasurer left by the communicating door. At the hospitality cupboard (normally in use only on Thursday evenings) the Secretary said,

'A thimbleful of Scotch and plenty of vodka.'

'Half a tumbler of vodka. Popular drink with the birds these days, isn't it ?' The President's face grew abstracted for a moment.

The Secretary got all his attention by asking, 'Do we do this or not?'

'We must. This very morning my wife said she'd know we were up to no good if things went this far and we refused to appear.'

'I'm with you. We can handle this. They've certainly sprung it it on us.' The Secretary's head came round hard. 'Open your letter.'

The President obeyed. 'Of course. Full details of arrangements. Apologies for short notice. Sending by messenger to save time. I see. My wife got it last evening, opened it in case it was urgent, put it in a fresh envelope and sent it round here by taxi. Supposedly I was at the lecture with everybody else. From her point of view she was being very sensible and helpful.' He looked up at the Secretary. 'I'm sorry I bit your head off.'

'That's all right. Now we've got to plan.'

The Treasurer came back with Cambuslang. 'On the air in half an hour. If we go on. Do we ?'

'We do,' said the Secretary. 'We'll decide what we have to decide in the next ten minutes. Cambuslang, guard the door. Now . . .'

They began to plan.

Friday, May 22nd, 7.17 p.m.

'Nice and quiet, everybody,' called one of the many men in charge. 'Let's have lots and lots of lovely quiet, shall we ?'

The Treasurer, standing with the President near the windows of the Lecture Hall, took some deep breaths. He glanced down the room to where the Secretary and Mordle sat facing Cambuslang and the dreaded Dr Pearson, the genuine, indeed expert, Egyptologist imported for the occasion by Lasker. Isham watched from the sidelines. In the mood that seemed to possess him these days he was clearly useless, even to waffle about art.

'Ten seconds.'

The Superintendent, whose gift for talking around, beside,

away from the point would have been invaluable to the Society in this its direst crisis to date, was simply not present and could not be reached. Froald, too, was missing, though his absence was felt less keenly. Boon, knocking back a tonic water in Mordle's company when Lasker's men appeared, had bolted wordlessly out through the Isis Room and into the street at a pace Mordle himself, with all his knowledge of the course, could hardly have bettered. This departure was later taken as a rough-and-ready withdrawal of the M.P.'s application to join the Society, and it never heard from him again.

'Five seconds.'

The Treasurer felt a bit like praying, and would probably have invoked the Egyptian goddess of love had he had any idea who she was. Instead of that, he put in a silent appeal to the shade of Nefertiti to see what she could do for them. Crossing his fingers, he glanced at the President and the two exchanged an ocular handshake.

On the monitor screen a few feet off Buck Remus, the popular fat ungenial head man of 'This Evening', turned his back on some anti-blood-sports people he had been ridiculing and said in his floor-of-the-mouth Canadian voice,

'Now as usual in this end-of-the-week edition of "This Evening" we wind up with something a little bit off the track. Here's Eric Lasker.'

'Good evening and indeed we are a bit off the track, six thousand years off, in fact,' said Lasker with that humble unpretentious insincerity which had endeared him to countless homes. 'That's how long ago the magnificent civilization of Ancient Egypt began to develop, with its pyramids and all its wonderful tombs. Some of us have been able to get a glimpse of it fairly recently in Elizabeth Taylor's spectacular film of *Cleopatra*.'

The Treasurer saw Dr Pearson's expression change from slightly resentful boredom to flatly unbelieving fury. One of the technicians nudged his mate and both doubled up in a fit of expertly noiseless laughter.

'But to just a few of us,' continued Lasker, 'the study of Ancient Egypt, known as Egyptology, is something between a hobby and a passion. I've come to the headquarters of the Metropolitan Egyptological Society here in London to find out what it is about

173

this long-dead culture that exercises such a fascination. Now you, he told the President, 'are the President of the Society. Tell me what gave you the idea?'

The President languidly rotated one hand. 'Chance,' he said. 'As with so many things in life that later assume a unique importance in one's world, the merest chance. Enjoying a quiet glass of claret with a couple of old friends some three years ago, I was prompted, though how or why I confess I am at this date unable to recall, to mention the fact, which had probably not recurred to me for two or three times as long, that, how much longer ago I very much dislike to think, I had been interested, in what was no doubt a very ill-instructed way, in the culture, understanding this to embrace other manifestations than the purely artistic, of the ancient dynasties of Egypt what was my surprise,' he pursued, jumping clean over the expected full stop and so forestalling Lasker, whose mouth had been opening more and more purposefully in the last half minute, 'to find that of the two friends who were with me on that occasion one had had a more or less keen interest in the topic for some time but had despaired of finding congenial circumstances in which to discuss it, while the other –'

'And so the Society came into being,' Lasker got in at last. 'But tell me, what was it about all these sphinxes and so on that attracted you?'

'There are many things about the Pharaonic culture of enormous –'

'Which one in particular?'

'To take simply the better-known –'

'What attracted you?'

The President shrugged thoroughly, seeming to recognize he had lost the initiative. He had every reason to feel satisfied with himself after holding Lasker off unaided for nearly a minute and a half. 'Romance. Call it romance. The romance of something beautiful and long dead.'

'Thank you.' Lasker turned to the Treasurer as the President slipped away. 'What about you, sir? Was it the romance of Ancient Egypt in your case too?'

'Well, I'm a rather hard-headed sort of chap,' said the Treasurer, smiling. 'Got to be, you know. Yes, I handle the finances for this little group of ours, and that's no picnic, I can tell you. No

174

ou need all your wits about you for that little job of work, believe
me. Why, just the –'

'What attracted you to Ancient Egypt?'

'Well, I'm afraid that's by way of being a long story. I –'

'Please be as brief as possible.'

'There's one very important point I want to make about the
financial side if I may, a vitally important point,' said the Treasurer, looking grimly into the camera as he spoke. 'Have we got
time for it?'

'Yes, if it really is important, because we don't have very –'

'I mean, do say if we haven't got time, because I wouldn't want
to –'

'We've got time,' said Lasker through his teeth.

'Thank you. Well, I just want to say this. I shouldn't like any
of the viewers to run away with the idea that starting an Egyptological Society is like starting a knitting circle or a debating club
or something. Oh dear no. You need money. The cost of building
up an adequate library and the basic historical charts and so on
is far higher than you might perhaps –'

'At any rate the money's been well spent,' said Lasker, walking
away up the room with a camera in pursuit, 'as I'm sure you'd
agree if you could see the fine collection of books and pictures here.
Well, we've heard something of what it's like to study Egyptology.
But what about the subject itself? What are Egyptologists up to,
what are the problems they discuss among themselves?' He sat
down between the Secretary and Cambuslang. 'On my right here
I have the Secretary of the Society and Mr Mordle, another of the
members. Tell me, Mr Mordle, what is your particular line of
country?'

While Mordle took a good ten seconds to say how much he
appreciated the form of the question because it stressed the
enormous breadth and variety of Egyptological studies, the
Treasurer looked at the electric clock the crew had brought. The
time was just coming up to 7.22. At 7.30 minus 15 seconds, come
what might, Lasker must close the programme. That sounded
good, but a single minute would be enough for Pearson to work the
Society's ruin. The Treasurer shuddered and tiptoed out into the
passage.

Mordle was saying, 'My speciality, if you can call it that, is

175

Ancient Egyptian writing and language. There are several sides to this. The actual symbols used have a primeval beauty of their own, an epic quality. Then of course there are the linguistic problems, working out the grammar and syntax of the language and so on. That sounds most frightfully dry, perhaps, but it can throw light on completely different questions in a rather exciting way. For instance, it's always been assumed that the inhabitants of Ancient Egypt belonged racially to what we now call the Middle East, rather than to Africa; but certain elements in the language contradict this. If – '

No doubt feeling that any moment Mordle would make a genuine point, perhaps even initiate a discussion, Lasker cut in. After informing Pearson of Pearson's name and professional status, he asked if he had any comment.

The expert had turned out to be about fifty years younger than any of them, brought up as they had been on the President's demonstrations, had ever supposed it possible for an actual Egyptologist to be. He had neither curvature of the spine nor speech-impediment. So human did he look, in fact, that Cambuslang, mistaking him earlier for one of the electricians, had been about to confide to him what awful balls Egyptology was and how proud he felt of knowing nothing whatever about it. Something in the other's demeanour, some hint of being able to get results by knowing things, had shut Cambuslang's mouth in the nick of time.

At the moment Pearson was certainly going on as if he knew a lot. 'Oh, that old rubbish,' he said in a gentle but penetrating voice. 'That was all cleared up by about 1900. You're like someone fiercely maintaining that heavier-than-air flight is possible.' He glanced irritably over his shoulder at the Treasurer, who was cautiously approaching with a piece of paper in his hand, then went on, 'What have you been reading, may I ask?'

'Well, Erman chiefly,' said Mordle, shifting in his seat, 'and that thing he did in lots of volumes with that man with the Russian name.'

Without replying, Pearson fell forward in laughter.

'Of course I – I don't set myself up as an expert, I merely – '

'Nice of you,' said Pearson. 'Very very good of you.'

Cambuslang had taken the piece of paper from the Treasurer, glanced at it and passed it to Lasker, who sat holding it on his lap without reading it. Now the Scotsman roused himself to carry out his part of the agreed plan. This was to lose his temper at every opportunity. The Committee had explained to him that he had been chosen for this role not because those who knew him thought he had had much practice at this activity, but purely and simply because the sight of a Scot losing his temper was normal and proper, would act as a powerful reassurance to the home viewer that what he was seeing was authentic. The President had recommended the injection of a 'yon' and a 'mon' or so to point up this effect.

Accordingly, after growling for as long as he dared – the Secretary had worked out that seven seconds was one per cent of the programme – Cambuslang said, 'You're earning yourself a wee ding of the toe of my boot, laddie, by havering in that strain. I'll abide no more of it, do you hear?'

If Pearson had fought back by any means at all Cambuslang would have been away for several per cent of the programme. But as if informed by some malign pacifist instinct, the expert faced Lasker with outflung arms and said, no less gently but rather more penetratingly than before, 'Please.'

'Isn't it odd,' said Lasker quickly, 'how even a subject as . . . as apparently remote as Egyptology can arouse strong feelings? Let's pass on. You, sir, you're the Secretary of this Society. What's your line of country?'

The Secretary's calm was as marmoreal as ever. Behind it, he was noting that the programme was barely half over and here he was, facing the enemy alone. Mordle showed no sign of recovery from his reverse. Cambuslang sat quite inert, a crack battleship torpedoed to driftwood after firing one salvo. Everything hung now on Lasker looking at the piece of paper in his hand. For the moment he seemed to have forgotten it altogether.

'Well, there's a lot of administration to be done, of course,' said the Secretary consideringly, trying to catch Lasker's eye. '*Paper* work. Letters and *notes* and such get *passed to* me, and I have to *deal with* them. So I –'

'So you don't get much time for Egyptology, is that it?' said Pearson, beginning to laugh again. 'Just answer me one question, will you? Were the pyramids built in the early, middle or late period of Egyptian history?'

The Secretary's knowledge of such matters was small, even for a member of the Society. It had happened at last, then, the simple ineluctable pistol pointed between his eyes. Well, he had had a good run for his money. He began doing his own laugh, the one with steam-engine sound-effects. 'You mustn't ask me things like that,' he said. 'Not right.'

'Try you on something else, then. Cults, ceramics, any of the dynastic – '

'Don't mean things like that,' puff-puffed the Secretary. 'Mean ask like that. Not in school now.'

Pearson flung up a hand. 'I knew it,' he said, smiling amiably now as well as laughing. 'I had a look at your books and periodicals. And your programme for the year. Great stuff. L. Stone Caton and Miramare and the rest of the chaps – I know my way round this stuff pretty well, and I've never –'

'If I may just interrupt you there,' said Lasker, 'it appears that in the last few moments, since we came on the air, we've had a most distinguished visitor from the other side of the Iron Curtain who's on a short visit to this country. Fascinating, isn't it? and reassuring too, to find culture and science reaching across political divisions in this way. We're very lucky to have with us, and to welcome to "This Evening",' – he looked down briefly at the paper in his hand – 'Professor Asimov from the University of Kraków.'

He was about half-way through this when an impressive figure began making its way over from the door, limping slightly and supporting itself on a bamboo walking stick, but maintaining good progress across the cables and between the light-holders. Arriving in shot, the Professor bowed briskly and settled himself in the chair that one of the men in charge had found for him. Asimov was perhaps seventy years old, with fringes of white hair edging a bald crown and a magnificent iron-grey moustache that partly concealed his mouth. He wore a heavy pair of tortoise-shell-rimmed spectacles of which the left-hand lens was smoked glass. 'Good evening, dear colics,' he said in a cordial rumble, and added into camera with remarkable aplomb, 'and good evening also to you se watching public. And now, to what stage have come our discussions?'

'From Kraków, you say,' said Pearson, with enough gentleness left in his tone to limit the offensiveness of his words. 'I have to tell you I've never heard of you, which is rather odd in a field in which – '

'Ass your great English national poet Milton has written, so on a very different occasion,' said the Professor good-humouredly, 'not to know me argues syself unknown. So much for sat. We were saying . . . ?'

'Well, there was a question about the pyramids.' Lasker gave Pearson an admonitory look. 'About the date at which these great stone structures were built.'

'A fairly elementary question,' said Pearson, undeterred, 'to which I didn't get an answer.'

'Se elementary questions are not always se most easy, my young friend, and sis is a case in point. Se evidence is multitudinous, but it is also conflicting. We have to – '

'Conflicting!' Pearson's voice was hardly gentle at all now. 'The attribution of the pyramids to the Old Kingdom, up to about 2,300 B.C., is absolutely solid and unshakable. Nobody's ever questioned it. It would be – '

'Nobody, sat is, until quite recently, until, in effect, se result of Leiber's experiments became known. Off course' – the Professor turned to Pearson with a smile – 'our sceptic here will tell us he knows nothing of Fritz Leiber and his new radioactive sorium technique of dating. But sis is quite likely, for Leiber, so full always of integrity, has refused to publish his results in se usual way, declaring say are not hundred-per-cent certain, and will consent only sat say will be circulated to twenty or sirty fellow-workers all round se world. And' – another smile at Pearson – 'our young friend will perhaps not expect sat he will today be one of such a company. Hiss time is yet to come.'

'Name some of the – ' began Pearson.

'And so,' Lasker broke in, 'as so often in the past, and increasingly often in the present, science puts its techniques at the service of history and culture. But tell me, Professor, what was it that drew you to the study of Egyptology in the first place?'

'Ah, you take me back many years. But se question is a good one because se answer is I sink a little surprising.' The Professor paused dramatically. 'Essence.'

'Essence of what?'

'Essence, Greece. I am for se first time as a young man in se city of all sose great names – Pericles, Sucydides and se rest, under se Mediterranean sky, and I say to myself –'

'Yes, yes,' said Pearson loudly, 'but what's all this stuff got to do with Ancient Egypt, for heaven's sake?'

'But everysing to do.' The savant from Kraków looked mildl surprised. 'As I am saying, I look around me at se Parsenon and se porches of se Erechseum and sis, sat and se usser, and se sought hit me like a blow – all sis from se East comes originally.'

Pearson sat up straight. 'You're not going to tell me there wa Egyptian influence in Athens, are you? Because if there's anythin; that's known for certain about the past it's that Egyptian civiliza tion had already begun to decline when the early Attic Greek; were still sitting about in mud huts.' Then he laughed. 'Oh, I can see what's coming now. Some Japanese who hasn't published hi results has found traces of hieroglyphics under the Parthenon friezes.'

'Not Japanese, no.' The Professor was patient. 'Se Bulgarian Hvoyev. And his discoveries relate to various religious objects But Hvoyev is perhaps not well known in sis country.'

Here the Secretary took a hand. 'I think you're right, Professor,' he said. 'I barely recognized his name when you mentioned it Would the others agree?'

'Yes,' said Mordle. 'I think I can say I've heard of him, but no more. I'm afraid I do stick rather exclusively to my own little linguistic backwater.'

Cambuslang snorted. 'He's a new one on me. Sounds a bit of a crackpot, I'd say.'

This throwaway manoeuvre (made possible by the Secretary's earlier insistence that any lead given was to be followed) shook Pearson severely. He sat for a moment with his mouth open.

'Once again,' said Lasker, 'we have a demonstration of the essential unity of all culture. Egyptians, Greeks, perhaps the Ancient Romans too in their very different way – all these historic civilizations were striving for the same sort of ideals. At bottom they were human beings like ourselves. All men –'

'But this is ridiculous,' said Pearson desperately. 'Nothing's been said about Egyptology at all. A lot of completely wild and unsupported – let's call it theorizing from the Professor and the others obviously don't know the first thing about it, have never studied the thing for five minutes, can't even –'

'Se first sing we must learn,' said the Professor in a kindly rumble, 'is sat we all know very little. And se second is sis. Knowledge is for everyone to pursue in his own way, whatever se obstacles may be. Sis is in my country taken for granted. I am a little surprised to find sat in England it needs to be insisted upon.'

'We've learnt something this evening,' said Lasker into camera, 'about the fascination of long-dead civilizations, thanks to officers and members of the Metropolitan Egyptological Society, Dr Pearson of London University, and our unexpected guest, Professor Asimov from Kraków. That's all from me. Have a good week-end.'

When, with varying emotions, all present had watched the credits roll up on the monitor, Lasker turned to the Professor and shook his hand. 'You saved the day for us,' he said. 'It was pretty poor stuff until you turned up.'

'You are very kind,' said the Professor, beginning to fill a small meerschaum pipe. 'It will be somesing to tell sem in Kraków.'

'There's the question of your fee. We usually offer five guineas for this sort of appearance. Where shall I send the cheque?'

'Please, no fee. Donate to se Society, my good hosts.'

'Certainly, I'll be glad to arrange that. I'm afraid we weren't able to get your name on the screen in any way – there just wasn't time.'

'Sank you, I wish no publicity. I am tired now. Good night.'

And, with the Secretary and the Treasurer supporting him on each side and Mordle and Cambuslang closely following, Professor Asimov departed.

19 Surrender Terms

CAESAR: High events as these
    Strike those that make them.

Monday, May 25th, 1.10 p.m.
Three days later the Society held a business meeting at its premises.
It had been convened not by the Secretary but, most unusually,
by the President, who had on the Monday morning summoned
the membership by telephone with an air of urgency equally
unusual in him. None (except Chester) failed to appear. They were
in any case in congratulatory mood. Six wives had been alerted by
Furze before the TV programme went on the air, it having been
agreed that failure to hand out this news would have been as
damning as almost any débâcle in front of the cameras. Five ladies,
the wives of the President, the Secretary, the Superintendent,
Isham and Cambuslang had watched the show and no response
more adverse than mild interest was reported. Mrs Cambuslang
had dubbed it instructive and very creditable. The Secretary's wife
had thought it perfectly smashing, with a rider about how riveting
it had been to see that little twit from London University put in
his place by that sweet old Hun or Hunk or whatever he was. The
morale of the membership had never been higher, and hard liquor
flowed like wine. Even Froald accepted a Vaughan Jones and
Angostura and soda at the hands of Cambuslang.

The President arrived last. He was dishevelled and looked
shaken, abruptly brushing aside compliments on his rendering of
Professor Asimov. He called for a large neat brandy and, standing
by the still unrepaired Nefertiti statue, at once called the meeting
to order.

'Good things first,' he said. 'Everybody on the programme did
magnificently. I'd like to mention Mordle in particular, but it was
really a collective effort. A lot of suspicions have been lulled for a
long time. Lasker was on the telephone this morning saying that
he and his chums were well satisfied with it, even that barbarian
Buck Remus. But Lasker had other news too.'

After a sip of brandy, the President went on, 'The B.B.C. received fifty-two telephone calls after the broadcast, all favourable. There were seventeen applications for membership in this morning's post – they open mail unless they're asked not to. All were genuine and most of them literate, I gather. More people rang up this morning. There's already talk of a follow-up show, with Asimov talking to members of the Archaeological Institute.'

Froald started to applaud.

'Shut up, you moron,' said the President, in a harsher tone than any present had heard him use before. 'Can't you see what this means? We've done too well for our own good. We're back where we started when Lasker got interested in us. Farther back. The editor of the *Listening Times* – I know the man slightly – rang me this morning and said he'd had a call from some Professor of Egyptology in the provinces saying Asimov was a fraud and he was drafting a letter about it and what had I got to say. I'm giving the editor lunch on Monday and I'll do my best to choke him off but I doubt if I can. Furze tells me at least a hundred people stopped in the street and watched the TV stuff coming in here and there was talk about it in the Red Lion on Saturday night. We're in the public eye now and no mistake. Even the –'

The telephone rang.

'I'll take it,' said the President, and took it. They all watched him in silence. 'Yes? Yes. Thank you. No, I'm afraid not. The list is closed. For ever.' He hung up with a crash and stared accusingly at the membership.

'That was a man wanting to join the Society. Or had you guessed? No doubt the first of many. Another thing Lasker said was that quite a few of the people who rang up wanted to know when we held our lectures and meetings.'

'But surely they weren't told?' asked the Treasurer.

'He says he can't be certain. He says his secretary took the calls and the fact that we meet on Thursdays is in his file on us. He says his secretary's new and he thinks he told her not to give information over the telephone but he can't be certain. He says he asked her if she did and she says she didn't and he thinks she's telling the truth but he can't be certain.'

'And with our address in the telephone book ...' supplied Mordle.

'Exactly. Every Thursday evening there'll be half a dozen *chums* on the doorstep asking if vis is vere vey does ve Egyptology. What do they think they'd get out of it? It must be some *mana* thing to do with Elizabeth Taylor. Attend a lecture on Egyptian sea-power and you'll find it easier to imagine yourself hanging round old Cleo wearing a blue head-scarf and with one of those little shaving-brush affairs glued under your chin. I don't know. Anyway, I move that the Society be disbanded forthwith.'

This last, coming so quickly after the *mana* digression, took a few seconds to sink in. Then, among a medley of noises, the Treasurer cried incredulously, 'At *this* point? Just when we're – '

'Yes, at this point. Last week was bad enough. We had a fresh crisis every few hours. But a hundred times as many people are interested in us now as last week. That makes us a hundred times as vulnerable. We'd be finished in a few days. And think what discovery would mean with the world watching – "Sphinx-Men Exposed as Sex-Men: Callous Deception, Says Judge." We'd be – '

'I'll hear no more,' interrupted Cambuslang. 'Contemptible poltroonery. Of course we're in special danger for the moment. But it won't last, don't you see? We'll fix a genuine lecture for Thursday and for the six Thursdays after if need be and we'll all turn up and bore the very heart and liver and lights out of any outsider who presumes to attend. Then, what the hell, we go into summer recess, postpone Project Nefertiti – there's always next year. If the Society can survive a twelve-minute TV show it can survive anything.'

'Hear hear,' said Froald.

Mordle rounded on him. 'Before you get *carried away*, let me just remind you that you neither took part in the show nor watched it on the telly-box. So you've no idea what it was like. Bloody but unbowed was what we were, exceedingly bloody, and within a pretty poxy little margin of being bowed. If Lasker had delayed looking at the message about Asimov one second longer we should have had it. How would that have gone down at home, eh?'

Froald's eyes and nostrils dilated,

'Just so. And answer me this. Could you go through another week like the last one, with everything that hangs on it?'

Froald shook his head.

'Then you're with us?' asked the President. 'Mordle and me?'

Froald nodded, then, looking in the general direction of the Treasurer and the Secretary, but without catching either's eye, burst out, 'I'm sorry, chaps, I don't want to let you down, but I've got more at stake than you. All you've got to face is a public scandal and a divorce and perhaps losing your jobs. With me it's much more than that. Look what she gets up to already. Pursuing me along the street shouting at me. Rows in buses and tube trains. Turning up at the office and throwing a scene lasting three hours. The last time I mentioned something she felt strongly about – you know, men or women or one of those – no food came my way for three days apart from what she threw in my face. You see?'

'That's three,' said the President briskly. 'What about you, Super?'

'I'll suspend judgement for the moment, old man, if I may. If you'd seen yourself and your two colleagues under the circumstances I first saw you under, I don't think you'd lose heart so quickly. But then on the other hand I rather fancy we haven't heard quite everything yet, am I right?'

The President ignored the question. 'Isham?'

The man addressed looked up hastily. His demeanour, furtive and somnambulistic by turns, reminded the Treasurer of what it had been for the first part of the journey to Peterborough. Isham said huskily now, 'Neutral.'

'So we're equally divided.' The President gazed at Isham a moment longer. 'Yes, the Superintendent was right. There is more. What I have to tell you can't be backed up with any solid fact, but you'll have to believe me when I say I have no doubt in my own mind that it's true. My wife is on to us.

'I hoped not to have to bother you with this, but you leave me no alternative. Consider the way we were finally frog-marched on to TV. My wife and Lasker deliberately engineered a situation in which – as she told me the previous day – to back out would be taken as an admission that we had something pretty hefty to hide. Oh, I don't mean Lasker knew the full story. No doubt he thought he was just being helped to manoeuvre some awkward academics on to the air. But I know she wasn't acting in good faith. A packet arrives which is so important it has to be sent by taxi, but it isn't

185

important enough for her to check that I've got it, which one minute on the telephone any time the next day would have settled. No. Cleverly planned malice.'

'Couldn't she have been – well, just sort of needling you in general?' asked the Treasurer. 'Without being actually on to us in full, so to speak?'

'No. You should have heard the hinting and the digging in the ribs over the week-end. A positive barrage of it. We'd got away with it this time but we mightn't always be so lucky: what did she mean?: I knew what she meant, ha ha ha. I must get Professor Asimov along for dinner unless perhaps he's had to fly back to Poland in a hurry. What did I think of the idea of starting a women's branch? and so on. Actually her tone was enough. It was exactly the one she uses when I – let's say stay away too long at a party.

'I don't know how much she knows. I have my ideas, but I don't suppose I could ever confirm them.' The President's glance moved casually over towards the window, near which Isham sat with bowed head. 'But whatever she knows it's too much.

'I move the immediate dissolution of the Society. There can be a cover story about a quarrel over the TV show. Our efficient Secretary will devise it. Well, gentlemen?'

Before any hands could be raised the Treasurer got up. 'You're forgetting the Society's aims. They are not those of self-preservation. I move the rejection of the motion and the acceptance of the resignations of any members who feel themselves unable to stand by our principles. We knew when we entered upon this undertaking that difficulties would arise. Our selection of members was based on the idea that they'd be good people in a tight corner. We don't want any fair-weather friends. If we've relaxed sufficiently to admit any such, their place is outside. Let them leave now.'

The Secretary smiled faintly, perhaps at hearing such militancy in the mouth of one given by nature rather to following the line of least resistance. But the Treasurer's motive had been mainly tactical. Isham and the Superintendent, in their different ways, seemed quite impassive, but Froald was visibly wavering. Even Mordle frowned in a troubled way, and his comment, 'Half-baked romantic twaddle,' carried little conviction.

After further silence, Froald said tentatively, 'Perhaps if just the

President resigned – after all, he's the only one whose wife's got on to the – '

'Christ!' yelled the President. 'The only wife we *know* is on to us! The word may be buzzing round among them as we sit here!'

Froald dilated his eyes and nostrils again.

'Come on,' said the President more calmly. 'Vote. The immediate dissolution of the Society. Those in favour ?'

He, Mordle, Froald and Isham signified at once. A moment later the Superintendent, with an agonized expression, slowly raised his hand.

'Against ?'

The other three responded.

The President nodded. 'Thank you, Carried 5–3. The Treasurer's motion is therefore out of order. I declare the meeting closed.'

He rose smartly to his feet. 'Right, let's be off. I'm going to have some lunch. We can make Biagi's if we get a move on. Mordle? Good. Anyone else ?'

'I'll join you if I may,' said Froald.

The three moved to the door. Froald halted there, looked over at the three Noes, shook his head sadly and left.

The Secretary had not been able to speak at all during the meeting. He now said in a tight voice to Isham, 'You have the Isis Room key, I believe.'

Isham, by this time appearing quite ill, handed it over and left in his turn.

The Superintendent drew near. 'It broke my heart to do it, but I'd no alternative. You fellows could get other jobs, but who wants an ex-policeman? And it's bad enough being in work with what I've got at home.

'It's such a pity, all this, though I think I knew all along it was too good to last. Anyway, thank you for all the good times. We'll knock back a beer together one of these days and have a laugh about it.'

When this drew no reaction, he added, 'I suppose you'll be starting again, will you, when and if all this has blown over and been forgotten ?'

A flicker came into the Secretary's eye, but soon died. 'No,' he said. 'The Society's campaigns will doubtless be waged again, but only by others. We aren't the three to keep the bridge any more in the proper style. That belongs to the brave days of old.'

Possibly not catching the allusion, the Superintendent judged it time to be off. 'Well, good-bye, old man . . . old man . . . old man,' he said, shaking hands with all three. 'You did a splendid job. I'll never forget the afternoon in the office and that record. *Ancient Egyptian Music and Musical Instruments in the New Kingdom* – oh dear oh dear.'

When he had gone, the Secretary said in a monotone, 'Life has used us and laid us aside.'

Cambuslang said suddenly, 'You know, I never really believed that laddie's tale about never seeing any good pornography and suchlike. I'll wager he's got a neat wee pile of Grade A tit locked up with that bottle of Scotch.'

'Well, I don't suppose we'll ever know now,' said the Treasurer. 'Did you mention Scotch?'

20 The Last Adventure

ENOBARBUS: Then world, thou hast a pair of chaps, no more.

Monday, May 25th, 1.55 p.m.
There was enough Bell's in the cupboard for three large tots.
Cambuslang poured them and handed them round.

'Quite right to choose it,' he said. 'The serious drink. Before and
after danger or exertion. The flask for the difficult journey, with a
swig to each man. Gin is for egotists.'

The Secretary drained his glass, then turned and made for the
door.

'Where are you off to?' asked the Treasurer.

The Secretary muttered something about Somerset, revenge and
centuries (or sentries) and walked straight out of the house.

'I suppose it's all right to let him go?' asked the Treasurer.

Cambuslang answered a little doubtfully, 'Yes, I should imagine
so ... He's got a sister in Somerset, I think. If he's thinking of
spending a few days in the country I should say it would be a very
good thing for him.'

They finished their drinks in gloomy silence.

A moment later Furze came in with cheese-and-Branston
sandwiches and Guinness for two. He seemed to know exactly
what had happened. 'A very sad business, gentlemen,' he said.
'Mind you, I could see it coming a mile off. A chain's only as
strong as its weakest link, if you know what I mean.'

'Too horribly true,' said Cambuslang. 'Who would you say
was the weakest link in this case?'

'You're not offering any prizes, sir, are you? That Mr Mordle, of
course. I must say I never took to him. Sly. Imagine him sneaking
in here to read up on pyramids and that. Not natural, is it, somehow? To express it briefly, he's the sort to go to pieces under fire.
I'd stake my oath he was the one really behind this decision to
disband.

'Funny, I never had a lot of time for Mr Isham either, now I

189

come to think of it. He was sly too, but in a different sort of way. I wouldn't have cared to trust him farther than I could throw him, quite frankly.

'There was no harm in Mr Froald, though, was there, gentlemen? Just a boy, is how I'd describe him. And the Superintendent – well, I don't trust policemen, but I have to admit in fairness he was very quiet and pleasant-spoken. And as for your President, I shall always admire him for his fine qualities. His mistake was paying too much heed to Mr Mordle.

'It'll have taken the Secretary hard, this, naturally. My view is, for what it's worth, that not much will be heard of him for a time . . . Well . . .'

'What about you, Mr Furze?' asked the Treasurer. 'What will you do?'

'Well, sir, it's funny, my only consolation for the Society breaking up is that I'm spared the disagreeable necessity of resigning my post here. Oh, it's been satisfying work as far as it went and I've enjoyed it, but it never – how shall I phrase it? – it never went deep enough. I think now I've got hold of something that does. On Friday I'm to attend an interview at Trinity House with reference to a vacancy in the Goodwin Sands lightship. Apparently I'm one of four candidates out of over two hundred. And if that falls through, so the fellow was telling me, it shouldn't be difficult to fit me in at one of the remoter lighthouses. They're tending to take older men for these posts now, he said. Seems they're steadier than the youngsters. They know what they're not missing, you see.'

'Congratulations, Mr Furze,' said Cambuslang. 'This calls for a drink.'

'I'm afraid there's no Scotch,' said the Treasurer.

'Oh yes there is.' Cambuslang took a half-bottle out of his raincoat and tore off the foil. 'One of my aunties had the second sight, so maybe it's in the blood, but probably the unaided light of reason would have sufficed to make me bring this along today. Here goes. Deceivers ever.'

After the question of his notice had been amicably settled, Furze left them. The sandwiches had been among his best, and the stout and Scotch set them and each other off very satisfactorily. By the time everything had gone but a couple of fingers of Scotch apiece,

190

the Treasurer was feeling more sanguine. He and Cambuslang were able to discuss some aspects of the Society's history with fair objectivity.

'One thing I'm a wee bit sorry about,' said Cambuslang, 'is that we picked on Egyptology for our cover. It's a kind of insult, a way of saying there's nothing more boring in the world. And that can't be right. Egyptology's status as 100-proof boredom is a matter of general agreement, public opinion almost, which is likely to be very inaccurate in such cases. Now I'd have thought Byzantine art, or pre-Columbian America, or *anything* Japanese, would have been far more –'

The front-door bell rang. The Scotsman went to answer it. The telephone rang. The Treasurer answered it.

A woman's voice with a foreign accent said pleasantly, 'Hallo, may I please speak with Professor Asimov?'

'I'm afraid he's not here. Who wants him?'

'This is the Cultural Delegation of the Polish Republic. Can you kindly tell me where we may find Professor Asimov? We wish to congratulate him, you see, on his appearance on B.B.C. Television.'

'Oh. Well, I'm afraid I don't know his address, but you might be able to contact him at the Chinese Embassy. He has an appointment there tomorrow.'

'The Chinese Embassy? But that is quite –' A man's voice spoke sharply in the background. The woman said, 'Thank you,' and rang off.

The Treasurer sat back and began to grin to himself. He had not finished doing so when he heard Cambuslang's footfalls on the stairs. They were very rapid, expressing no doubt his eagerness to share with his friend some tiding of good fortune – the return of the President begging forgiveness and reconstitution, say, or the death of Lasker.

The door burst open. 'Out at once – Isis Room – police,' roared Cambuslang.

Accelerating vividly, the Treasurer ran. Twenty seconds later the pair were out in the lane, pounding heavily through a substantial drizzle. By the merest chance in these purlieus, a taxi now came chugging slowly across the intersection before them. Cambuslang reached it first and shouted something to the driver.

As he tumbled in, the Treasurer heard a motor-bike being started up in his rear.

The taximan turned ponderously. 'Where did you want, guv?'

'King's Cross station,' said Cambuslang, perhaps prompted by vague instincts of escape over the border.

The Treasurer looked out of the side window and saw, a hundred yards away, a police officer wearing a blue crash-helmet sitting astride his machine and just beginning to move in their direction. He turned to the driver and said in a fairly admirably controlled voice,

'And as you can see we're in a bit of a hurry. If you could make it as quick as possible we should be very grateful.'

Almost at once they scraped through at the end of an amber light and saw the policeman beginning to infiltrate a dozen miscellaneous vehicles held up by the red before the taxi swept round a bend.

'Do you think it's important enough for him to be authorized to jump lights?' asked the Treasurer.

'No idea. Is there a scale in these things? Is what important enough?'

'Christ, how should I know? You let him in, didn't you?'

'Did I buggery! What happened was this. When I answered the door there was a bloke in a green leather jacket wanting to join the Egypt Society. Struck me as confoundedly odd. It's as if what I might call the sexual component in our dealings had by some telepathic alchemy got itself across to some members of the public, though what a laddie of that sort would want with an alibi I just can't . . . Hey, that must be it. Not a sexual alibi. He thought we'd cover up for him and his mates while they went down to Brixton and did a garage or a sweet-shop. But how he could have –'

'Cut it out, will you? What happened then?'

'I told him we were closing down for lack of funds and he took it very nicely. Said he was sorry to hear it and so forth. These youngsters are much more polite than they're given out to be, you know . . . All right: I was just closing the door when this cop came farting round the corner and set about stopping outside the house. Can you see him, by the way?'

The Treasurer had been peering out of the back window. 'No. But he could be only a dozen yards off for all I can tell.'

'The point, or part of the point, was I recognized him. You remember that gorilla-faced bastard who led the raid on us back in March? The Inspector?'

'God, do I not? I thought I saw him on the canal the other day, you remember. But isn't he Vice Squad?'

Cambuslang nodded grimly. 'Exactly. I thought at first it must be the Chester perjury rap, same as you probably did. But I'm afraid it looks more like the Isis Room. Only thing I can think of. Keeping a disorderly house.'

'I thought the Superintendent had secured that flank, didn't you?'

'Seems he hasn't. How are we doing now?'

The taxi, throbbing unevenly, was halted at the Praed Street traffic lights. A couple of scooters were nosing up the column, but no motor-bike. The lights changed and they were on the move again.

'I think we've lost him.'

'In that case let's improve the shining hour.' And the resourceful Celt thrust a hand into his raincoat pocket and produced another half-bottle of Scotch, which he skilfully divested of its seal. 'Here.'

The Treasurer began pouring whisky into the cap of the bottle, which held about a pub double.

'To hell with that,' said Cambuslang. 'Put the neck in your teeth and chuck your head back. What you get in the next ten minutes may have to last you five years.'

Coughing violently, the Treasurer returned the bottle to its owner. 'Is that what they give you for keeping a brothel?'

'Search me. It may be twice as long for all I know. Perhaps we'd have done better with making a false statement to the police.'

'If things go according to form we'll wind up with both of them. With any luck the sentences will run concurrently.'

'No, with two quite different charges like that it'd be bound to be consecutively.'

'D'you think,' asked the Treasurer quaveringly, 'that we could get abroad if we shake off pursuit?'

'Maybe. Anyway, we must hide for a day or two. And the place to do it has just occurred to me – down in Somerset with the Secretary's sister. He'd certainly get her to put us up.'

The Treasurer at once took the point. As the taxi halted at the first lights in the Marylebone Road, he rapped at the communicating window and said to the driver, 'I'm afraid we've left it too late and we'll have missed our train. Would you take us to Paddington Station instead?'

The driver's shoulders rose and fell in a manner expressing resignation.

'You know,' said Cambuslang, 'any secret service in the world would be proud to have us after the way we've been trained.'

'Mm . . . You don't happen to know the Secretary's sister's address, by any chance? Or the town she lives in? Or her married name?'

'No, but I'll probably remember on the way. The main thing is to make for Taunton or somewhere and at least get clear of London. We'll find the place somehow. Then the three of us can try to get a plan together. We might go down to Brixham and have ourselves taken over to France by motor-boat. I've a friend in Brixham.'

'Could he manage that?'

'Bruce'll fix it if anybody can.'

The taxi, having turned right, was moving fast down Seymour Place. The Treasurer took a swig of Scotch and said almost cheerfully,

'Well, this detour should have flung our friend in blue right off the scent.'

As he spoke a motor-bike came into view and shot up the street towards them. It was – yes! 'Down!' yelled the Treasurer, but too late. Although the two vehicles must have passed each other at a combined speed of eighty miles an hour, the Inspector caught his eye for a second.

'Him?' asked Cambuslang.

'Him. And he saw me. He must have lost the trail and have been making a wide sweep in the hope of picking it up again.'

'Which by the most damnable ill-fortune he has now succeeded in doing. Give that bottle here.'

To their mounting astonishment they reached Paddington without incident. They attained almost the pitch of incredulity on finding that there was a train for Taunton in fifteen minutes. While Cambuslang kept a look-out the Treasurer bought the tickets. Waiting for his change, he remembered how Mordle had wanted the Seminar to depart from here on grounds of Paddington's higher social standing. Mordle ... Had Furze been right? Had Mordle, who no longer needed or respected the Society, exercised decisive influence on the President to get it dissolved? Might Cambuslang's scheme of going underground for a few months have had a chance of working? They could have had themselves taken out of the telephone book on the plea of evading TV fans, found new premises, signed up for crash courses in Egyptology ... Useless. It was all past history now.

The pair hurried towards the barrier. 'Any sign of him?' asked the Treasurer.

'I thought so once, but I couldn't be sure. With his crash-hat off he'd look much like anyone else from a distance ... Let's get near the restaurant car. I intend not to be able to remember arriving in Taunton.'

They found an empty compartment in the desired part of the train and huddled back into the corner seats. For a minute or two a shaky silence prevailed. Then Cambuslang said,

'I've just remembered the address. It's at Exmouth.'

'But that's not in Somerset. Why did he say Somerset? He must have –'

Cambuslang interrupted, 'To hell, let's get out of London anyway now we're on the train. There's probably a connexion at Swindon or ...'

His voice died away. Following his gaze the Treasurer saw the Inspector in the corridor, looking at them. The policeman threw the door aside, advanced, and stood with hands on hips, still looking at them. Eventually he said.

'What's the matter with you gentlemen? Guilty consciences or something?'

'Certainly not, Inspector,' said the Treasurer with dignity. 'Have the goodness to state your business, if any.'

'I'll state it when I see fit. Meanwhile I'd be obliged if you'd account for your behaviour of the last thirty minutes approximately. Just out of curiosity.'

'I don't know what you mean. This gentleman and I have come here by taxi in a perfectly normal manner, and are now –'

'Normal manner! I'd hate to see you in your abnormal manner. Dodging to and fro like nobody's business, going east off Edgware

Road and then doubling on your tracks ... You saw me back in Old Lane and then again in Seymour Place, didn't you?'

'I may have done,' said the Treasurer, shrugging his shoulders. 'I think probably you've got one of those faces that just don't stick in people's minds, Inspector.'

This was a gross injustice, especially at that moment. The officers's jaw was moving back and forth in a direction parallel to his line of sight and for a distance of a couple of inches each time, threatening to snap its pinions at the temples and become so much dead weight. Its owner said with his best Piltdown intonation,

'Where do you think you're off to, anyway? Where's your luggage?'

This was too much for Cambuslang. 'Look here, my good man, either you're arresting us for an act of gross indecency, in which case clap on the darbies, or you're trying to sell us tickets for the Police Ball, in which case there'll also be an act of gross indecency involved somewhere along the line. If you go on like this I'll call the guard and have you removed.'

The oscillations of the Inspector's jaw slowed and decreased in amplitude. 'I've a message for you from my superior,' he said at last.

'Oh, our friend the Superintendent. What does he want?'

'No, not *your friend* the Superintendent.' The jaw started up again. '*Your friend* the Superintendent had me ... I mean I transferred to the C.I.D.'

'What is this message?' asked the Treasurer, keeping his voice steady.

'It concerns the Mr Chester who as you know disappeared recently. Well,' said the Inspector disgustedly, 'we've solved the case. There's nothing in it. He just ran away from his wife and went to the West Indies. None of our business, though his wife still seems to think it is. The Chief Inspector thought you'd like to know, and wanted to thank you for your co-operation. A written copy of this message will follow in due course,' he ended in a monotone.

'But why all the urgency?' The Treasurer felt behind him for the whisky-bottle. 'You don't send Inspectors careering over London to deliver that kind of thing, do you? What's your Chief up to?'

The Inspector pointed his chin and bent close. Clearly a greater cause for hatred had displaced the two Egyptologists. 'You may well ask,' he hissed. 'Off his nut, that bugger. His officers aren't going to get rusted to their chairs, oh dear, no, not they. They're going to get out in the real world, keep in touch with life and improve the public image of the police at the same time. Which doesn't just mean dragging bloody canals for the bodies of blokes who've had the sense to clear out to the West Indies. It means you get into uniform and take the bike down to Camberwell to tell some old bint she's got another week to pay for her dog-licence. That was me last Friday afternoon. Didn't even get asked in for a cup of tea.

'Have you wondered why there are all these brutality cases in the police these days? I'll tell you why. You get so desperate you've got to take it out on somebody. You get in such a state with these bullshitting bastards round your neck all the time that you're at flash-point day in day out. If you didn't let yourself go now and then you'd go barmy. See? That's confidential, mind.

'Well, I'll be getting back to the Yard. Uh . . . have a good trip.' He said this with a puny and hesitant malice that was no doubt his version of good grace. He went.

The Treasurer drank whisky until he felt a jet of it might come shooting out of the base of his neck. Then after a minute or so of deep breathing it occurred to him that they now had no need to take the train. He leant across and shouted as much, a lot louder than he had intended, in Cambuslang's ear, but got no more response than a couple of blinks and a grunt. The Scotsman seemed to have gone into a state of deep shock. The whistle blew. The Treasurer tried again, with no more result, as the train began to move.

A thought struck him. He shouted 'Somerset!' and with a desperate burst of energy dragged Cambuslang to his feet, opened the door, pulled him along the corridor, got the outer door open and jumped with him on to the platform. The speed of the train was enough to send them staggering for a yard or so. Fetching up at the end of this against an empty luggage-trolley, they sat down on it.

There appeared an official with a moustache so wiry that it set the Treasurer's teeth on edge to look at it. The man explained to them that passengers must not jump off moving trains. The

Treasurer gestured complicatedly at Cambuslang, trying to convey some notion that his friend was unwell. After bending and sniffing and nodding, the official said, 'Like that, is it? Well, don't do it again.'

Cambuslang, emerging from his trance, said, 'What do you mean – Somerset?'

The Treasurer sprang up, quivering with urgency again. 'Come along – no time to waste – explain on way.'

They trotted off and were soon panting too heavily to contemplate speech. At the taxi-rank Cambuslang asked for the Scotch and was handed it. For some moments he clearly endured a fierce mental conflict as desire for a swig battled with reluctance to cough it up again instantly. When this was finally resolved he said,

'Where are we going? And how can there be any hurry now?'

The Treasurer said excitedly, 'He mentioned Somerset and something about revenge for centuries of something. That business of yours about his sister's place was a false lead. If you wanted to revenge yourself on marriage what would the Somerset connexion be?'

'Oh God, Somerset *House*! . . . He's gone off his rocker. He'll be going to assassinate the Registrar-General or something. Hell, he'll be there by now. Maybe we're too late already.'

Grabbing Cambuslang by the arm, the Treasurer ran with him to the head of the queue. Almost without thinking he said to the elderly woman who was about to take the next taxi,

'Excuse me, madam, we're police officers. Did you notice anything about the man who's just been driven away?'

'Well yes, he did have something funny, spectacles or a moustache or a pipe or a –'

'That's him! Thanks for your help, madam. Come along, Sergeant.' Lowering his voice a good deal to tell the driver Somerset House, the Treasurer followed Cambuslang into the taxi's interior and they were off.

For a few minutes nothing was said. Then, as they circumnavigated Marble Arch at a speed sufficient to recall faintly Poe's vessel caught in the maelstrom, Cambuslang gloomily offered,

'The trouble with our Secretary is that he can't forgive the world for not being as he'd like it to be.'

'For once I'm prepared to listen to your heavy Scotch moralizing.'

'Freudian, surely, rather than Scottish, though it is true that many of the most distinguished exponents of those doctrines have had the Caledonian stamp upon them. If there is such a thing as a national temperament . . .'

'Then I can't face hearing about it now. Go back to moralizing.'

'I was merely about to say that our friend seems never to have discovered the reality principle, or at least he's never come to terms with it.'

'Emotionally still stuck with the pleasure principle? But aren't we all?' The Treasurer pondered. 'He doesn't look like a pleasure or sensuality man to me. It's all power, I should have thought. I don't know how that fits in with Freud, but . . . You know what I think? It wouldn't surprise me if he spent his Thursdays quietly reading a book at his club. Running that organization was what appealed to him. Not girls.'

Cambuslang was shocked. 'I think that's a dreadful thing to say about a friend,' he said, and relapsed into a silence that lasted until they were approaching Aldwych. Then he revived and declared,

'We must go round by Charing Cross Road on our way back.'

'Why?'

'Because there's a statue of Brigitte Bardot outside the Cameo this week.'

'Ah.'

'Rotating,' Cambuslang added after a pause.

'How do you mean?'

'On a rotating pedestal,' the Scotsman explained.

They paid off the taxi before entering the circuit round Bush House and ran the remaining hundred yards. At the portico of Somerset House notices directed them to an entrance on the right. They rushed through it and found themselves in a tallish room that, apart from the overhead gallery that ran round most of it, reminded the Treasurer of the general post office in a medium-sized provincial town. There was a general impression of green-and-red leather-bound books and high writing desks.

As a grey-uniformed attendant approached, inquiring courteously if he could help them, the Treasurer caught a flash of spectacles from the gallery up on his left. He motioned to Cambuslang and they hurried up the iron stairway, trying with fair success to accommodate silence to speed. The Secretary was down on one knee doing something with and around his brief-case. Cambuslang reached him first and grabbed him from the rear, imprisoning his arms. The Treasurer caught him by the wrist and in so doing dislodged from his grip a quart beer-bottle, which rolled slowly along the gallery spilling some pale fluid. A smell of petrol arose. By the time a man in formal attire and two attendants had reached them, the bottle was stoppered and back in the brief-case and the Secretary, his face expressionless, had been hauled to his feet.

'And ... just ... what ... on ... *earth* is taking place here?' asked the formally attired man.

'This gentleman is a psychiatric patient of mine at the Blomfield Clinic,' said Cambuslang. 'I apologize on his behalf for this disturbance. I'd be most grateful to you if you'd allow my assistant and me to remove him without fuss or delay. I appeal to you as a human being.'

'Are you a doctor?'

'I am.'

'Have you any identification?'

'Certainly.' Cambuslang dug in his breast pocket. 'My driving licence, my discount card from John Bell & Croyden, my prescription pad with my name and that of my clinic on it, a pharmaceutical circular addressed to me and a letter from the Librarian of the British Medical Association. Will that be sufficient?'

'Perfectly, Doctor ... Cambuslang. Of course we will consider the matter closed. Can I help you in any way? You've only to ask.'

'I think we can manage between us. Thank you most warmly.'

A minute later the trio were emerging into the street. 'Good job that laddie didn't know we only do kidneys and bladders at the clinic,' muttered Cambuslang.

The Treasurer held up his hand to a taxi representing itself as FOR HIRE, but the driver shook his head in angry disgust, as if entreated for alms, and swept by. The next one proved more amenable. As they got into it the Treasurer noticed flickers of tentative sunshine reflected from the wet tarmac. It was going to be a fine evening.

The Secretary's brief-case proved to contain altogether two quarts of petrol, a box of kitchen matches and a few handfuls of shavings. Not perhaps what might have been expected of the

Secretary – a couple of thermite grenades or a kilo of napalm would have been nearer the mark – but practical enough to have done for, say, R A M to S H I 1899–1924 if properly employed. The would-be incendiary sat between the other two looking fixedly ahead, though there was nothing in that direction but the back of the taxi-man's neck, less thickset than that day's average. It seemed that the Secretary had entered a dazed state similar, in kind if not in intensity, to that which had afflicted Cambuslang at Paddington. A psychologist, reflected the Treasurer, might have used this likeness in response to stress as basis for a generalization about likeness in personality structures among those who had been members of the Society.

When the taxi arrived at Badgett Street (Brigitte Bardot had been deferred for a more appropriate occasion), nobody had any money to pay for it. The earlier rides and the tickets to Taunton had emptied the Treasurer's and Cambuslang's pockets; the Secretary, when searched by the other two, had no more than a few pence, all that remained, probably, after some unimaginable taxi-borne tour in search of the fire-raising stores. After a short delay the fare was raised out of the petty-cash box. Three pound notes and some silver and copper remained. The Treasurer divided this among them. What they had been up to in the preceding couple of hours could certainly be considered Society activities, even though the Committee might well not have ratified the Secretary's project, had it succeeded.

'Chester's run away to the West Indies,' said the Treasurer as the three sat apathetically about in the Club Room. 'So that's cleared up.'

The Secretary gave no sign of having heard.

'A coward's way out!' said Cambuslang admiringly. He distributed the last of the Scotch.

'It's isn't really what you're thinking,' said the Secretary abruptly. 'The collapse of the Society, though that did sort of touch it all off. It happened on Sunday after dinner. We were talking about the T V programme and I suppose I must have said it was a great strain. My wife said I'd been looking so worried lately that she thought there was something I ought to know. And it was this: she'd been wise to what the Society was for from the very first time I mentioned it to her. Don't ask me how.'

Cambuslang stared at him. 'And she let you go on with it, knowing that?'

'Encouraged me. Bought this house for us, if you remember. It gave me something to do, you see. An interest in life. A hobby. I was the kind of person who enjoyed planning and plotting and people were nicer if they were allowed to do what they enjoyed doing, so I was given my head to plan and plot.'

'Why did she tell you all this?'

'To stop me worrying. In future if there was a crisis, especially if it involved any of the wives, I was to consult her and we'd dope out a plan together. You see what that makes me, don't you?'

'Indeed I do,' said Cambuslang. 'A bit of a bloody twot is what it makes you, laddie.'

'I felt life had become impossible. So I made my gesture. Even then I was stopped. Though I see now that that was for the best and I want to thank you. But it's what happens next that I can't see. I can't go home, and I can't live here because she paid for it.'

'Why can't you go home?'

'She doesn't know yet that the Society's been disbanded. Think of the sympathizing and the commiserating and the we-must-find-you-something-else.'

'Mm,' said the other two.

'And for the rest of my life any project I start up will be suspect from the word go.'

'Mm.'

'So what am I to do?'

'I'll tell you what to do,' said the Treasurer. 'Tell her everything and ask for help in devising a really horrible revenge on the President and Mordle and whoever else you fancy. It's a worthwhile enterprise in itself, it's something to occupy your mind, and above all it gives you time.'

'Time for what?'

'For devising a project she won't be able to shake.'

'But I've just told you she'd be on to anything I could –'

'*Anything?*'

Cambuslang said weightily, 'Are we to take it that a problem of this kind will be too much for the man who conceived and carried through the Week-end Seminar, who was equal to all the difficulties inherent in Project Nefertiti (shelved through no fault of

202

his), who guided the Society safely through weeks and months of tension and crisis, who fell at last only by treachery?'

After nodding pensively, the Secretary finished his drink. He went on being pensive for the next ten minutes, by which time he was being put into a taxi and sent home by Cambuslang and the Treasurer. The tendency of the Secretary's pensiveness was inked in when he said over the lowered window,

'The first step would be to send them mutually contradictory cover stories about the dissolution of the Society.'

'And there's the Chester angle. Don't forget that none of them has heard about him turning up out there safe and sound.'

'Christ, that is a point. Well, see you.'

The taxi drove off. Cambuslang said they might as well go and start the evening at the club off Berkeley Square he belonged to.

The Treasurer acceded. He hoped that his scheme for rehabilitating the Secretary would succeed. It would be nice to think that, at the onset of some unprecedented, as yet inconceivable crisis in the future, a Cincinnatus of such a calibre would be available for recall from the rustic contentment of his farm.

21 The Unbearable Secret

ANTONY: O whither hast thou led me, Egypt?

Early the following week the ex-Treasurer found himself at a loose end at the junction of Shaftesbury Avenue and New Oxford Street. He had been visiting, in an attic in St Giles's Circus, a 'brilliant young' and hitherto unknown designer who had submitted a revolutionary lay-out for a three-way stretch. He now had in his pocket a signed contract disadvantageous to the young man. He felt no qualms about this: to his mind males so fanatically devoted to designing female clothing were a repulsive lot. He wished that the pubs were open, so that he could wash away the taste of the catch just hooked – in particular, the memory of that sweeping gesture of two long forefingers to sketch the estimated effect upon thigh and hip of the device in question.

Other items lay alongside the contract in his brief-case (a much slimmer affair than the ex-Secretary's, which had looked as if it carried a substantial gelignite booby-trap against unauthorized opening). There was a sheaf of cheques, postal orders and cash to the value of £27 0s. 6d., donations to the defunct Society sent as a result of his remarks about financial problems on the TV programme. They would have to be returned when he could summon the energy.

There was a letter from Lee Eddington Schwartz which he had picked up that lunch-time in the course of a clearing-up visit to Badgett Street. It said, in part, that she appreciated his burst of frankness about the Society but that she liked her frankness spread out evenly from day to day, not in bursts. It would have to be destroyed before he went home.

There was a postcard from Chester, picked up at the same time. The stamp on it was of the Benedictine Republic in the Caribbean, and the reverse side bore the likeness of a moustachioed person, his name (Etcheverria) and the word *Libertad*. The text read, 'Wish you were here. Will write.' There followed the signatures of Chester and a certain Battersby, a friend of Chester's who had once tried to join the Society but been turned down on the grounds that he was 'unmarried'. Beneath the names were a couple of barely legible but evidently feminine scrawls. This missive too could not be allowed to remain where it was, but Cambuslang at least must be allowed to inspect it, if only to confirm or deny that it smelt just perceptibly of Bacardi rum.

Finally there was a letter from the ex-President dated the previous day, imploring the ex-Treasurer to ring a stated telephone number at exactly 11.30 the following morning. No names were to be exchanged on the line. It could be deduced that the ex-Secretary, with or without the assistance of his wife, had already made solid progress with his campaign of vengeance. For him, at least, communication with some sort of imaginative or imaginary world had been kept open. For others there was nothing left except life as it had always been.

Crossing New Oxford Street, the ex-Treasurer thought he would have a drink at the Museum Tavern if it were open yet. He was reluctant to go home.

'What are you going to do now your Society's packed up?' his wife had asked him at Sunday lunch.

'I might put up for the Institute if they'll have me. And I shall do my best to keep up with the periodicals and so on.' He gloomily foresaw a couple of months, at any rate, of bringing home and affecting to peruse *Egypt*, *The Middle East Archaeological Journal* and the rest of them without, as heretofore, the afflatus of tangibly rewarding deception.

'I shouldn't bother if I were you. And I didn't mean that. I was wondering if you were thinking of going in for model railways or politics or something, so that you can go on having your Thursday evenings like always. She'll have something to say if you don't, I expect.'

'She?' The replacement for Miss Schwartz had been going to be a girl in his accounts department, amiable enough, but on the whole not as nice. 'What do you mean, she?'

'I mean she, whoever she is. Your steady, if it is a steady. Mm, I've known for over a year.'

Denial had plainly been useless. 'How?'

'By using my tiny little mind, mate. Watching and listening and thinking.'

'I see.'

'I wouldn't have brought it up, only Brenda's going to South Africa next week, so I shall be at a loose end on Thursdays too.'

'Brenda? Oh yes, your pal at the hospital.'

'That's right, my pal at the hospital. Only he's six-foot three and a nerve specialist and an ex-Rugby international and he isn't called Brenda.'

'Oh. Supposing I'd asked you to produce Brenda, called at her flat to pick you up or something?'

'Then she'd have had to go on the night shift to stand in for her friend Marjorie who'd been taken ill suddenly, and she hadn't been able to let me know in time because Matron wouldn't put up with even staff nurses using the phone for personal calls when they were on duty and as much more of the same as you'd been able to stand. I learn fast, you see. I never even used to have to write anything down. It made me laugh like hell when you went on about your professors and lectures and then sat back while the funny little woman prattled away about her funny little concerns. Of course, it was easier for me than for you, because you thought I might be listening and I knew you weren't. Now you'd better have a nice long think about things in general, only not too long because Brenda might be coming back in the autumn if he doesn't like South Africa.'

How many more of them had known the score? the Treasurer had wondered then, and wondered now. Apart from the bloc formed by the wives of the former Committee, what about Mrs Cambuslang? Mrs Isham? Mrs Froald? – not she, at any rate. If anything these days could be counted an irreducible fact, that could.

The pub was still shut. But the Museum itself, opposite, was open. It would fill in the necessary few minutes. He mounted to the Egyptian galleries, and was passing down the long halls with what he felt to be an admirable detachment, when he was brought up short by coming eye to eye with the bust of Queen Nefertiti – in fact the original, for a plaque on its pedestal read, *On loan from Ehemals Staatliche Museum, W. Berlin*. (Earlier that day he had seen the torso of the Society's version of her, still minus one breast, in the otherwise bare Club Room. The head had presumably been removed by Isham.)

206

He bent close and said with a venom that surprised him. 'You bitch. Look where you've brought us all. Why have you done it? Why are you what you are?'

Nefertiti stared levelly to her front, as she had done for thirty-three centuries.

Well, what next?